"Has the passion and resolve of a brilliantly played symphony. Elizabeth Oness's characters are like graceful, complex melodies you will want to memorize and recall for a lifetime. This is one beautiful book."
——Alyson Hagy, author of *Keeneland*

"In detailing the seemingly ordinary lives of three sisters, Elizabeth Oness has created a vivid, deeply realistic portrait of contemporary women. Unmoored and each in her own way anguished, these three characters are bound to stir debate. *Departures* is ultimately a highly charged novel, political in the most personal sense."
——Julianna Baggott, author of *Girl Talk*

"An affecting and absorbing novel of loss and recovery, a contemporary story that digs into the inner recesses of its characters with tact and skill. I admired in particular the swift, unerring prose, which carries forward with an intensity and clarity that is heartening. A wide audience should find its way to this artful novel by Elizabeth Oness, a young writer of considerable promise."
——Jay Parini

continued on next page . . .

Praise for the work of Elizabeth Oness:

"Oness is a highly skilled writer whose stories are freighted with unique messages and perspectives. Since her work is already familiar to readers of literary quarterlies and of the 1994 O. Henry Prizes, Oness should broaden her audience with this collection."

—*Publishers Weekly*

"*Articles of Faith* has a strange and amazing range: her work is impressive for what it risks, and even more for what it achieves. She spares her characters nothing, because she loves them; she spares the reader nothing, either, which is, of course, the mark of a real writer . . . A moral puzzle . . . weighty and intricate . . . each character is complicated and real. She is a tremendous and heartfelt and gutsy writer."

—Elizabeth McCracken

"Compellingly and beautifully written. I cared about these characters—not only about what happens to them but about what Oness shows us about being human. These stories were so good that I just placed myself in her hands and kept on reading."

—Judy Troy, author of *From the Black Hills*

"Written with deceptive simplicity . . . A wonderful collection of insight and empathy."

—Anna Esaki-Smith, author of *Meeting Luciano*

departures

Also by the Author

ARTICLES OF FAITH

departures

Elizabeth Oness

𝓑

BERKLEY BOOKS, NEW YORK

𝔅

A Berkley Book
Published by The Berkley Publishing Group
A division of Penguin Group (USA) Inc.
375 Hudson Street
New York, New York 10014

Berkley trade paperback edition: May 2004

Visit our website at www.penguin.com

Library of Congress Cataloging-in-Publication Data

Oness, Elizabeth, 1960-
    Departures / Elizabeth Oness. —1st Berkley trade ed.
        p. cm.
    ISBN 0-425-19590-2
    1. Divorced mothers—Fiction. 2. Mothers and daughters—Fiction. I. Title.

PS3565.N56D46 2004
813'.6–dc22

2003063863

PRINTED IN THE UNITED STATES OF AMERICA

10   9   8   7   6   5   4   3   2   1

For Chad, for everything—
and for the Shines.

I am grateful to the following people in more ways than I can say: Chad Oness, a poet in the house makes so many things unnecessary to explain—especially the necessity of the work. Drake Hokanson, for his eye on photographic matters; he and Carol Kratz have been inspiring friends in all weathers. Special thanks to Jim and Laura Armstrong for their careful reading, friendship, and urbane sense of style—life in Winona would be less without them. Leona Nevler for her astute identification of the gaps in the original manuscript; it's been enormously helpful to have a steady guide. Rolph Blythe, who was generous to take the time to read. And Jennifer Carlson, for her good humor and faith.

one

one

ZEKE STEPPED OUTSIDE AND HER BREATH TURNED TO SMOKE in the autumn air. Overnight, it had turned cold, and the smell of damp leaves and sudden chill made her remember being a child, watching plumes of breath rise from her mother's mouth as she and her sisters waited for the school bus. When they were small, their mother waited with them, her hair loose, rippling over her jacket, her breath a benediction, as if she had breathed them out of herself, made her daughters out of moist expiration and smoke.

When Zeke got into her car, it seemed colder than outdoors. The engine caught on her second try, and she waited as the car warmed up, the pearled condensation on the windshield sealing her off from the larger world. She was glad she had stayed at her own place last night. Marcie was pissed off, brewing about something, and Zeke didn't feel like fooling with her. After a few minutes, a clear crescent revealed the road in front of her and she pulled out of the drive. In the hilly, sheltering landscape there was the feeling that you didn't know what lay beyond the next hill or curve. Hardscrabble Road had been here since the time of the Revolutionary War, but the name didn't fit at all. The homes were stately and well maintained, the land lush and private, studded with small ponds and pine forests. Toward the end of the road, in the middle of a long descent, a plaque and small American flag marked the place where John Andre was captured on his way to meeting Benedict Arnold. As a child, in the long summers, she raced by on her bike, feeling the wind on her face and arms. There was a history here that meshed with hers obliquely. A traitor had walked here. Even in these lush and serene surroundings, there was a thread of betrayal.

Zeke turned into the university. At the base of a wooded hill, a small farm bordered the north side of the campus. The university had purchased the property so their pre-Vet students might get some practical experience, but before Zeke came it was haphazardly run and underutilized, in danger of being paved over for a parking lot. The Environmental Center, as the farm was now called, felt removed from the bustle of campus, although Zeke could see the Student Center from her office window.

As soon as she got out of the car, she felt something was wrong. She looked over the fences; most of them were visible from the gravel courtyard where she parked. The posts and rails had weathered to silver over the years, but everything seemed secure—Mr. T and Romey were out in the field, the sheep scattered at the bottom of the south pasture. The chestnut-colored rooster, a mean, greedy bird, pecked at some grain near the edge of the barn. The barnyard was quiet.

She yanked on the barn door and was filled with the smell of corn and leather, saddle soap, the scent of warm bodies and breath, mute exhalation. The rhythmic sound of chewing carried through the barn. At the end of the aisle, in the half dark, she saw a pony's rump. Ebbie's head was in a grain bin. She cursed under her breath.

"Ebbie, how did you get out?"

Ebenezer Scrooge was a shaggy Shetland pony whose springy flaxen mane made Zeke think of Tina Turner's hair. He lifted his head from the grain bin and gazed at her, sweet feed dribbling from his lips. He could have been here for hours. A pony would literally eat itself to death. How had he gotten out? Who had left the grain bin open? She'd kill whoever closed up last night.

She grabbed a lead rope, looped it around his neck, and he followed her without resisting. She felt a nervous weight in her stomach. If he had just started eating, he would have dug in. She put him in his stall and latched it tight.

Zeke walked to the cottage, glancing at the withered garden on her way in. The garden plot looked odd in the front yard, but it was the only spot with enough sunlight. A huge black walnut tree in the back yard shaded the long grass. The cottage was part of the original farm, and the weathered shingles needed repair. Inside, the painted floors and old-fashioned kitchen made it feel more like an artist's workshop than a house. She sat down to call the vet, punching through the series of numbers that would page him. As she waited for him to call back, she checked her e-mail, which was usually of little consequence: messages from the university administration that she deleted without reading, one or two friends who occasionally sent chatty notes. She punched SEND AND RECEIVE. There was a message from her mother and she cursored down to read it.

Zeke:

I'm leaving the country for a while. Don't look for me. Don' t
worry.

Love, Mom

What the hell? Her mother lived in the next town, and they saw
each other fairly often. What did she mean—"leaving the country"?

The phone rang and she jumped, imagining it was her
mother, but it was the vet, and she explained about Ebbie getting into the sweet feed.

"Well, you know the drill." His voice was calm. "Start
walking the pony. I'll be by this morning."

She muttered a reply, still thinking of her mother. Was she
supposed to get in touch with her sisters? Her mother wouldn't
have left her to tell them. If she had only told one of them, it
would have been Pagan. There must be an obvious explanation,
one she couldn't think of right now.

PAGAN CREPT OUT of the baby's room and moved quietly down
the hall, turning off the upstairs phone in case it rang while
Maud was napping. At times, she still thought of Maud as a
baby, although she was almost three years old now, her chubby
fingers becoming dexterous in a thousand confounding ways.
Pagan turned on the kettle, took coffee from the cupboard, then
stood still for a moment, gazing out the window at the maples
at the edge of the yard: scarlet, yellow-orange, vermilion. Pregnant again, she felt a sense of stillness, as if she could stand and
watch the brilliant trees for an hour without boredom or rest-

lessness or worry. The house grew quiet around her. A breeze rippled in the trees, sending a few leaves to the ground. Pagan turned off the kettle. She felt most like herself when the house was empty or Maud was asleep. She knew this was silly, because she understood, in the practical sense, that she was most real in relation to others now, but she needed quiet to sense her relation to the larger world.

A thump sounded by the front door. She poured her coffee, then walked to the foyer where a pile of mail lay on the floor. Although she wasn't big yet, she felt so tired that almost any action required a conscious directive. *I have to bend over now and pick these up.* She gathered up the mail and moved to the living room to sit down. She blew on her coffee, still too hot, and wished it wasn't decaffeinated. She flipped through the stack: bills, mailings from stores she wasn't interested in, a letter from Gerber with a cellophane window. She tossed it aside. She knew what was in it, she'd opened one once. What nerve they had, trying to sell life insurance to expectant mothers. Pagan picked up a baby catalog, glanced at the cover, then set it down. She wanted to make a nursery upstairs, but planned on waiting, after last time.

She lowered herself into an armchair, thinking about names. She had protested about Maud's name, but Tommy was insistent. What could be wrong, he argued, with naming a girl for a great Irish beauty? No one would mispronounce it, not like Nuala or Siobhan. Pagan said she wanted a simple name, a name that didn't need interpreting, but finally she relented, thinking that naming her daughter Maud was different from her mother's impulse in naming them.

She and her sisters were named for different stages of their mother's spiritual seeking: Pagan, Zhikr, and Prana. Of course, it was the sixties then, lots of kids had hippie names, but her mother had changed, left all that behind. Now their names were like clothes out of fashion or pants that were too short, a reminder that time had moved past them.

At home, Pagan was called Pag for short, but in the presence of outsiders the long *a* was softened, transmuted into *e,* so she became known to the outside world as Peg. When she first met Tommy, at a friend's wedding, he bent down to hear her name amidst the noise and the music and thought she had said Pegeen. She smiled to herself at his misunderstanding, at how his upbringing showed, an Irish-Catholic boy to be sure.

She pushed the mail from her lap, but stopped when she saw a small envelope addressed in her mother's neat handwriting. For a moment, because of its diminutive size, she thought it was for Maud. Pagan ripped open the envelope with her finger.

October 15, 1998

Dear Pagan,
 I'm taking a trip & I'll be out of the country for a while. Even though I'm not here, I'll be with you in spirit. Don't look for me. Try not to worry.

Love, Mom

Pagan read the letter again. She looked at the date, two days ago. Where had her mother gone?

PRANA ADJUSTED THE place mat, the ever-so-neatly tossed napkin, and stepped out of the way. The lights were hot; the lettuce was going to wilt. The cobalt blue plate was too dark. She had mentioned this might be a problem, but now the food was on it, and the chef had left in a snit, so something else had to be changed. The art director kept wandering in and out, muttering that no one really valued his eye. Wounded and imperious, he insisted they keep going. Prana felt a thrumming in her throat; she needed a cigarette. She suggested a different place mat, of course she'd brought several, maybe moving the glass of wine so the red would be less distracting? White would look better, but you'd hardly serve that with beef bourguignonne. Maybe just the edge of the bottle in the corner, turn it so he wouldn't shoot the label. The photographer bent down to get another look. He smiled at her.

"Prana, sweetheart, you've saved the day."

She forced a smile and made a motion with her fingers.

"Yes, of course, go have a smoke." He bent down to look through the lens.

She went out back and sat on the iron steps, looking out into the alley. On certain days in autumn, the sky in Washington, D.C. became a soiled white, the color of the monuments. Leaves swirled in little gusts through the alley, tiny twisters that lost momentum and filled the corners near the steps and the wells of basement windows with leaves. Her life consisted of arranging things to look beautiful. Could anything matter less—selling dishes or food, or whatever the product might be? This subtle arranging was something she did almost instinctively now, but she was tired of managing things, tired of trying to make disparate things come together. She blew a long stream of smoke into the air.

At the end of the day, she walked through Dupont Circle, then down Rhode Island Avenue toward her apartment.

The weather would be cold soon; she felt it in the wind. At the building door, she fumbled for her keys.

"Hello, darlin'."

She knew the smoothness in his voice without turning around. She hadn't heard him come up behind her.

"Hi, Joe."

Joe stepped forward and opened the door for her. He wore an expensive-looking overcoat, and he looked pleased and energetic, even at the end of the week. He had lived across the hall for several years now, and they partied together when they were on their own. He had his friends and girlfriends; she had her friends and Stephan. In the foyer she opened her mailbox and stuffed the mail in her bag.

"You're looking dapper," she said.

"Long week?" He raised his eyebrows.

"Yes," she sighed. "What are you up to this weekend?"

"Big day tomorrow. Meeting Marian's kids." He shook his head, grinning. "Don't know what I'm getting myself into."

"Oh, I'd say you do." She smiled and waved good-bye at her door.

As soon as she walked into her apartment, she checked for the light on her machine. He hadn't called.

She hung up her coat, took a glass from the rack, and poured herself a glass of wine. Her bag tipped on the counter, and she gathered the mail and carried it into the living room. Fashion magazines, photography magazines, announcements for gallery openings. A postcard slid out of the pile and she reached for it, hoping for word from him, although he never sent postcards. It would be ridiculous, a photographer sending someone else's bright version of another place. The postcard was from Manhattan, Rockefeller Center, an image of the large bronze statue of Atlas holding the world on his shoulders. She turned it over and saw her mother's handwriting.

Dear Prana,

I'm taking a trip, leaving the country, and I'll be away for a while. Don't let Pagan drive herself crazy looking for me. There's no point. I love you. Mom

Prana flipped over the card and smiled. Every year, when they were kids, they went into New York on Christmas Eve. They saw the tree at Rockefeller Center, went ice skating, and Marco took them to dinner. What was her mother up to? Would she have gone somewhere with Marco? No. After all these years, it was impossible. The postcard was a sign, a private joke. Prana swirled the wine in her glass. Whatever it was, she hoped her mother was having fun.

two

ZEKE WALKED EBENEZER AROUND THE PADDOCK, ROUND AND round the inside of the fence, thinking of her mother's message. She held a riding crop lightly in her hand. The pony was sweating, moving slowly from the drugs the vet had given him. The danger wasn't the colic itself. The danger was that, left alone, he would lie down and writhe around, try to alleviate the pain. He could twist an intestine, and then he'd have to be put to sleep.

When Zeke called the student who'd closed up last night, she claimed to be studying for an important test. Zeke explained that horses can't throw up, that Ebbie might die unless she walked him, so Sally had grudgingly agreed to come. That was hours ago. Where the hell was she?

Yolanda, wearing high-heeled shoes and a bright pink

sweater, tottered up to the fence. Her shoes sank unevenly into the gravel, and looking down at her muddy heels, she cursed in Spanish. Zeke grinned. Yolanda had attitude. She taught a few Continuing Ed classes at the cottage, and her presence made Zeke feel that she wasn't the only adult around.

"Your sister's on the phone. She says it's urgent."

Zeke studied Yolanda's shoes and long fingernails. "Which sister?" Zeke asked.

"You have a sister named Pagan?"

Zeke sighed, with Pagan it was always urgent. "Tell her I'll call as soon as I can."

WHEN SALLY FINALLY arrived, Zeke handed her the lead rope and the crop.

"You can't let him lie down," Zeke said. "If his knees start to buckle, you've got to hit him. Keep him going."

Sally took the lead rope without looking her in the eye, and Zeke walked back to the cottage. Inside, she took a sandwich from her pack and called Pagan.

"Did you get a letter from Mom?" Pagan asked.

"E-mail." Zeke's mouth was full.

"Don't you think it's weird? Can you go to the house and look around?"

When Pagan was anxious, she organized things to do. The trouble was that Pagan's ideas usually involved other people, and once she conceived of a plan, she expected everyone to fall in line.

"What's the point?" Zeke asked.

"I just think it's important to check on things."

Zeke took another bite of her sandwich. She didn't think it

was necessary to go, but Pagan lived thirty miles away, and Zeke knew it was a hassle for her to pack up Maud and all her kid stuff, and drive up in the car. It would take Zeke only a few minutes to get to her mother's.

"I'll call you when I get there," Zeke said.

AT THE END of the day, Zeke set off for her mother's house. She glanced in her rear-view mirror at Sally leading Ebbie in the fading light, his tiny hooves tapping around the paddock like a drunken cartoon. Sally's slump-shouldered walk, the hood of her sweatshirt bunched up, half-caught beneath her coat collar, gave Zeke an uncomfortable twinge.

She had an extra key to her mother's house, in case of emergencies, but she didn't really know what to consider this. The odd thing about her mother's disappearance was the open-endedness of her return. Before leaving, Zeke looked at her mother's message again: "*leaving the country for a while.*" What did *a while* mean? One month? Two? A year?

On the way to her mother's, Zeke passed her own apartment: a renovated carriage house belonging to a couple who worked in the city. The carriage house was set across the road from a property that had fascinated her when she was younger. Lillian Hellman and Dashiell Hammett had owned the farm across the way. The large rambling home, hidden by trees, had been renovated since the famous couple owned it, but Zeke liked to imagine their embattled glamour still lingered. In middle school, she had done a report on the McCarthy hearings for social studies, and she was impressed by Hellman's statement that she wouldn't cut her opinions to fit that year's fashions. Zeke liked her defiance and bravery and was fascinated by Hellman's book photograph: the prominent, elegant nose, the jutting face that was not pretty but fierce, the cigarette she brandished like a gun. At twelve, Zeke didn't understand why she found the woman so compelling.

The landscape had changed very little since her adolescence. There were a few developments of upscale suburban homes, but they were built on roads that sprouted from Hardscrabble, so the enclaves of suburban modernity were visible mainly to themselves and didn't intrude on the atmosphere of lives lived out quietly, separate from others. This was not a place where people turned to neighbors when trouble found them. In case of tragedy, you were heavily insured; you called your attorney, not your friends. Neighbors were for socializing: maintaining the illusion of cultural equilibrium, creating the impression that life could be lived in a serene fashion.

The white wooden fence with a sloping top, which she had walked like a balance beam on her way home from the bus stop every day, had recently been replaced by a metal guardrail. The houses were the same, but they were owned by people she no longer knew. She drove past the Leitholds' with its elegant Georgian facade. She could picture the sun room in back, the grand piano in the living room, the acres of apple orchards behind the house. She passed the marshy undeveloped woods studded with saplings and hummocks of marsh grass, the Swim & Tennis Club, where she and her sisters spent summers in the chlorine-soaked pool. They went every day, regardless of the weather. She remembered lying on the sunny cement, feeling the warmth radiate up through her body. Lifeguards shouted in the wind, ordering kids not to run on the deck, their cries repeated so often that the words were reduced to a shrill but remote sound, like seagulls squawking in the distance. She and Prana grew blond in the sun. Pagan's dark curls never changed.

Zeke turned onto her mother's street, which had a mix of older, elegant homes set in terraced gardens and more modern homes built on wooded lots. As soon as their mother earned enough for a down payment, she moved them into their own house: a contemporary three bedroom with large windows and wood floors. Zeke loved the openness of the house, the sense of living in the trees. She felt something ease in her mother when she finally bought her own home, as if she had delivered them to safety.

She unlocked the door and stepped inside. The air was still. The furniture was in place, everything looked the same, but something was missing, some element removed.

Her footsteps echoed on the floor as she walked into the kitchen. No plates in the sink indicating a hurried departure, not even a single empty cup. The dishwasher was empty, the dishes stacked neatly in the cupboards. What was so different? Zeke looked around. The plants! The array of plants that filled the floor space in front of the large south window, the ceramic pots that cluttered every window sill—all of them were gone. The house looked bare without them. The thermostat was set to fifty-eight degrees.

She climbed the stairs to her mother's bedroom. The bed was made; clothes hung in the closet. Zeke opened a few drawers. She didn't pay attention to her mother's clothes, so she didn't know what might be missing. She went into the bathroom and opened the medicine cabinet. Nothing seemed unusual or out of place. Her mother's toothbrush was gone.

Zeke sat on the bed and looked around. The quiet filled her. She thought she knew her mother, but maybe she hadn't been paying close enough attention. Her mother's jewelry box was on the bureau, a few photos, the picture of them, wait—the photo of the three of them, taken one summer at the beach—was gone. She checked to make sure. It was a small photo in a square brass frame. Her mother had given each of them a copy because it captured them in a way that photos rarely do, their three bodies so close together it was hard to distinguish the lines between them. Pagan, the worrying eldest, her hand over her eyes as if looking off to sea, trying to chart the safest course. Under the shadow of her hand, her eyes were dark; above her raised arm, her dark curls lifted in the breeze. Zeke, leaning against Pagan's shoulder, looked boyish even then: her head thrown back, throat exposed, hair streaked by the sun. She seemed caught in forward movement, as if she were going to burst from the group and move forward out of the frame. Prana, delicate and fairy-like, the silent bloom inside her still nascent.

Her mother always kept the photo on her bureau.

She opened the jewelry box. Her mother didn't have much jewelry, most of it was old hippie stuff, turquoise and silver, which would have been out of place with the more muted, suburban style she had adopted, but she had inherited a few pieces from her own mother, which she kept but never wore. Zeke poked through the box and felt a tingle of shock when she realized the expensive pieces were gone. Her grandmother's brooch was missing: a large gold disc with a raised cornucopia-like basket. As a child, Zeke had been fascinated by it. A mass of gemstones representing different fruits overflowed the top of the basket: emerald, ruby, garnet, opal, topaz, sapphire, pearl, aquamarine. It was far too ornate for her mother to wear. Zeke looked again. It wasn't here. A thick gold chain and a bracelet studded with sapphires were also missing.

Where could they be? Her first thought was that they had been stolen, but that didn't seem likely. Her mother would have told her. Had her mother given them to her sisters? Zeke felt a twinge of jealousy, then told herself it was silly. She'd never wear anything so femme. She started to close the jewelry box when something caught her eye. Ticket stubs. She picked them up. Carnegie Hall. She couldn't see what the concert had been. Funny, she didn't recall her mother saying anything about going into the city.

Zeke walked downstairs and into her mother's study. The answering machine was disconnected, but her mother had left it on the desk with the cord wrapped around it, as if the machine were bound. The implied suppression made Zeke nervous. Then she saw an envelope with her name on it. Inside, her mother's familiar hand:

> *Zeke—*
>
> *I guessed you'd come out to check on things. Please don't worry, everything's fine.*
>
> *Love, Mom*

Zeke picked up the phone and dialed Pagan. "So I'm here. Everything's cleaned up, turned off, the refrigerator is empty, the dishes put away."

"You didn't find *anything?*"

Zeke heard the implication that she hadn't looked carefully enough. She imagined Pagan on the other end of the line, fiddling with the phone cord.

"She left a note," Zeke said.

"What kind of note?"

The fear in Pagan's voice irritated Zeke. In the absence of information, Pagan always assumed the worst.

"Not that kind of note. She just says 'don't worry.' But here's a strange thing: she gave away her houseplants. All of them. Why wouldn't she just have someone come in to water them? Here's the other thing—"and Zeke felt herself framing her question cautiously. "Has Mom given you or Prana any of her jewelry?"

Pagan took a breath. "No, why?"

"Well, I looked in her jewelry box. You know that big brooch with all the gemstones, her gold chain and stuff? They're gone."

"Are you sure?"

Zeke was silent, annoyed by Pagan's question.

"I'm sorry," Pagan said. "Do you think someone stole them?"

"I don't think so. I don't think her stuff is that valuable. It's just—"

Maud started to wail in the background. Pagan cursed under her breath, dropped the receiver with a clatter, then returned a moment later. "Sorry," she said.

"Yeah, sure," Zeke said. "Look, will you talk to Prana tonight? I've got to get back to the barn and check on this sick pony. I left a student walking him around the paddock. She's probably freezing to death."

"Okay, bye."

Zeke was startled by Pagan's rapid hanging up. Sometimes, in midsentence, Pagan would say "gotta go!" and hang up before Zeke had a chance to respond. Later, she would explain that Maud had figured out how to climb over the gate or was working on getting the child safety plugs out of the outlets or had learned to open the door to the basement steps. Pagan had been unexpectedly mellow when she was pregnant with Maud, almost a different person, but these days she seemed breathless and constantly exasperated. Of course, she'd been throwing up for months, which was enough to make anyone crabby. Sometimes even her curls looked tired. How had their mother managed alone with three of them? Zeke looked out over the yard, the birches dark in the autumn dusk. To all appearances, her mother had arranged everything very neatly and left. Why hadn't she told them where she was going?

ON THE DRIVE back, she thought about what the vet had said. Ponies tended to founder, and that was another mess. Too much sweet feed was heatening, and their hooves almost melted, turned and curled up like old-fashioned Turkish shoes, the navicular bone sinking down toward the bottom of the hoof. It was painful for the pony to walk. In a bad case, you couldn't correct it, even with shoeing or trimming, and the farm didn't have money to shoe a pony anyway.

Zeke pulled into the yard, saw the vet's car parked by the paddock, and felt a nervous tingle in her stomach. When she got out of the car and saw Ebenezer standing up, her nervousness subsided. Sally was talking to the vet, probably telling him how annoyed Zeke had been. He nodded as the girl spoke and seemed to weigh what she was saying. The skin above his eyes drooped a little, hooding them, but there was nothing hidden there—his eyes, a shade between pale green and blue, looked back at the world directly. Bert looked to be in his mid-thirties; he was not especially tall, but compact and strong. He traveled up and down both sides of the Hudson to the smaller, back-yard barns. A number of the students who helped at the farm went out on calls with him. Zeke had noticed that, although he possessed the authority that came with specific knowledge, he wore this authority easily. He seemed to enjoy listening to people, rather than hearing himself talk.

She pulled herself up on a railing and swung her leg over the fence.

"How's he doing?"

The vet had a syringe cover in his teeth, and he plunged a shot into Ebbie's shoulder while Sally held the halter.

"This is the last shot of Demerol the little guy is going to take." He squinted at the pony and then addressed Zeke. "You might as well put him in a stall and cross your fingers. It's getting cold out here. You can't walk him all night."

Zeke reached for Ebbie's halter. "Look Sally, don't worry, this happens," she said.

"I have to get back and study for my test." Sally huddled in her sweatshirt.

"Go on then, I'll let you know how he's doing in the morning."

After the girl was out of earshot, Zeke said, "I was a little hard on her. Had to twist her arm to get her out here. What she did was stupid, but these kids don't know."

The vet nodded. "She does feel bad." There was no disapproval in his voice, but he didn't try to alleviate Zeke's remorse.

"I didn't expect you to come back," she said. "You didn't have to."

"I was just up the road. Had to stitch up a horse that got caught in some wire."

She led Ebenezer into his stall. Usually so nimble, his legs seemed loosely fastened; he barely got over the door jamb.

Zeke stood in the stall with her hands in her pockets, her mind back at her mother's house.

The vet came up behind her and waited at the stall door. "You can't stay out here," he said.

She shook herself a little and came out of the stall.

"You all right?" he asked.

"Had some weird family stuff going on today. I don't know what to make of it."

She walked him to his car so he could write up the bill. Usually, Zeke didn't care what people thought, but she hoped Sally hadn't made her out to be a monster. He reached for his receipt book, scribbled something on a pad, and handed it to her. The only thing she could make out was the printed header: Francis Bertelli, D.V.M.

"Francis! New stationery. All this time I've been calling you 'Bert.' "

"Everybody does."

"You write like a doctor. The university bean counters will ask what this means." She looked over the trunk of his car, which was tightly packed with syringes, hoof testers, stethoscopes, and medicines.

"You fill them in." He worked efficiently in the dark, tucking his instruments away. "You know, I'm starving," he said. "Do you want to go into town and get some dinner?"

Zeke was startled by his suggestion. She couldn't see his face in the dark. At the thought of food, she realized how hungry she was.

"I could eat," she said.

He suggested a pizza place in town, and suddenly she could almost taste melted cheese and olive oil, pepperoni. As far as she knew, Marcie wasn't expecting her for dinner tonight. "I'll meet you there," Zeke said. She felt in her pocket to make sure she had her wallet, then headed for her car.

Driving out of the farm, she wondered if she'd overreacted to Marcie's mood last night. Suddenly, she didn't feel like navigating an evening with someone unfamiliar. She wanted to turn her car in the opposite direction, go to Marcie's, ask what to do about her mother. Marcie had a way of ferreting out secrets. She worked as an administrator at St. Joseph's Hospital, just a few miles away. She had learned about the university acquiring the old Brownwood Farm, even before the sale had gone through and somehow knew about the university's desire to appear more progressive and environmentally correct. Zeke remembered how she had put it: "Look, they hire a lesbian to run their new Environmental Center. They don't say it that way, but it gets them *big* diversity brownie points. Then they don't have to feel so guilty about going overbudget on the football team."

"I don't really want to compete on that ticket," Zeke said.

"You don't have to," Marcie said. "Trust me, they put it together themselves."

Marcie had been right. She knew how to make things work to her advantage. Part of it was her beauty, Zeke supposed. People wanted to impress her. Zeke had gotten her attention by refusing to court her.

She met Bert at the restaurant, which was half-empty on a Tuesday night. She ordered a glass of red wine, then leaned back and stretched her legs to one side of the table.

"The pizza, actually all the food here, is pretty good," he said. "I have a mother who makes calzone from scratch, so I'm picky."

"Where are you from?"

"Upstate, but I moved here a few years ago. I'm still getting used to the idea that my kids are growing up in a town called Pleasantville."

Zeke snorted.

"When we first moved here, I gave some friends the address and they thought I was kidding."

"I guess I'm used to it," she said.

"You grew up around here?"

Zeke nodded. "Over by Hardscrabble Road."

"There are some nice places there."

He was being diplomatic, but she felt a twinge. She had never outgrown her discomfort with people assuming that because she grew up in Shady Grove, she was rich.

"We weren't what you'd call fancy," Zeke said. "Do you work any of the big barns in the area?"

"Some, but mostly the routine stuff: inoculations, worming. It keeps life simple."

Zeke had heard there was more to the story than that, but it didn't seem polite to probe it. "Have you been to the Rockefellers'?" she asked.

"I was up there last week. They have a nice place."

"The Estate is beautiful," Zeke said. The trails were open to the public and stretched for miles, from Briarcliff into Pocantico, almost to Tarrytown. A rider could go for hours on cinder-covered bridle paths that wound through woods and orchards overlooking the Hudson. The groundskeepers were trained to work around finely bred horses, so when a rider approached on a thoroughbred, or a horse that looked skittish, they would turn off their engines, set down their rakes, and wait for the horse to pass.

The waitress brought their food, and Bert smiled, rubbing his hands together. The smell of melted cheese, oregano, and tomato sauce, made her feel almost faint.

"So why did you start a practice around here?" she asked.

"I used to be at the Bronx Zoo, but after we had kids, we wanted to move out a bit, and there seemed to be room for an equine practice up here. Of course, once we got settled, my wife, now my ex-wife, took a job in the city."

She winced. "I'm sorry."

"I am too."

"How old are your kids?"

"They're seven and ten. Actually, the whole thing is not as bad as it could be. My ex-wife is . . ." He paused, taking a sip of beer. He did not seem reticent, simply taking the time to say the truth of the matter. "She's a good person. She knows I adore the girls; they kept the house, and I have a little apartment outside of town. Three days a week, I pick them up after school, take them to gymnastics or ballet, or take them on calls with me."

"It all sounds so amicable. Why did you split up?"

He smiled at her bluntness.

"I could say it's complicated, but it's not." He leaned back in his chair. "I went to college when I was sixteen. I was still pretty young when I finished vet school. What can I say? We were young. She was beautiful. She wanted kids and thought she loved me."

Zeke could imagine him younger, a little surprised and awkward, stunned that a beautiful woman would marry him. She reached for the pizza, burning her fingers a little.

They ate pizza and talked about horses. Pagan used to tease her, saying that Zeke talked horses the way men talked sports, until Zeke pointed out that riding jumpers *was* a sport. It was instinct now: to analyze how a horse moved, decide whether he would make a decent jumper or not. The talk was judicious and unhurried, calling up the scent of dry leaves, the fragrance of liniment and hay. They talked about an old jumper Zeke had retired on the farm; she'd seen him jump at Madison Square Garden when she was a kid.

"A weird thing happened to me today," she said.

"What's that?"

"My mother disappeared."

He stopped chewing and looked up.

"We don't think there was any foul play or anything. *Foul play*. I can't believe I used an expression like that! She left an e-mail for me, saying she was leaving the country."

"And this is unusual for her?"

"Absolutely. I went to her house and everything's straightened up. Empty. She left a note, telling me not to worry."

"Maybe your mother has a secret life," he said.

"Apparently so."

WHEN ZEKE LET herself into her carriage house that night, she felt relaxed and pleasantly full of pizza. Bert was interesting and didn't seem rattled by petty things. It would be nice to have a sane friend. Almost everyone she knew was on edge these days. Pagan, pregnant again, was tired and touchy. Marcie was increasingly unpredictable. A few weeks ago, she had gotten drunk when they were out together, and it definitely did not suit her. Her defiance, which was brave and even admirable at times, became hostile and belligerent. Over the past year, there had been a number of minor scenes; Marcie would say things that were uncomfortably true, insulting her own friends. Zeke started to wonder if there was more to Marcie's drinking than she had realized. And now this thing with her mother. She wondered if Prana had called and hoped she'd been satisfied to talk to Pagan.

She was pulling her sweater off when the phone rang. Static crackled around her as she tugged the wool over her head.

"Zeke, it's Eleanor—" the child's voice was a sob. "Mom cut her wrist and it's bleeding all over the place."

Zeke heard Marcie cursing and shouting in the background.

"What happened?" Zeke asked.

"She was going out the back door, she put her hand through the glass." Eleanor sounded panicky and breathless.

"She's been drinking?"

"Yes," and Eleanor started to cry.

Zeke imagined calling an ambulance, having it show up with Marcie drunk and the kids in a panic.

"Wrap a belt around her arm. Don't let her get in a car. I'll be there as fast as I can." Zeke hung up the phone and ran out the door.

three

WAKING, PAGAN MOVED TOWARD TOMMY, HER SKIN SUFFUSED with warmth. He slid his hand along her side, down her back.

"When you're pregnant, you feel even softer, like you have—" and he touched her with his finger gently, "an extra layer of skin below your skin."

"Are you saying I'm puffy?" She smiled at him sleepily.

"No, I like it."

She settled back into the pillows, stretching beneath his hands. She missed being able to sleep late, wake slowly, shelter in his warmth before moving out into the day. On weekdays he left so early, and on weekends, with a child's perverse radar, Maud woke at dawn. Tommy moved toward her, and she felt him against her and smiled.

"I don't think we can this morning," she whispered.

"What? It's going to show up on the ultrasound?"

"I guess it won't." She smiled and leaned into him, listening to make sure Maud was still asleep. The bedroom door was closed.

WHILE TOMMY WAS shaving, Pagan sat on the couch, sipping a large glass of orange juice. She was scheduled for an amniocentesis late in the morning, and Tommy had taken the day off to go with her. Ever since the doctor suggested it, she had been dreading the procedure, but she told herself that getting through it would mark the end of the fourth month, the end of nausea and fatigue. She was supposed to be past all that now, but weariness surrounded her like a heavy coat. Sometimes, when Maud called for her in the middle of the night, Pagan stumbled out of bed with a sense of dread. How would she ever manage the nights with a new baby? Tommy would help, but he slept the heavy sleep of a man not expecting to be called, where Pagan heard the slightest cry and moved toward the call without thinking.

When she was pregnant with Maud, Pagan couldn't understand how pregnant women coped with having toddlers. Now she knew: they didn't cope very well. Or at least she didn't. It was inevitable that Maud asked for something the moment she sat down, and fulfilling any small request seemed like climbing Mount Everest. One day, Pagan asked her to pick something up off the floor, and Maud told her: "I can't Mommy, I too tired." Pagan wanted to weep, thinking that Maud would look back on these early years and remember only Pagan's exhausted refrain: "I can't. I'm too tired."

Maud tucked up against her on the couch as *Sesame Street* started.

"Can we go to Aunt Sheila's today?" Maud asked.

"Not today, but we'll go again soon."

Last night, Tommy's sister Sheila had them over to dinner. She lived just a few miles away, not far from where she and Tommy grew up. Pagan had never gotten used to Tommy's family. There were eight Gallagher children and, especially at holidays, the clan was overwhelming. They congregated for christenings, first communions, graduations, and birthdays. Pagan sometimes felt that if she had no friends at all, their calendar could be completely filled with Gallagher family events.

Sheila was forty-two, pregnant with her third child, and had chosen not to have an amnio. They were standing in her stenciled kitchen after dinner when Sheila said, "It wouldn't make any difference if there was a problem, we'd still have the baby." Her tone was even and airy, as if having no particular aim, but Pagan understood the implied criticism.

Pagan leaned down and smoothed Maud's hair. The Muppets danced across the screen as Ray Charles sang a song about numbers.

"Why does he do his head like that?" Maud wobbled her head from side to side and grinned.

"He just does, sweetie," Pagan answered.

"But why?"

"Shh," Pagan said. If she said Ray Charles was blind, Maud would ask questions about blindness for a week. When she told Maud that she shouldn't run out into the street, it had spawned two weeks of questions about being hit by a car. "Bumped" was the word Pagan used, because the harsh sound of "hit" and the photo-like image of her child's broken body lying in the road frightened her too much to say. Maud's questions were constant, flowing from previous questions with slight variations, like a self-renewing fountain. Would she die if she was bumped by a car? Would a baby die if it was bumped by a car? Would a tree die? Would grass die? Would Santa die? Could baby Jesus die? What if you were bumped by a teeny-weeny car? What if you were bumped by a garbage truck? What if you were bumped by a school bus? What was die? Oh it was endless. At a certain point, usually halfway through the morning, Pagan would lose her temper and tell Maud: No more questions for at least an hour! And Maud, chastened, would play quietly for a few minutes, and then, transparently surreptitious, she would begin a new line of questioning.

The monsters danced across the set singing about the letter O. Pagan kissed her hair, which still smelled sweet from last night's bath.

She had come to feel that embarking on a pregnancy was like preparing for war. You were uncomfortable for months, your food was restricted, a simple misstep in the form of medication or exposure to something toxic could be disastrous, the whole outcome was unsure, there would definitely be pain, a thousand things could go wrong. Even if everything went right, after the baby was born there were months of exhaustion and anxiety, that heart-stopping fear every time she looked at the soft sleeping lump and waited for the tiny chest to rise and show evidence of breath. Just as it was all getting easier, the baby started walking, suddenly able to get into new and terrifying situations—and then the terrible twos set in. Planning to get pregnant was like setting out on a voyage from which one might return so changed or scarred by love that the familiar might never be the same again.

So why do it? Pagan couldn't quite explain, even to her sisters, how every cliché, like every ridiculous love song she'd ever heard, seemed suddenly, blazingly true. In the course of an ordinary day, she would look at Maud and feel an overwhelming joy in her presence: her soft perfection, her lovely smile. Pagan felt the abundance of such feeling was impossible to contain, as if her love, tinged with protectiveness and an awareness of passing time, was so extreme that her happiness crested over into something painful. Ordinary life seemed unbearably sweet.

TOMMY'S FOOTSTEPS SOUNDED on the kitchen floor above them as he made himself a cup of coffee. It was nice to have him in the house on a weekday. She couldn't think of the last time he'd taken a day off. After she had Maud, she couldn't bear to go back to working full time, and Tommy had been surprisingly amenable to her staying home. They sold their nice cars and bought a used Volvo. They spent little on child care. She still felt surprised that she had changed from being the woman who could persuade Tommy to take a long weekend in Napa, to becoming a cloth diaper, coupon-clipping sort of mother.

"Daddy home?"

"Yes, and you're going to Mrs. Dudley's for a little while."

"Why?"

"We're going to the doctor's."

"I go." Maud stuck out her lower lip.

"It will be boring for you, sweetie."

"I GO!" Maud flounced away from the sofa.

Pagan rolled her eyes and grabbed the remote. She clicked off the TV.

"Elmo!" Maud said.

"We'll see Elmo in a little while." Pagan rose slowly. "Isn't there an Elmo doll at Mrs. Dudley's?"

. . .

TOMMY LIFTED MAUD into her car seat. He was becoming thicker as he approached forty, his body starting to take the shape of a middle-aged man. She felt a rush of tenderness for him. Fatherhood had called out a patience that had not been necessary before. The largest of his brothers, she knew he had muscled his way through his youth, playing football and lacrosse, masking his intelligence with a certain obdurate force. His older brother, Mike, was the serious one. Kevin was wiry and wild. The children had taken up their allotted roles, and Tom was the defensive end; his intelligence revealed itself when he chose. Beneath Tommy's gravity something delicate in him turned, like one of those fragile holiday toys that revolves by the heat of a candle flame. He cajoled Maud into sitting still as he snapped her into her car seat. He was playful with her, better at deflecting her insistence than Pagan was. She waited in the car while he settled Maud with the babysitter, then they headed for the hospital.

"I wish we were doing something more fun than this," Pagan said.

"Maybe some night we could drop Maud at my sister's, go to a movie or something."

"Is work any better?"

"A little, but everyone's jumpy." He shook his head. "Sometimes I wonder if I'm in the right business."

Pagan felt shocked. "What else would you do?"

"Don't worry, I'm not quitting yet. But lately, everything seems like a house of cards."

Pagan liked him talking to her like this. She was often curious about what Tommy was thinking, not because she suspected he was keeping things from her, but because he was tired when he came home and didn't like to rehash the day. After the most recent correction, the market was bouncing like an electro-shocked eel. She knew his clients were nervous, work felt grim.

When they met, she worked in pension planning for a large department store. She had been a business major in college, choosing a practical route because she never wanted to be in the position that her mother had found herself in: broke, no easily marketable skills, and children to support. Pagan had always liked the clarity of numbers: she thought of them as comforting, a dispassionate way to figure the odds or measure possibilities. She found it reassuring that variables could be plotted and fig-ured: no messy problems of belief, no questionable lines between cause and effect.

THEY SAT IN the waiting room. She'd been told to drink a quart of liquid before the ultrasound, and her bladder was uncomfortably full. She didn't feel like chatting, and hoped she wouldn't run into anyone she knew. Before Maud, she had thought that being a mother would give her something in common with other women, but at times, it seemed just the opposite. Over the past few years, she had lost touch with certain friends because she found—even the ones who went back to work after they had children—that their thinking had become almost predigested. One college friend, a girl she used to drink beer with, became a fundamentalist Chris-tian and barely seemed to have an original thought. Another became obsessed with making her precocious children into gifted and talented types, and Pagan felt a distance spring up between them. She couldn't say to Karen, "Your kids have the intelligence of well-fed, upper-middle class people. Could you just be grateful instead of trying to make them Mozart and Pete Sampras rolled into one?" She leaned against Tommy and glanced down at the *Wall Street Journal.* It didn't hold her interest anymore.

When the nurse called her name, Tommy helped her up. The nurse led them down a hallway and into a small room with curtains around it.

Pagan didn't want to see the ultrasound. Her friends' gray and white pictures—the images half-formed, fishlike and floating—frightened her. She didn't like to picture the baby unfinished. She lay down on her back, and the nurse put cold, transparent gel on her stomach.

Once the ultrasound started, it was hard not to look. Pagan saw tiny vertebrae floating in the dark, all smoothly in place.

"How can the doctor avoid poking the baby with the needle?"

"We locate a pocket of fluid. That's what we're doing right now." The nurse looked at Pagan carefully, then turned back to the monitor.

When the doctor came in, Pagan closed her eyes in mock fear. "People told me not to look at the needle." She tried to joke, but her voice came out flat and humorless. Friends had warned her the anaesthesia was the worst part.

The doctor looked to be almost sixty. Even in the darkened room, the edge of a bright Hawaiian shirt was visible beneath his white coat. "They're right," he said. "But I want to look at the ultrasound first, so you have a minute or two." He looked down at his clipboard. "Pagan," he said, taking in her name. He seemed to reflect on something for a moment. "Is there anything you want to ask me before we start?" His voice was kind, and he looked at her directly.

"I don't think so. I just—"and she paused. "I had a miscarriage last winter and I'm nervous about this."

"I am very, very careful."

Pagan tried to smile.

He gazed at the screen, and asked the nurse for some measurements. He looked back and forth between the screen and his clipboard, making notes. "Very small." He looked at Pagan over his glasses. "This shows that you're actually a bit early to do this test."

Pagan felt stunned. "I'm sure of my dates," she said.

"And your last period was—"

She gave him the date.

He frowned.

"Well, the only problem is this: If we do it too early, the sample of fluid is young and it's hard to get the cells to reproduce." He looked at the monitor. "The worst thing that would happen is that we'd have to repeat the test."

"Whatever you think is best," Tommy said.

"I want to get this over with," Pagan said.

"All right," he nodded. "You look off to the side while we numb you up."

She clutched Tommy's hand and looked at the shadowed wall. A sharp sting seemed to go deep into her, and then the doctor said, "All done." She turned to look at Tommy who was somehow pale and flushed at the same time.

THE DOCTOR HAD suggested she stay in bed for the rest of the day. At home, Pagan sat in bed, propped among her pillows, listening to the clink of plates and Maud's squealing rise up from downstairs. Tommy must be letting her wash some dishes. They had a dishwasher, but Maud loved to stand on a chair and splash in the water, making bubbles with the dish soap. Pagan didn't usually have the patience for the mess she made. *Mommy, mommy, mommy,* Maud jabbered, and in her gleeful chant, Pagan remembered listening to her own mother sing while she washed dishes, singing a song about the moon. What was the song? Pagan lay still, trying to summon it. Blue Moon? Harvest Moon? That wasn't right. She hummed a little to herself. She had taught it to Maud. *I see the moon and the moon sees me, the moon sees somebody I want to see* . . . As her mother worked, her long hair fell forward, looping over her shoulders, hiding her cheeks. She would flick the suds from her hands at Pagan and Zeke, who giggled wildly, then reach back and gather up the loose strands, letting her hair fall down her back. How beautiful she was, how full of music.

Her mother played the harp, the piano, almost any instrument with strings. She moved through the world touching things, making them sound. Pagan remembered fragments from that early time, but it was hard to separate images of the sixties from what she truly remembered. From their names it was clear her mother had dabbled in women's groups and witchcraft, Sufi ceremonies and yoga, but after the death of their father, and Marco's abandonment, she had done what she said was necessary: she sold her instruments to pay the rent, cut her hair, put away her gauzy skirts and clogs. She had to find work.

Pagan sank down among the pillows. Her mother was practical, certainly she wasn't easily fooled. Pagan couldn't imagine anything terrible had happened. When she said it out loud, *"My mother has disappeared,"* the words sounded dramatic and far-fetched. There must be some obvious explanation. What did "out of the country" mean? Mexico? Canada? Europe? The real question was not where had she gone, but why she had left without telling any of them. Her mother wasn't the secretive type. That was Prana. For a moment, Pagan felt a flash of recognition, as if her mother might have inherited her daughter's mysteriousness. But that was backwards. How foolish. Of course not. Pagan wondered if her disappearance had something to do with the past, with her life before them, but it didn't seem like her mother to go off to India or trek into Tibet. The sixties was a phase, and her mother was young then, that was all.

f o u r

PRANA SHIFTED THE GROCERY BAG IN HER ARMS AND
unlocked the apartment door. Pushing it open, she held her
breath, as if he might appear before her. What was marvelous
about him, what she never truly got over, was his presence in
her own surroundings. He belonged, in a very real sense, to the
public world, and yet he had chosen her. It wasn't that he was
powerful, so much as he was known, connected to people in far-
away places because of his work and reputation.

Whenever she came back to her apartment, she felt the gap
between the outer world and her inner life. To the outer world,
she had a fashionable job; her work consisted of finding objects
that would please others, creating the impression of a luxuriously
arranged life. She sometimes told people that she shopped for a

living, a comment designed for a laugh, but unfortunately, it was true. Of course, the central product was prescribed—plates, towels, glassware—so she had to find the right props to surround whatever was for sale. For her most regular job, a series of cookbooks, it was up to her to find serving dishes and cutting boards, ceramics, place mats, candlesticks, and silverware—the accoutrements of familial life.

Her apartment was a place of contemplation. The walls were white; the charcoal-colored leather armchair and sofa were deep and comfortable, but did not draw attention to themselves, except that one might note their quality. There were no knickknacks. When she found a photo or an object she admired, she set it on an empty table where it occupied a place of prominence. Her apartment was filled with little altars—objects or pictures that reflected what was inexpressible. She chose to worship something she could not say aloud. She didn't know how to define it, or could define it only by a lack: a lack of falseness, a lack of commercialism, the absence of clutter. She had recently purchased a hand-blown glass vessel, spun with turquoise and dark purple, a few strands of honey-colored amber swirling through the bruised colors. Slightly asymmetrical, pleasing to look at, it would occupy a place of honor on her table until she set it aside in favor of something else.

Her real life was here, with him, in private, and the dichotomy between her outer life, so visual and apparent, and her true, hidden life disturbed her. For him, her apartment, her very being, was sacred, a place of renewal and reflection. She knew this, and thrived in it, although she sometimes felt the burden of being adored.

•   •   •

SHE TOLD HERSELF not to depend on his arrival, international flights were often delayed, but she had bought a good bottle of wine. She carried her bag to the counter, put the wine in the rack, food in the refrigerator, then sat down for a moment. What would she make tonight? At the market, she had debated between chicken and linguine, then bought the makings for both. She would prepare something simple, in case his flight was late. He was flying out of Brussels, into New York and then down to Washington. She wanted to call the airline, to check on his flight. Instead, she touched the edge of the vessel, her finger tracing the undulant line of the rim.

They had once spent a few days in Bruges when he was on assignment in Belgium. In January, Brussels was damp and foggy, but she felt warm beneath her coat, as if lit from within. They had stayed in an old-fashioned, elegant hotel, their first night alone in several weeks, and she still remembered the timelessness of the night, how they made love and slept, made love and slept, as if they were making their own rhythm beyond the world around them. The following morning, breakfast in the ornate dining room was surprising and lush, and the sheer variety of foods and different tastes on her tongue seemed an extension of the night.

Their hotel was at the edge of the business district, not far from the train station, and after breakfast they walked through a wispy fog to take the train to Bruges. As the train clacked out of the city into the countryside, it felt as if they were moving back in time: rocking past signs in Flemish, the unfamiliar combinations of consonants magical and strange, materializing and disappearing in the pearly air. She was traveling with him, they were together. This was her life.

• • •

THEY HAD MET when she was dating a self-important young man named Damien. She had only been out with him a few times, but she quickly saw that his bravado was a facade, and she was not interested in what lay behind the persona he was aiming for. Damien taught painting at the Corcoran and had intrigued her at first, but she quickly understood he was pretentious rather than intelligent. When he introduced her to people, he jokingly referred to her youth as if it were a condition to be ashamed of, although he wasn't so old himself, perhaps twenty-eight or twenty-nine. He had introduced her to Stephan at a reception. There was a tone of reverence and gravity to the evening; the exhibit was a tribute to photographers who had died during the Vietnam War.

Stephan stood out to her immediately as interesting. He was neither tall nor short, but solid, as if he might have once been a wrestler, but had stopped working out, so a familial thickness had settled around him. His face was round, the planes of his cheeks broad. Later, he would tell her that he looked like his mother, who was Dutch and had emigrated to the United States as a young woman. Stephan's light curly hair was beginning to turn gray, but his curls were messy, springy and fine, and seemed to have a life of their own, at odds with the lines around his eyes. When he smiled, deep creases ran down onto his cheekbones, which made it all the more startling when his face settled into reflection, and she could see his eyes: clear and deep brown, tired, as if he had seen more than he wanted to. He looked as if he'd spent years in the sun and rain, waiting and watching.

He had about him the aura of fame, which is to say that he didn't need to move outside himself for attention, to explain to Prana, or anyone else, who he was. She noticed later, as she pretended not to watch him from around the room, that a number of people came up to him and thanked him for coming. In the way he would casually put an arm across their backs, lean toward them to say something in confidence, she recognized they shared a certain history and recognized each other as valuable.

When he was out of earshot, she asked who he was, and Damien explained that Stephan was a photographer, a photo-journalist really. He had worked for *Time* and *Life,* had taken pictures all over the world. His images were famous. She would recognize them, he said. Stephan freelanced now, and did a lot of work for *National Geographic,* which was based in Washington, D.C. Her glimpse of him spoiled Damien for her, who would have been spoiled anyway, and when they left, she told him she was tired and would like to go home.

SHE RAN INTO Stephan at a reception at the Washington Project for the Arts a few months later. She was there with a woman from school, part of an assignment for their beginning photography class. When her friend went off to flirt with someone, Prana got a glass of wine and began to look at the work, a group show. Her assignment was to write a review, but she didn't know where to begin. In any discussion of aesthetics, she felt as if she were floating, as if she'd walked into a conversation she wasn't old enough to understand. She was filled with a sense of things, but didn't know how to articulate her ideas.

It was surprising to see Stephan at WPA that night. The crowd was mostly younger artists, skinny types wearing black clothes and metal accessories. Stephan seemed large and distant, out of place, as if he'd dressed in clothes for another season. He strolled through the room, looking at the pictures, barely pausing in front of anything. She was standing in front of a picture, pretending to study it, when he came to stand beside her.

"So what do you think?" he asked.

"I think they're mostly bad."

He didn't say anything for a moment, and she felt frightened that she had offended him.

"You're right." He sounded reflective, slightly surprised, as if recognizing a kind of intelligence most people didn't see. "Why?" His question was a test.

She was quiet, not wanting to fumble out loud. She looked at the photo in front of her: half-naked store mannequins haphazardly arranged in odd, supposedly erotic poses. The picture was harshly lit against a red background.

"I don't know how to talk about things," she faltered.

He waited, and she knew that admitting ignorance was not enough. If she could not rise to this, she would lose him. He would not be charmed by her youth.

"It's contrived," Prana said. "Someone arranged all this to make a point, instead of finding something in the world and actually seeing it."

He nodded. "So you're a student at the university?"

"Just starting," she said.

"Well, I suppose I'll see you in the fall. I'm supposed to come and give a talk to Carter's class," he said it casually, but she felt herself seize this detail, as if it were something to hold onto.

PRANA ROSE OUT of her chair to get ready. She took out her softest pair of cotton sheets, almond, cool, and clean. In late afternoon, the sunlight fell into her small bedroom, small world.

She loved the autumn sun, how warmly it pooled in her room. She changed the sheets, smoothed the comforter, decided to shower before doing anything else.

She liked hot water, never hurried in the shower. It took time to wash her long hair, and she gave herself over to it. The ritual of shaving her legs, making herself smooth, was something she enjoyed. She could never understand why some people had radios in their showers. She liked the buffer of sound, the beat of water on ceramic, plenitude and warmth. News, even music, would seem intrusive. She ran the razor around the curve of her leg, behind her calf, taking her time.

OUT OF THE shower, wrapped in a towel, she wandered into her room to decide what to wear. She hadn't seen him in more than a month. She wanted to wear a piece of clothing with sentimental importance, although she knew this was foolish. He liked her in anything. She chose a white shirt, a pair of jeans. She knew, without vanity, that her beauty didn't require special clothes. People still told her, all the time, that she should model, but she had never been interested. She felt that, if she allowed herself to be photographed, she would be reduced by the lens and silenced. Her power was that she made her own silence. People waited to hear what she would say. To put her silence in someone else's hands was impossible.

FROM THE BEGINNING, he came to see Prana on his departures and returns, giving his wife a date earlier or later so he and Prana would have time, even a night together, on the incoming or outgoing leg of his trips. Apparently his wife never suspected because, for the outgoing part, it was too much trouble to pack up three kids to take him out to Dulles, and his incoming international flights were so often delayed that it simply wasn't practical to try to meet him.

Prana moved to the kitchen and looked at the clock. She wanted to prepare dinner, but knew from experience, almost nine years now, from having prepared and thrown out so many meals, that starting dinner would not be a good idea. She put the kettle on to boil. She wanted to tell Stephan about her mother, whose disappearance was definitely odd, but not worrisome. She felt the weightlessness of it all. He had never met her mother, or anyone in her family. He knew the names of her sisters, what they did for their livings, and a fair amount about their lives. She had never met anyone in his family, but knew the names of his children, their ages, his worries for them, and his pride. She rarely asked about his wife, because he loved her.

His wife had gravitated toward the children since he was away from home so much. It was natural, he said. He had told Prana, any number of times, that his wife was a wonderful mother, and Prana knew he meant this as high praise, not as if mothering were simple. His older daughter was seventeen, wanting to be on her own. His son, at fourteen, was a mystery to him. His younger daughter had cerebral palsy, not too severely, but enough to complicate the already difficult task of guiding a child through the world. Prana had never seen him with his children, but she had seen pictures of them. She wanted to. Walking to her bookcase, she decided to pick out something to read while she was waiting. Some books she read completely, over and over, others she read parts of, vowed to finish, and never did. The light flashed on her phone machine.

He must have called while she was in the shower. She heard

his voice, crackling from Kennedy airport, saying something about his wife and daughter, how they'd made arrangements to meet him, something about looking at colleges. Inside, she went gray and hollow; he hadn't bothered to call her cell phone. He had left a message here, so he wouldn't have to listen to her forlorn protests.

five

ZEKE SWUNG INTO MARCIE'S DRIVEWAY AND RAN INTO THE house. The hallway and kitchen were empty. She hurried into the living room where Amy lay with her head in Marcie's lap, sucking her thumb. Marcie had a narrow belt pulled tight around the top of her forearm, and a towel pressed against her wrist. Her cheeks were flushed beneath her dark hair.

"Eleanor, get your coat, and Amy's too. Let's go!" Zeke said.

"We're not going to Saint Jo's," Marcie said.

"What?"

Marcie looked up, her gray eyes bleary, but intent. Zeke recognized her expression: an insistence that made no sense, like dream logic.

"Eleanor, take Amy out to the car," Marcie said.

"Mom," Eleanor started to cry. "We have to go to the closest place!"

"Shut up!" Marcie yelled. "Do what I say!"

"Be quiet, Marcie." Zeke's voice was firm. She looked over at Eleanor, whose face was crumpled with tears. Her stance made Zeke think of a toddler's helpless grief, and this somehow upset her more than Marcie on the couch with her towel. Zeke felt a pounding in her head. She moved toward Marcie and lifted Amy from her lap. "Let's see this."

Slowly, Zeke pulled the towel from Marcie's wrist. Blood had soaked through the thick cotton, and Zeke examined the scrape on the inside of her arm, the short deep gash above her wrist. Marcie was so slender, there wasn't much cushion. She must have twisted her arm as it went through the door, because the cut was toward the bone at the top of her arm, rather than the soft underside of her forearm. Zeke bent closer and, pulling lightly on the skin above the cut, saw the dull white of bone. She let go. Dried blood smeared underside of Marcie's forearm. She felt Eleanor hovering behind her.

"You're damn lucky you didn't cut the tendon," Zeke said.

Marcie tipped her chin at Eleanor, indicating that she wanted to say something out of the girls' hearing. When the girls walked out the door, Marcie stood up, slightly unsteady.

"We can't go to where I work," Marcie said. "We'll go to Mount Kisco."

Marcie struggled with her coat while trying to keep the towel against her wrist. She held the towel as if it were the sleeve of a sweater—trying to keep it from bunching up beneath her coat sleeve, but the towel was too large and Marcie spun in a circle as if this would squeeze the towel under her coat. It would have been funny if it weren't so absurd. As Marcie turned around the room, Zeke suddenly understood: Marcie couldn't show up drunk in her own emergency room.

"Listen to me," Marcie said. "You were here when this happened."

"What?"

Marcie dropped her coat on the floor, wrapped the towel awkwardly around her wrist, and walked towards the front door.

"What the hell are you talking about?" Zeke followed her.

Marcie turned. Her eyes were bloodshot. She smelled like wine. "If a mother is drinking, while taking care of her kids..." and her chin started to tremble. "They report it to Social Services, Zeke. It's a thing we do."

"Can you brush your teeth without bleeding to death?" Zeke asked.

"Zeke, please," Marcie said. "This will never happen again. I promise."

"I can smell you from here," Zeke said. Marcie flinched. "Brush your teeth and comb your hair. I'll be in the car with the girls." Zeke went out to the car, and snapped Amy into her seat belt.

"Is Mommy okay?" Amy asked. Her hair was standing up in odd places like a warped filament halo.

"She's going to be fine," Zeke said. "They'll put some stitches in her wrist, and it will heal up like new."

Amy seemed satisfied. Zeke reached over and cupped her hand against the curve of Eleanor's cheek. "It's going to be okay, Ellie," Zeke said quietly.

Marcie got into the car, arm in the air, and Zeke felt calmer once she pulled out of the driveway. It would take twenty, maybe twenty-five minutes to get to Mount Kisco. She wanted to yell at Marcie, ask her what the hell she'd been thinking, but the girls' presence stopped her. The night was dark, moonless, and Zeke had the odd sense that she'd been driving from one unsureness to another all day.

She turned up the Saw Mill River Parkway. She was angry with herself. It had taken her too long to realize Marcie drank. In the exciting, early part of their romance, everything seemed worth celebrating. They were incredible in bed, each of them leaving work at lunchtime and going back to Marcie's while the girls were at school. In the beginning, Marcie must have been on good behavior. But as the weeks passed, Zeke did notice that whenever they went out together, Marcie and the girls would pile into Zeke's car so Zeke would be the driver. Even a mellow outing called for a beer or two at lunch or a glass of wine. No one in Zeke's family was really a drinker, so it didn't seem to matter at first. Marcie simply seemed careful about not drinking and driving.

"You won't believe what happened today," Zeke said to Marcie in a low voice. "My mother disappeared."

"What?"

"She sent me an e-mail saying she was leaving the country for a while."

"Wow." Marcie sounded reverent and surprised.

"Why did she leave the country?" Eleanor asked from the back.

Zeke sighed. She changed her voice, tried to sound brighter.

"I don't know. I guess she wanted to take a trip."

Zeke wished they could remain in this warm, suspended space, moving through the dark. They passed the railroad station and climbed the hill above Shady Grove. Between the pines, the lights of the town pierced the dark. The parkway was empty. She didn't want to expose them to the hospital's light. Amy was quiet, starting to doze. Eleanor hiccuped softly in back.

When Zeke turned into the hospital parking lot, Marcie turned to the girls.

"If you tell them I was drinking, they'll take you away from me. Do you understand?"

Zeke felt as if she'd swallowed an entire glass of freezing water. "Marcie, stop!"

"I was taking out the trash. It was an accident. Got it?"

Eleanor was silent. Amy was asleep.

"Ellie," and Marcie's voice softened. "This is not a big deal. It could happen to anyone, okay?"

Zeke felt light and hollow. She picked up Amy, resting her on her shoulder like a baby. Inside, it was bright. The emergency room was empty, except for them.

AFTER MARCIE WAS stitched up, a nurse came into the waiting room and said the doctor wanted to talk to Zeke.

"Keep an eye on Amy, okay?"

"I want to go home." Eleanor's voice was angry and petulant. She held a torn *Highlights* magazine in her lap, while Amy leaned against her, looking at the pictures.

"I know," Zeke said. "I do too."

The doctor was youngish, perhaps in his early thirties, with thinning hair. Zeke felt a pounding in her chest.

"I understand this was an accident." He was holding a clipboard and glanced up at Zeke.

"Yes," Zeke said. She looked him in the eye.

The doctor made a mark on this paper, and looked over at Marcie. "Your friend was with you at the time of the accident?"

"Yes," Marcie said.

He studied Zeke for a moment. "You're fine to drive?"

"Absolutely," Zeke said.

When they got back to Marcie's, Zeke felt as if the day, stretched beyond its allotted hours, had suddenly snapped, like a rubber band pulled too tight. She wanted to sit down, put her feet up, not talk to anyone. Instead she told Marcie, "Sit still. I'll take care of the girls."

Amy had fallen asleep again on the way home. Zeke carried her to her room and laid her on the bed. Her wide mouth and high cheekbones resembled Marcie's, but Amy's cheekbones were softened with a child's flesh. She had what Zeke imagined to be her father's temperament. Even-tempered, she followed Eleanor's lead. Zeke unsnapped Amy's pants, reached for her cuffs and tugged at her pants from the bottom. Amy muttered something unintelligible, then rolled over. Zeke looked in her dresser for a clean nightgown, but couldn't find one. She sighed and figured that Amy might as well sleep in her T-shirt. Zeke knew it didn't really matter what she slept in, but the neatly painted dresser without clean clothes in it depressed her.

Eleanor changed without being asked. Zeke heard her brushing her teeth in the bathroom. She was so well behaved, perhaps too much so, afraid of setting Marcie off. Zeke went into Eleanor's room, decorated with unicorns and wallpaper clouds, to kiss her good night.

"Will you stay here tonight?"

"Yes, of course," Zeke said.

"Zeke?" Eleanor looked up. Her gray eyes were tinged blue, a shade darker than Marcie's. "You know how some kids have cell phones?"

"Yeah?"

"I wish I had one."

Eleanor had the covers pulled up to her chin. Zeke started to say how ridiculous it was for a ten-year-old to have a cell phone, then realized what Eleanor was asking.

"You can always get ahold of me, Ellie."

"What if you're out riding?"

Zeke sat down on the edge of her bed. The smell of stale sweat wafted up; the sheets needed to be washed. Zeke felt suddenly furious with Marcie, who kept up appearances at the expense of everything else. She thought for a moment, took a deep breath, but didn't want to get Eleanor out of bed and upset her. "Even if I'm out on the trails, I have to ride back in."

Eleanor nodded, her eyes filling. Zeke brushed the hair from her eyes.

"Look, I'm going to talk to your mother. Things will be better from now on, okay?" Zeke bent down and kissed her forehead, smoothing her hair back from her face.

She went into the living room where Marcie lay on the couch, staring into space. Zeke stood over Marcie and spoke quietly so the girls wouldn't hear.

"They know they can't depend on you."

Marcie looked startled, as if she'd been slapped.

"What if one of them got hurt and you were too drunk to drive to the hospital?"

Marcie's face crumpled into an expression of acute grief. She started to cry, almost silently, gasping for breath. Zeke stood above her.

"Zeke, I'll stop. I promise." Marcie pulled herself upright and reached for a box of tissues. "I know what I need to do. Stay here tonight, okay?"

Zeke felt as if she were looking at her through the wrong end of a telescope. Marcie seemed small and unbeautiful, her features distorted by tears.

"I'm serious. I'll stop. Please just be with me," Marcie said.

Zeke moved to the couch and held her, hoping the worst was over.

s i x

THE SUMMER AFTER HER FRESHMAN YEAR AT COLLEGE, PRANA
had her mother to herself. Zeke had stayed at school in Santa
Barbara to take an oceanography class; Pagan was working in
Manhattan and had her own apartment outside the city, but
Prana had returned home, discouraged by her freshman year,
unsettled by meeting Stephan. She wanted to tell her mother
about him, but what would she say? I met a man who's astounding? Who barely knows I exist? She had looked up his work, and
he had been everywhere: Beirut, Pakistan, Belfast, South America,
El Salvador, and Nicaragua. His photos had appeared in *Time*
and *Life* during the Vietnam War. The wartime photos, mostly
black-and-white, captured people in extremity: a boy howling
over the body of his mother whose hands had been hacked off; a

girl picking through the rubble of a house, reaching for a broken bucket; a woman lapping water from a rut in the mud. Each image implied a story she could barely stand to know.

The pictures of stillness were a different kind of story: a portrait of Robert MacNamara, his thinning hair combed back in wet, even furrows. He gazed at the camera as if seeing beyond it, the weight of judgment in his eyes. And then there was a shift, and the later pictures were all in color, reproduced in *Smithsonian* or *National Geographic:* a Norwegian fishing village, the Blasket Islands, Berlin when the wall came down, lighthouses in Nova Scotia, an air show in Wisconsin where people flew homemade planes. The pictures were bright and billowing, movement caught at its apex, rather than its aftermath. It was as if the black-and-white wartime images were taken not by someone else, but by a different self.

Her mother was waiting for her at the train station in Shady Grove. Her hair was loose down her back, and she looked pleased and relaxed, as if Prana's arrival signaled the start of a vacation. Her mother had retained a youthful slenderness, but she disdained what she called "women wearing kid clothes" to show off their figures. She wore a pair of linen pants, a white shirt open at the throat, a slim gold bangle on her wrist.

Prana hadn't seen her mother since Christmas, and was relieved to see that she looked just the same. After Christmas break, a number of girls on her floor had mentioned that, after being away for just a few months, they could see their parents aging. Prana didn't like to imagine this; she thought of her mother as immutable. Partly it was her mother's voice, which was measured and calm. She had a cultivated cheerfulness, hewn from difficulty. She moved toward Prana and hugged her.

"Well, you did pack light!" Her mother picked up one of her bags. "You got the apartment?"

"Starting September first, but Miranda let me put my stuff there. It wasn't much really—winter clothes and books."

"That was nice of her. Where's she moving to?"

"Albuquerque."

They walked across the parking lot. The circular garden outside the train station was bright with azaleas. Beyond the shaded lot, a row of stores lined Greeley Avenue. Prana had once asked her mother how they came to live in Shady Grove, and her mother said she wanted to move to a place where the unexpected seemed less likely to take hold of her. The towns in this alcove of the Hudson River Valley—Tarrytown, Briarcliff, Pleasantville, and Shady Grove—bore the conservative stamp of New England with a bright touch of money from the city. From the highest point in Shady Grove, you could look west and see Sing Sing Prison and Maryknoll Seminary. The Hudson was a bright sliver in the distance.

Prana hitched the strap of her bag up onto her shoulder and pulled her suitcase behind her.

"We really should have looked into buying a condo down there," her mother said. "But you didn't give me much notice about moving out of the dorm."

"I know." Prana smiled apologetically. "But who knows how long I'll really be there." She sensed her mother looking at her, registering her discouragement, but her mother let the comment go.

They set her bags in the trunk of the car, an old Mercedes painted a color between cream and yellow. Prana called it The Creampuff. Her mother had always chafed at the fact that it was necessary for a realtor to drive an expensive car. The fact that the Mercedes was older, classic, was her mother's small rebellion.

At the end of May, it was already warm. The trees and lawns were green, but hadn't reached the fullness of summer. Prana remembered being little, feeling there was a certain time in August when everything became greener, as if the trees had grown more leaves overnight.

"Do you need anything from town?"

"I'm fine," Prana said, and settled back in the car. Sitting in this enclosed space, driving along the wooded roads, Prana realized how much she was looking forward to this time alone with her mother. When Pagan was around, she required a lot of attention, not necessarily in a bad way, but she was intense, often irate about some situation that couldn't be helped. Zeke was either clowning or taciturn, and her arrivals and departures were accompanied by flurries of activity that involved the entire household. She would show up at the house with a ferret or a litter of kittens or three friends who needed to be fed and put up for the night. She breezed in from the stable, the pool, the ocean, then disappeared out the door. Prana and her mother moved in a quieter rhythm.

Inside the house, the windows filled with the gray tint of evening light; the trees gave a sense of shelter. Living in a dormitory hadn't suited her. The other freshman girls seemed frenetic and silly, thriving on one another's petty dramas. They swirled around her like midges. Prana's preoccupations—her classes, what to major in, why she felt so unmoored—these topics didn't seem to enter their conversations at all. The girls chattered about boys and changed their clothes; they touched up their makeup before dinner.

"Are you hungry?" Her mother asked. "I put together something light. I didn't know what you'd feel like."

"Anything would be great," Prana said. "I'll put my stuff in my room."

She carried her bags upstairs, then hesitated on the landing. There was a framed photograph she'd never seen before: Pagan pushing her in a stroller. Tiny, slumped a bit sideways, Prana didn't look like herself; she could have been any pudgy baby. Pagan's thick curls were instantly recognizable, and she was grinning broadly, both her front teeth missing. Her dress, with a large strawberry pattern, seemed familiar; Prana must have worn it herself.

Until she was five or six years old, she believed that her father was the same as Pagan and Zeke's. The knowledge that this was not true had seeped into her consciousness slowly; she couldn't accept all that it implied. When she finally understood that Marco was her father, that Pagan and Zeke had their own father, she somehow got the idea that she slept in a separate bedroom because she had a different father. As she grew older, the knowledge that Pagan and Zeke's father had died, while Marco lived in the city and saw her once or twice a year, was like a private chasm between her and her sisters that only Prana seemed to notice. Her isolation felt large because it didn't seem to matter to the others. By the time she understood her thinking was wrong, she also knew it was foolish, and it didn't seem like the sort of thing she should confess.

As they grew older, Pagan started demanding a new room arrangement. She didn't want to share with Zeke, who was supposed to leave her equipment in the basement, but whose saddle, boots, hardhat, crops, and other horsey implements all ended up in their bedroom in spite of Pagan's protests. Finally, Prana and Zeke switched. Zeke moved into the small bedroom, and Prana moved into the larger room with Pagan. Prana liked the new arrangement, which seemed to consolidate her position. When Pagan went off to college, Prana had the room to herself, although she had left their shared belongings in place.

Prana pushed open the door. It had only been a year since she lived here, but it felt longer. One of their posters had come loose from its thumbtack in the wall, and a corner curled in the darkness. The posters were idyllic images of waterfalls and forests with poems and quotations printed on the landscape. In middle school, Prana thought they were cool, but now they seemed childish, although they were exactly the kind of thing that girls at college bought for their dorm rooms. A black-and-white poster of James Taylor and Carly Simon hung behind the door. She had been privately thrilled when Pagan confessed that she thought James Taylor was cute.

Prana set her bags down next to a shelf filled with books and records. All their childhood books were here: *Harriet the Spy, The Hobbit, A Wrinkle in Time, The Little House on the Prairie* books. Pagan had cried when Mary went blind. They didn't argue over books, but they had bickered over records. Pagan had played that *Boston* record over and over. Prana smiled to herself. Pagan had seemed so grown up. After she got her driver's license, she would drive them up to Caldor's to look at records. Prana had loved speeding up the parkway in the summer air.

When she came downstairs, her mother was setting out a light supper in the living room: French bread, roasted peppers, Greek olives and Camembert, a large green salad. She poured sparkling water into wineglasses. Her mother didn't usually drink, claiming it made her sleepy and maudlin. She speared a piece of pepper and laid it on bread.

"I listed a house for the Coppersmiths today. Do you remember them?"

Prana felt a spike of envy, her thoughts tugged in a direction she didn't want to go. "I think The Amazing Emily was a grade ahead of Zeke."

"Yes, Carolyn does go on and on about her." Her mother's mouth puckered as she mimicked Carolyn Coppersmith. "Emily can't decide whether to study at the Sorbonne, or to go to a special program in Japan where her Japanese will become really fluent. She's been offered an internship with the new minister of culture." Her mother rolled her eyes at the Coppersmith's well-rehearsed quandary.

Prana picked up a small knife and cut a wedge of cheese. She was intimidated by the combination of talent and ambition so apparent in her peers. Shady Grove was a town of achievers, and the precocious children of those achievers, so her dilemma about what to major in at college was diminished by those with more lofty ambitions. It seemed that certain people were blessed, superior beings. Emily Coppersmith was one of the anointed.

"What's wrong?" Her mother asked.

Prana split open an olive with her thumbnail, carefully removing the pit. "I feel like I've wasted a year of school. I don't know what I should *do*. I can't draw. I'm not interested in ceramics or painting. Sometimes I wonder if I like photography because it doesn't require me to actually *make* something." She broke off a piece of bread and pulled out the soft inside. "I have this friend, Jesse. He was in my photography class. He actually sees things differently. He sees things I don't see." She was quiet for a moment, thinking of how Jesse noticed odd juxtapositions, the irony in found objects.

"But it's like anything—" her mother's voice was soft and encouraging. "Your eye can be trained, certain kinds of seeing are learned."

Prana made a face.

"It's true. It's like music." Her mother leaned forward in her chair to emphasize her point. "All those parents who brag about their kids having perfect pitch—it's not something they're born with, it's something they learn. Besides, you have time to decide what you're interested in."

"I feel weird about spending money on tuition when I don't know what I want to do."

"Don't. Really, most people figure out what they want to do like pinball."

"What?"

Her mother smiled. "You know—you bump into one thing, you don't like it, you bounce off it, you bump into something else, you don't like that, you do something else."

"That's crazy," Prana said. "Besides, if you know how it all works, why didn't you go?" With the words out of her mouth, she felt stupid. She knew the answer.

Her mother looked at her for a long moment, as if deciding whether to be annoyed or not. "My parents said they'd pay for school if I stayed in Ohio, but there was no way I was going to Kent State, so I moved out to Eugene and started taking classes. But then I met Pagan and Zeke's father, and neither of us had any money. We figured, especially after I got pregnant with Pagan, that we'd go to school one at a time. He'd get his degree first, and then I could go back when Pagan and Zeke started school."

"Did you mind putting it off?"

"Not really. Most of our friends were taking classes, and all of them worked, so I *felt* like I was in college. It wasn't like here where people go to an Ivy League school and push through in four years."

Prana felt foolish for having raised the subject. Anyone else would have said: *How would I go back to school when I had the three of you to feed?*

SHE GOT A summer job at a department store in the Mount Kisco mall. She worked as a sales clerk, suggesting clothes combinations, gently encouraging the women, all of whom could afford it, to indulge their taste for summer whites, or espadrilles, or whatever the store was pushing that week. It was pleasant enough work, air-conditioned and quiet, and as she placed clothes out on the racks, she thought of her work as a kind of penance, earning money to compensate for her indecision about school.

Pagan and Zeke had always been clear about what they wanted. Pagan had been a business major, and she had breezed through statistics, micro-economics and macro. Prana remembered her coming home for the holidays, and thinking *macro* sounded cool, tossed from Pagan's lips with such authority. Zeke's direction was a foregone conclusion: she would do something outside, something with animals, and she had gone off to the University of California at Santa Barbara to study pre-veterinary science and then oceanography. She had trained horses at a stable in Goleta while she was in college, and in almost any picture of her taken during those years, she was wearing the same gray UCSB sweatshirt and jeans, her hair streaked by sun. She looked happy. Thinking of her sisters, Prana wished for an obvious predisposition. She had the energy for something, but no clear direction.

In the long summer evenings, Prana worked for the local summer theater. She wasn't interested in acting, but she helped build sets and paint them, found or borrowed props. The cast and crew were mostly college students home for the summer. Each year a few students from SUNY Purchase or Yale Drama School came down to audition. For Prana, and those who had grown up in Shady Grove, it was a way of being in their home town that didn't feel childlike. The play that summer was *Two Gentlemen of Verona* done in a modern setting.

At night, after rehearsals, the cast and crew drifted into the parking lot to discuss their evening plans. Occasionally, there would be a gathering at someone's house, but most often the college-age students split up into groups, the formation of which depended on whether a person liked to drink beer or smoke pot or both. Most people went off to Mullane's, the unofficial town pub. When they had more money in their pockets, they sometimes went to the bar at a local restaurant, The Fishmarket. Prana liked mingling with grownups in the air-conditioned dark, the air thick with the scent of steamers and melting butter. Most often, she went with a few friends to a marsh preserve outside of town. They called it Yellow Brick Road, or YBR, a boarded walkway raised above the marsh on stilts. At the end, there was a deck with benches, intended for bird watching, and other wholesome pursuits, but Prana had never been there in daylight. At night, in the quiet, they could smoke pot and talk. Her friend that summer was Clark, the musical director, who was in love with James, who was impossibly straight, so of course it was hopeless, impassioned, and thick. They sat out at YBR under the stars. James rolled, because he was best at it. They were adrift in a small circle of desire. Clark passed her a joint, and she took a long hit, then passed it to James, holding and holding her breath. The night stars flanged around her as if they could talk. It was like that movie, what was it? Where the stars talked? *It's a Wonderful Life.* She didn't like the movie, something about it irked her—except that scene by the telephone, where Jimmy Stewart was falling in love. The woman's face was beautifully lit. He had stayed. Anyone else would have left. Prana looked up. The stars were thick. There was no moon yet. She would like to take a picture of this place at night, but she'd have to wait for a full moon. The deck had a phosphorescent glow, as if the path were raised up out of nowhere, floating above a watery darkness thick with life. She leaned back and closed her eyes. She was biding her time, waiting to go back to Washington. She would see Stephan at least once. He would come and speak to her class. It seemed such a slight thing to hope for.

THE SUMMER FLOATED along, and Prana felt as if she moved between different worlds that didn't intersect except for her transit through them. She worked at the department store during the day, went to rehearsals at night, partied afterward. She saw her mother in the mornings, before they went off to work. Sometimes, if Prana woke late, her mother would be out in what she called her garden. Prana called it an interrupted lawn. Behind the house, her mother had planted clumps of prairie grasses, some of which had thrived and spread. A line of tall, heavy-headed grasses rippled up to the trees. In front of the house, in more neatly tended beds, she had planted snapdragons, marigolds, hyacinths, and irises, and the flowers bloomed in bright profusion.

In the evenings, her mother was sometimes still showing houses or writing contracts. Prana didn't like coming home to an empty house. One afternoon, on her way home from work, she stopped at the library for a novel, or something absorbing, for the nights her mother was out. But once inside, instead of browsing in fiction, she looked up "Photojournalism, Vietnam. The Saigon Four." Had Stephan known them? Skimming through a collection of photos, she found what she was looking for: a picture of part of the American press corps. Although he must have been fifty pounds thinner, Stephan was unmistakable. His cheeks were grimy, his curly hair in disarray, and he was half-turning, his expression urgent, his mouth open, shouting. He looked almost mean, intrepid. His eyes kept people out.

ONE SUNDAY IN June, Prana woke late. Her throat was dry, her head ached. After rehearsal, after YBR, they had gone to Mullane's. She stretched her arms above her head, and tried to reconstruct the end of the night. James had said he was going swimming in a neighbor's pool; he tried to persuade her to come. Even foggy headed, Prana thought this sounded like a recipe for the police. She sat up slowly, wanting tea or something fizzy to drink. When she went downstairs, her mother was already up, reading the business section of the *New York Times*. A familiar record, Chopin etudes, was playing on the stereo. Prana sat down on the couch and reached for the local newspaper, not feeling ambitious enough for the *Times*. The paper sounded loud as she pressed open the fold, and when she finally got it open, she saw it was Father's Day. Her mouth felt unbearably dry. She never sent Marco a card, it would be ridiculous. Prana sat up. The specter of Marco's failure rested on her shoulder, but she pushed it aside.

"Hey, look at this," Prana said. "Next weekend there's a big festival up in Croton Point Park."

"It's probably the Great Hudson River Revival," her mother said. "Pete Seeger and that crowd. They do it every year."

"Didn't you take us to that once? When we were younger?"

"I did." Her mother set down the paper; she seemed pleased that Prana remembered. "But you must have been really little. It was years ago."

Prana scanned the ad, looking at the list of musicians. "I'm supposed to be taking pictures this summer. Why don't we go? It's two days long, but we could go for just one. Do you have an open house next weekend?"

Her mother looked up, as if considering an invisible calendar. "No," she said.

"Let's then," Prana said. "On Sunday. You can take care of whatever business you need to do on Saturday, and then just tell people you won't be available on Sunday."

"People don't like to hear that a realtor isn't available on a weekend."

"Tough shit."

Her mother laughed.

Prana felt lightened, even with her head so fuzzy. As a child, she remembered her mother being subject to the whims of impatient buyers and sellers, but over the years, partly because she'd worked so hard, partly because her deference had paid off, she'd been very successful. She took more time for herself now, although Prana knew it sometimes cost her money. She remembered a few occasions as a child when her mother couldn't make it to a class play or school event because clients insisted on seeing a house on short notice. They flew in from Aspen or Antigua, and if they wanted to buy a quarter million dollar home, well, what could her mother do? As her mother got older, more financially stable and less desperate, it seemed she kept her clients on a shorter leash, and didn't let herself be pushed around in quite the same way.

THE FOLLOWING SUNDAY, the weather was clear and hot. The air shimmered along the road, and cicadas buzzed in the grass. When they got out to Croton Point, late in the morning, a huge stretch of land was already filled with lines of neatly parked cars.

Prana felt self-conscious with a camera around her neck, carrying extra film in a small pack. A woman with a Snugli, a sleeping child against her chest, was sitting at a card table outside the entrance. She took their admission fees, and Prana and her mother walked in.

The vast field was lined with small tents, canopied booths and stands. There were tables devoted to environmental concerns: cleaning up the Hudson River, GE's resistance, PCBs, information about solar power, organic foods, and renewable resources.

"I forget this world is here." Her mother looked out over the crowd, which was composed of people of all ages: bearded men, women in long, flowing skirts, teenagers in baggy clothes, lots of Birkenstocks and Guatemalan clothes.

They walked toward the first stage where a man with a gray mane of hair was singing and playing the piano.

"Oh God," her mother sounded shocked. "Look at Arlo Guthrie!"

Prana looked carefully. "I think his hair is prematurely gray."

"Oh, you're right." Her mother's expression relaxed.

They stood at the back of the crowd, listening to him finish a song. When it was over, and he made a joke, his clear, nasal voice was familiar.

"I remember when 'Alice's Restaurant' came out," her mother said. "He was just a skinny kid. God, we loved it."

The crowd was sitting on blankets in front of the stage. From a distance, Prana couldn't get any good pictures of the musicians, so she focused on the audience: children sitting between their parents' legs, toddlers pulling at grass, mothers doling out food as they knelt on their blankets.

Prana and her mother moved companionably through the crowd, looking at ceramics, handweaving, handmade soaps, and candles.

"Did you go to lots of concerts back then?"

"Not as many as we wanted, but of course we listened to everything. Bands from the Bay Area came up, and we all listened to folk music."

"Would you like to have done that?"

"What?"

"Been a singer-songwriter, travel around."

Her mother smiled. "We all wanted to be Joan Baez or Joni Mitchell. Some people wanted to be Grace Slick. I loved to sing and play, and I did—with friends—but you have to remember, I had Pagan, and then Zeke was on the way. I certainly didn't want to travel."

Prana heard what her mother would not say. *I loved their father, I loved him more than yours.*

Her mother studied her expression. "What?" she asked.

"Nothing."

"Please," her mother seemed to guess what Prana was thinking. "You were the best thing I got from Marco." Her tone

was slyly funny, as if Prana were now old enough to speak to
this way.

"The only thing, you mean."

"The best thing," her mother said firmly. They were walking, and something on a table caught her mother's eye, but she
looked at Prana before turning to examine it, as if determined to
make her point first. "You know, some women hate being pregnant, but I loved it. I was calm, happy, I had something to look
forward to. You came along at just the right time. You should
never doubt that."

Prana looked at her, wanting to believe her. She nodded,
silent.

They strolled along, looking at wood carvings, handmade
toys, and stained glass. The air was warm, and Prana felt happy,
looking at what people had made, stopping to examine whatever intrigued them. They paused outside a tent of musical
instruments: "Timothy Story, Luthier." Prana peered inside. The
instruments were long and narrow, made of pale wood, like
elongated, neckless guitars. Dulcimers. The curving lines made
Prana think of paintings of tall, elegant women, dressed in tints
of flesh and peach. Her mother stepped inside. Prana followed
her into the tent, and watched as her mother reached out and
gently touched a manicured finger to the strings. The sound was
magical, transparent, with an undercurrent drone. For a
moment, Prana imagined her mother younger, solitary, but the
image quickly faded. On a table in back were larger dulcimers
with trapezoid-shaped bodies. A pair of wooden hammers
rested beside each one.

"Go on," Prana said. "Try one."

"Oh," her mother smiled. She seemed embarrassed. "It's
been too long. I don't know how to anymore."

The luthier was a red-bearded man, sitting in a corner. Prana watched him watch her mother. He didn't speak. Her mother gazed around her, then smiled and moved on.

AT THE END of the field was another stage, empty now, where the waiting crowd seemed restless and expectant. Prana uncapped her camera lens as they moved forward, up to the edge of the stage, so she could shoot back into the crowd as well as the musicians on stage.

"Holly!" The crowd called. "Holleee!"

A woman with a friendly face and blond hair walked onto the stage carrying a guitar. She looked like a person anyone could know. A sign interpreter in flowing clothes followed her. From somewhere offstage, a loudspeaker voice introduced her: Holly Near.

The crowd, which was mostly women, applauded wildly. The women seemed less predictably dressed than the hippie types, although there were a certain number of ear cuffs and butch women with tattoos. They looked up, attentive, and without the usual stage patter, she began to sing.

The song was a simple, hymnlike melody, and by the time she reached the refrain, the audience was with her. "We are a peaceful, angry people, and we are singing, singing for our lives . . ." Prana and her mother stood in the crowd, and after once through, her mother started to sing along. She had a low, contralto voice with a slightly grainy edge. Prana rarely heard her sing and felt surprised by how easily her mother blended with the women around her. Prana's own voice was higher, more breathy; she couldn't reach down to that fullness. By the time the refrain came around again, her mother matched it effortlessly, a third above, following the line of the melody, like water running over stone.

After a few songs, a woman joined Holly Near on stage. She had long, fluffy gray hair and moved easily across the stage, beaming broadly, and Near reached out and put an arm around her shoulders. Together, they sang a duet in Spanish, but in the verses where the woman sang alone, Prana was amazed at the fullness of her voice; she really threw back her head and sang. Prana glanced over at her mother, who seemed transfixed.

"Who is that?" she whispered.

"Ronnie Gilbert," her mother said. "She sang with Pete Seeger and the Weavers, back in the fifties. As far as I know, she's been doing this seriously—singing political music—for most of her adult life. She's really held the course."

Prana was watching the stage as her mother spoke, but when she turned to look at her, Prana saw an expression that contradicted almost every casual denial her mother had made that day. Her mother dipped her head and put on her sunglasses, running a finger beneath the lenses. Her lips were pressed together, her nostrils flaring slightly, as if she were trying not to cry.

THE FOLLOWING DAY, Prana brought her film to a store in the mall. A real photographer would develop film herself, but the teacher said that if you didn't have access to a darkroom, you should simply have the film developed and see what you'd composed. When Prana picked up her pictures, she didn't look at them in the store; she carried the packets home and up to her room. Turning the bedspread inside out, she spread them against the white background.

Prana felt a grinding weight in her stomach as she surveyed what she had done. The pictures were terrible, all of them. If she'd had a decent subject, the light was wrong. If the light was right, the subject seemed odd or ill-considered. Details she'd imagined to be interesting didn't show up. The images were small and insignificant. What she'd hoped to capture was actually diminished by her vision. She felt a terrible helplessness. Not one picture was worth thumbtacking to a bulletin board. She felt a hot stinging behind her eyes.

Her mother stood in the doorway and knocked softly.

Prana started. She reached to cover the pictures before her mother saw them.

"What?" Prana said, not looking at her.

"Are these your pictures?" her mother said, coming into the room.

Prana swept them into a pile.

"Don't look! They're terrible."

"What do you mean?"

"Nothing's right! Not any of them!"

Her mother retreated, sitting in a chair by the desk. Prana stood, looking dumbly at the heap of pictures on the bed.

"I know it was just practice, but they're terrible. They make everything look small and stupid!"

Her mother didn't speak for a minute, then she sat up in her chair.

"Prana, I don't want to hurt your feelings, but in light of what you've been saying about school, and your reaction to this . . ." she gestured toward the pile of pictures, "I need to say something to you."

Prana turned to face her, dreading what she would say.

"You know, from the time you were little, people would look at you and smile, and tell me how absolutely beautiful you were. They were right, of course, but they would always say I should take you to modeling auditions down in the city." Her

mother sighed and ran her finger around the edge of the drawer
pull. "But I didn't want you to lean on your looks. I wanted you
to develop in other, interior ways. You have to realize that learning anything worthwhile doesn't come easily. It takes messing
up, and figuring out what you want to do, and trying again, and
probably messing up differently."

"So you're saying I'm spoiled!" Prana knew she was being
obtuse, she couldn't help it.

"No, no!" her mother said. "Don't be dramatic! I'm just
saying that certain things have come to you easily. This is an
art—" her mother swept her hand toward the bed. "Nobody
learns an art overnight."

Prana plopped down amidst the photos.

"I just feel like everyone around here is so *good* at everything."

Her mother looked suddenly tired. "You're not the only one
who feels that way." She shook her head. "I had no idea what I
was getting into when we moved here. I just hoped I could make
our lives normal for a while. I thought there was enough money
in town that the economy wouldn't be depressed, and I'd be
able to get by. But after you girls started school, I realized how,
I don't know, how competitive this place was."

Prana felt suddenly ashamed of herself. "I don't mean to
whine," she said. "It's just that everyone else seems to know
what they're doing."

"I think that's an appearance more than anything else. This
is an unusual place. There's just a high concentration of talented
parents, who have talented kids, and some of them push those
kids. Most of the country isn't like this." Her mother stopped
and gazed at her with such love that Prana felt embarrassed.
"You're doing fine," her mother said. "Believe me."

Later, when Prana remembered this conversation, she knew her mother had been right—she'd been expecting everything to come too easily, but understanding didn't make her bold.

AND THEN, WHAT she had never expected, what had seemed most outrageous to expect, did come to her easily. She had returned to school that fall, and Stephan came to give a lecture at the university. He spent a long time talking to her class.

She had her own apartment then, and when she saw him again, when she realized the thickness of the feeling between them, she couldn't quite believe it. She felt as if she'd been moving in a private fog that was invisible to him and everyone else. He told her he couldn't. He said he was married. She hadn't protested. She stared at him, just looked and looked, forcing him to look back, forcing him to see what he wanted, to see what he would miss, would never have, and she just stood there, as if imprinting herself on him, because part of her beauty was her reserve, because she knew that he was right, that words would not persuade him, only his realization that she was here, was finite, would be gone if he did not hold her, and what she imagined, but did not know, was that he was aware of his aging, of time passing, so that something in him knew he would never again have a girl who seemed so perfect in her youth, and finally, after what seemed like an eternity, why had he even come up to her apartment after all—finally all she had to do was to step toward him, move closer, and once they had kissed, once he stepped over that line between what was permissible and what was not, she had enclosed him in this private place, and they existed here.

seven

MAUD WAS AT THE SITTER'S, AND PAGAN STEPPED INTO THE shower with a sense of relief. She was going to a bridal shower for a friend and felt pleased at the prospect of getting out and talking to other adults. Turning, she let water run over her face and shoulders, soaking in the warmth. She ran her palms over her belly; the amnio hadn't left a mark.

Tommy wouldn't say it, but he was hoping for a boy. His own father, bemused and worn, acted as if his children were something surprising that had happened to him. He referred to them in the plural—the boys, the girls—and Pagan suspected Tommy wanted a son because he wanted to be a different kind of father.

She let water run into her mouth, a narrow stream filling it like a cup, a hollow sound against the inside of her cheek.

The term *morning sickness* had become a bad joke. She'd been throwing up for weeks, at odd times of the day, with no predictable relief. Last night, she had made spaghetti for Tommy and Maud, but the smell of meat sauce made her queasy. She carried a small bowl of buttered noodles into the living room.

Tommy followed her. "Stomach again?"

She twirled noodles on a fork.

"I can't stand this," Pagan whispered. "I'm exhausted beyond words, and I feel so damn awful all the time." She looked up and held his gaze to make sure he understood. "This is it, Tommy, this is the last time."

He nodded.

SHE DRESSED FOR the luncheon with a sense of anticipation. She felt as if she'd been wearing baggy jeans and an old Notre Dame sweatshirt for weeks. Deliberating in front of her closet, she pulled out a dove gray dress.

The bridal shower was a luncheon at a small, local restaurant, and Pagan felt a sense of familiarity as she stepped inside. Her friend Lauren was the matron of honor, and she led Pagan into the room, introducing her to the women she didn't know. After two children, Lauren still looked like an ad for J. Crew. She was tall and athletic, just as she'd been in college, but her breezy manner had been replaced by maternal caution. Ashley, the bride-to-be, was excited, exclaiming over everyone. Her hair was blow-dried, coiffed in a suburban style, and she looked brittle, like someone, Pagan thought, who did not enjoy sex. Pagan had worked with Ashley a few years ago, and it was only by chance they discovered they had Lauren in common. Pagan greeted her friends, felt the quickening, the scents, the humor of the well cared for.

At lunch, she was seated next to Ashley's most eccentric friend, Maria, who worked as a massage therapist. Pagan ran into her once or twice a year, and usually felt compelled to promise she would call for a massage, but she never did. They were eating their salads when Maria, reaching for the butter, told Pagan that she was pregnant too. Pagan smiled wearily. She wanted to talk about anything except being pregnant right now.

"Are you having an amnio?" Maria asked.

"I did last week," Pagan said, pushing a cherry tomato off to the side.

"Well," Maria said, "we talked about it, and decided that, if there was a problem, it really isn't right to bring a child into the world like that. It's really a form of pollution."

Pagan turned over a halved cherry tomato. Its green inside and pale seeds made her feel queasy.

Maria must have taken her silence as confirmation. "I mean, a Down syndrome child really has nothing to contribute to the world. You consider what a single person in the U.S. consumes in a lifetime and—"

Pagan simply stared at her. Lauren, who had organized the lunch, stood up to say a few words.

She tried to focus on Lauren, but felt herself shaking, amazed at Maria's bluntness. Beyond the social niceties, Pagan saw again that being pregnant was a true and concrete test of what one believed. You had the medical tests or you didn't. You went on faith or you didn't. You believed in vitamins, meditation, visualization, or you didn't. There was no hiding in abstraction. She sensed, although she knew it was superstitious, that facing a dangerous possibility head-on could prevent something bad from happening. It was why you bought a safe car, a good car seat, as if bad things happened to people who weren't vigilant. Difficulty was visited on them as a reminder that no one was exempt from random bad luck. She knew her reasoning didn't quite make sense, because she didn't believe in God, or in a force that mysteriously allocated good and bad luck, but somehow the feeling persisted.

AT HOME THAT night, as they were getting ready for bed, she told Tommy about Maria at the shower.

"Isn't that a Nazi-like argument? She was so matter-of-fact! If she'd said, 'We decided that we couldn't handle a kid who was retarded,' you'd have to say she was honest. But, God, it was so strange, Miss Chakra herself talking about human pollution."

Tommy slipped his hand around the back of her neck, under her curls; his touch felt warm and soothing.

"People can surprise you," he said. "Stop fiddling with things now, come to bed."

She turned and leaned up against him, feeling his solidity and warmth. She loved his steadiness, not simply because he took care of them, although it was partly that, but she trusted his judgment. He was willing to see things as they were.

Once they were in bed, Pagan was restless. She hated this feeling—physically tired, her mind busy. A scent of chemical sweetness drifted over her. She lifted her head. Over the past few weeks, she'd had a heightened sense of smell, and things she didn't normally notice—car exhaust, perfume, air fresheners—intruded on her attention. Pagan sat up.

"Did Sheila give you any kid clothes today?" Pagan asked.

"Huh?" Tommy was already half-asleep.

"I'm sorry, did Sheila give you any clothes for Maud?"

"Yeah." Tommy sounded annoyed now. "Bag's in the corner," he mumbled.

Pagan climbed out of bed quietly. She carried the plastic bag out of the room and set it outside the back door. Sheila gave them beautiful hand-me-downs for Maud, but she used a cloying fabric softener, and Pagan had to rewash everything to get the smell out. She lay back down and curled herself around Tommy. Fake floral scents disgusted her; they were too concentrated. The smell of sun and air was missing; there was no smell of earth. She turned onto her other side, tried to think of something calming.

One spring, when Pagan was very little, her mother said she'd make a sunflower house. When Pagan asked what that was, her mother only smiled, but that May, she marked off a small rectangle in the corner of the vegetable garden. She put a thick bed of straw in the rectangle, and planted sunflowers around it. By early summer, thick stalks had grown up like the frame of a little house, and her mother planted sweet peas to fill in the walls. Pagan would lie on her back and watch clouds scud across the sky, or sit cross-legged in the midst of the silver-spined stalks and twining sweet peas, while her mother worked a few feet away. She felt thrilled and proprietary in her airy enclosure. Zeke was too little to play in the garden, and her toys were scattered outside on the lawn. Her mother would bring out lemonade for all of them, and she would sit with Pagan in the green leafy house. It seemed stunning, magical, that her mother could imagine this, and then summon it into being. Pagan wanted to know where the sunflowers were, and her mother simply said, "They'll come," by summer's end, they did, growing bright and impossibly high against the summer sky.

eight

PRANA WISHED SHE COULD BE LIKE ZEKE, WHO NEVER GOT entangled, whose lovers were shed like encumbering jackets. If Zeke knew about Stephan, she wouldn't care that he was married, but she'd find it pathetic that Prana longed for him so. When the phone rang, Prana reached for it, hoping it was one of her sisters, but it was Joe, his voice excited, almost jarring, asking her to come over. She guessed what he had, said she'd be over in a little while.

When Prana was younger, she didn't understand that beauty had a certain liability, that her presence charged the air in a room. She had proceeded in her friendships simply as friendships, and it was easy to stay casual; she simply stepped back if someone became infatuated or called her too much. Her beauty kept men from crossing a certain line. By the time she reached her late twenties, the line became harder to maintain. Men assumed she understood the consequences of her beauty, that their attraction didn't have to be masked.

Joe never pressed that invisible line. Every few weeks, they got together and drank a bottle of wine, or Joe got some coke and they talked late into the night. He'd lived in Washington since the sixties, been active in the Civil Rights Movement, and Prana liked his stories. Now he worked for the government in some mid-level job, and he had his little formalities. He never knocked on her door unannounced. He always called, asked if she wanted to come over for a drink or a smoke.

WHEN SHE OPENED the door to his apartment, the room was dark. *Sketches of Spain* was playing on the stereo.

"Prana, come here. You have to try this."

She looked down at the coffee table: the glass pipe, the tin-foil, the matches.

"It's not like they say. Won't make you all jumpy like coke."

She was afraid it would take her over some edge inside herself, but she wanted something to stop the terrible thrum-ming inside her chest, the anxiety that beat inside her, like a trapped bird, ever since Stephan had left his message on her machine.

"In a little bit maybe," she said. "Do you have any wine?"

Joe walked to the kitchen and returned with a large glass of red wine.

"Thanks," she said.

"What's wrong?"

Prana looked around the room. Joe's shelves were filled with carefully ordered albums and CDs, pictures of his friends and extended family, a carefully ordered bachelor's apartment.

"Did you ever know someone who disappeared?"

"Disappeared how?"

And Prana told him about her mother.

Joe gave her a long look, then turned away, gazing at the floor. He wore a long-sleeved yellow T-shirt, which was bright in the dark room. He leaned forward, his elbows on his thighs, focused on something she couldn't see. For a moment she imagined him leaning over a potter's wheel, fashioning a vessel. He stretched his hands, opening and closing his fingers. "Your mother wasn't real political in those days, was she?"

"Well," Prana said. "I think she was political like most hippie types: you know, protesting against the war, a fan of Bob Dylan and Joan Baez, that sort of thing."

"So she didn't blow up buildings or anything like that?"

"No, of course not!" She took a sip of wine, feeling shocked. Never, not her mother, not that.

Joe raised his eyebrows. "Didn't mean to scare you, but you know, people change their identities, leave everything behind. Turns out some Girl Scout mom was a real radical. I had a friend who went away for that shit."

Prana shook her head. "My mother was pregnant, living out in the country. She's not that—" Prana searched for the word, "intense."

"Well, for someone who's not intense, she did give you all some unusual names. What's your middle sister's name?"

"Zeke."

"And what's it short for?"

"Zhikr."

"Damn," he grinned. "It's like naming a kid 'Dweezil.' Does it mean anything?"

"It means 'remembrance,' spiritual remembrance. You know, keeping your mind on God."

"What kind of Maharishi thing was your mom into?"

"I don't know exactly . . ." and Prana paused. "I think she named us for spiritual ideas rather than any specific religion."

"Can't have spiritual ideas without religion," Joe said.

"Well, she seemed to." Prana felt edgy. She didn't want to go round and round on this. "What about you? What were you raised?"

"Me? Baptist. Don't really go to church anymore, unless Marian wants to, but that stuff sticks with you—"

"Oh, it sure does." She couldn't resist teasing him, gesturing to the pipe.

Joe nodded, then rubbed his fingers over his eyes. "I made you uptight. You look upset."

She thought of Stephan, his failure to show up, his failure to care. She wanted a world he couldn't see into, a world without his images, his hands, his voice. It was like trying to escape the sky.

"Stephan," she said.

Joe nodded. The topic needed little explanation.

She thought for a long moment, then sat forward on the couch and lifted the small, glass pipe to her lips. Joe picked up a lighter and fiddled with something in the bowl. She waited, and then, when he nodded, she pulled the silver, metallic air, a cool chemical taste, into her lungs, then let it out.

"Now," he said. "Take a deep breath, and let it out slowly."

And she felt, as the breath slipped out of her, a swirling silver bloom exploding behind her eyes, and the blooming filled

her, and filled her, and as it dissolved, everything unnecessary
was cleared away. She saw the molecules that made up the chair,
the pillow, the table. The individual particles minutely linked,
hovering in place. The room was a pointillist painting in mono-
chromatic colors. How beautiful the dark. Everything was as it
was, but it was more. The music, wine-red and foreign, pressed
in on her. Everything in her life had brought her to this particular moment. It was perfect.

THE NEXT MORNING Prana felt like a kicked-in bucket. She
woke curled tightly in her bed, wondering what she had done
the night before, then remembered and felt hollow and light-
headed. She had slept only an hour or two. Thank God it was
Saturday. She tried to stand up, but as she started to rise, everything went black and she sat back down. She needed something
cold to drink. She got up slowly and walked to the kitchen.
Orange juice seemed impossibly thick. Seltzer, fizzy juice, she
wanted bubbles.

She found some apple juice on a shelf and looked at it
doubtfully, how long had it been here? What had possessed her
to buy it? Thinking of Maud perhaps. She poured herself a glass
and sipped it gingerly. She thought about last night. It had been
astounding. They had talked all night. And in talking she
revealed what she was just allowing herself to admit: that her
time with Stephan, once precious and inviolable, had become
tinged with the ordinary: last-minute phone calls, arrangements
to make overseas, odd pieces of equipment he needed to pick
up. When he returned from his trips, he was exhausted, his back
hurt, and she could tell he wanted to stretch out on her bed and
sleep as much as talk or make love. How could she blame him?

He was getting older, although this diminished nothing of what she felt for him. Sometimes she watched him while he slept and remembered their beginning, when he soared across thousands of miles to make that clear trajectory to her and her bed.

In the beginning, she had wanted to tell her sisters about him. She felt that knowing Stephan made her life exceptional, as if she were a different person through her connection to him. But time went on, Pagan got married, and she was afraid that Pagan would be horrified she was having an affair with a married man—especially an affair that had gone on for so long. Zeke would snort through her nose and tell her to get a life.

Prana sat down at the kitchen counter. When they had first met, she was young, which she had confused with being directionless. Her misunderstanding could be excused, but the sad thing was that she had continued in this way. Her jobs kept her distracted for a few months at a time. When one project was over, there was another in the wings, but the hard part was that she had believed in Stephan—not in a conventional sense, not that he would marry her—but his ideas were the ones she had listened to and rebelled against. He had been the large, overriding principle of her life, and because of her reserve, he did not fully realize the position she had put him in. If he had understood, he would not have allowed it.

nine

WHEN PAGAN WAS PREGNANT WITH MAUD, HER MOTHER HAD told her that she couldn't imagine how much she would love her child. Pagan was surprised, a little offended, and protested that she loved Tommy very much. "It's not the same thing," her mother said. "You'll see."

Her mother had been right; so Pagan's reaction last winter, when she started to bleed, had surprised her. At three and a half months pregnant, she thought she was safe. She went to the bathroom one evening and noticed she was bleeding, not a lot, but not a little either. In February the night-blackened windows were icy, the wind came in gusts, and the cold seemed like an animal that could knock her over. She didn't want to rush off to the hospital in the dark. She whispered to Tommy that she was bleeding, and he looked up from the newspaper. She could see from his expression that he was still focused on what he'd been reading, he'd only half heard her. "I'm bleeding," she whispered again, and his eyes went wide and then he rose from the couch and took care of her usual nighttime chores—giving Maud a bath, putting her to bed—so Pagan could be still. They had only hinted about a baby, but all Maud needed to hear was the word "blood" and she'd start asking questions. Pagan cursed and dug around in a closet for sanitary napkins; it had been months since she'd used them, then she sat in the playroom, on the couch where they watched TV, and tried to stay calm. She felt herself starting to cramp, small cramps, like menstrual cramps, and occasionally she would get up and go to the bathroom to see if she was still bleeding.

After putting Maud to bed, Tommy paced around the playroom.

"We should go to the hospital," Tommy said.

Pagan explained why staying still was best. Tommy seemed to hear what she was saying, but he moved around the room, putting Maud's toys away. Pagan called the hospital and spoke with the doctor on call, but the doctor confirmed what she already knew: there was little anyone could do if she were miscarrying.

She had always thought that a miscarriage, although sad, was a kind of mechanical correction, nature intervening when there was a problem, so the idea that this was happening seemed unbelievable, but not truly frightening. Tommy picked up the remote and, with the sound on low, flicked through the channels. Staring at the bright images, Pagan knew that wishing for this not to happen would not change anything. Early in both pregnancies, she had thought to herself *I want a healthy baby, if there's a problem, let this one go*. She thought this almost like a charm, a way of warding off bad luck. She hadn't thought it would happen. She tried to stay very still. Outside, the trees creaked in the wind. Tommy kept asking if he could get her something.

"Stop," she said. For a moment, he looked angry and penitent, like a child being scolded. She softened her voice. "Just try to be still. If there was anything they could do, we'd go to the hospital." She didn't want to go out into the freezing night, then simply wait in a hospital and bleed, letting Maud be exposed to germs, bacteria, God knows what. She called the doctor at two- or three-hour intervals, feeling the cramps getting worse, the bleeding not much worse. The last time she called the doctor, he sounded as if he'd been sleeping, and she felt annoyed that someone could be sleeping during her crisis.

When they finally went to bed, Tommy was restless beside her. The doctor had said she could take something for the pain, but she didn't want to: the habit of self-sacrifice during pregnancy was too strong. She lay in bed, turning from one side to another, feeling the small, muted labor. Her body was doing it alone, her being was not engaged. Turning onto her left side, she felt a small, sharp pain in her abdomen, something tearing loose inside. She got up to pack a diaper bag for Maud, in case they did need to go, and went into the bathroom one last time. Sitting on the toilet, she felt a little gush, which she recognized as water breaking, and then a gush of something she didn't want to think about. She breathed out. It didn't hurt, but she felt something pouring out of her. The cramping slowed almost immediately, and she sat still for a long time. She didn't want to look into the toilet; she was afraid of what she would see. The bleeding slowed. The cramping stopped. She didn't know what to do.

She didn't want to flush the toilet; it seemed criminal somehow. She didn't want to look, but she wanted to know. She got up and went into the bedroom.

"Tommy, wake up."

Tommy stirred, groggy, and then turned over quickly.

"It happened."

"Oh sweetheart," he tried to pull her down to him.

"No, I've got to fix myself up. I'm still bleeding a little. Tommy, I can't look. I can't flush the toilet, but I can't just leave it."

He got up out of bed. She heard him walk into the bathroom, a pause, the toilet flush.

"Did you look?"

"Yes."

She didn't ask him what he saw.

ten

LATE SUNDAY AFTERNOON, THE LIGHT HAD DIMMED AT THE windows, and Prana sat cross-legged on the wood floor, rearranging her books. It was something she did periodically, based on her progress in reading, although this wasn't something she would say aloud. One of her walls had built-in bookshelves, and she had arranged her books into sections. Photography was divided into two parts: technical books occupied one space, and large-format books with pictures had their own shelf. There was also a miscellaneous group of books she thought of as aesthetics or philosophy. The art history section was small, mostly biographies of different artists. There was a place for books and magazines she hadn't read yet—new arrivals—like a shelf at the library.

She had just finished reading *Let Us Now Praise Famous Men,* which she'd bought at a yard sale for fifty cents. She'd been smitten by the opening essay, "James Agee at Thirty-Seven," and she gazed at the wall of books, trying to decide where it belonged.

Taking her mug of tea, she knelt next to a stack of books she had started but never finished. Some books she might find useful later on. Others she had tried, but found the prose too convoluted. If she found a book that she simply couldn't get through, or didn't like, she sold it back to one of the used bookstores in town. She didn't like her apartment to be cluttered.

Along the bottom shelf, where the dust gathered, was a series of Time-Life cookbooks she'd had styling work in. She'd gotten a number of other books—pictorial essays, best photographs of the decade—cheaply through work. *Life* had issued a book of Larry Burrows' photographs. Stephan had been only nineteen when Burrows and three other photographers had been killed in Vietnam, and Stephan spoke of Burrows with reverence. In Stephan's wartime photos, she could see the influence of the photographers who'd gone before him. Or perhaps the subject, the imprinting of grief, had made its own stamp.

Prana stood up and stretched. When she looked at the shelves of books she was pleased—they were a record of what she had been thinking.

She hadn't planned to leave college. It had simply been a matter of one thing following another. In February of her sophomore year, Stephan had to go to Brussels on assignment, and then on to Bruges. When he asked her to meet him in Belgium, she simply decided not to enroll that winter since she'd be away in the middle of the semester. Their time away had been extraordinary, but when she returned, she had to find work. She got a job doing photo-styling for a Time-Life cookbook, *Fresh Ways with Vegetables*. She seemed to have a knack for setting up a picture, for smoothing disparate elements and discordant personalities. The photographers told her she had a good eye, although in retrospect she thought it was simply that she was willing to work hard. The series went on and on: *Fresh Ways with Fish & Shellfish, Fresh Ways with* . . . , and it seemed she had a permanent job, and then there were other jobs from that. At first, she stuck with it because she wanted to be free to travel with Stephan again, but after a while it seemed that going to college was ephemeral, like being part of a play—a distant scenario visited, particular to its time, impossible to return to. They had traveled together only once more. Four days in London before he set off for Egypt and the Far East. It was the first leg of a trip that would last for two months.

When the phone rang, she jumped, knocking over a pile of books as she reached for the phone. It was Stephan, asking if he could come over. She felt a vast relief, which she was careful to keep out of her voice. When she hung up the phone, she felt the familiar flutter of preparation. Her life seemed to pick up speed when Stephan entered it, as if the season changed from sleepy summer to autumn.

When Stephan walked in the door, she felt as she sometimes did when she hadn't seen him for a few weeks. For a moment he seemed smaller, as if she were looking at him from a distance. He looked like an ordinary, heavyset man, distinguished only by his curly unkempt hair and the deep wrinkles running down over his cheekbones. And then it was as if he snapped into focus, became himself, as if his vision, his past, created an aura around him, and he filled the apartment with something larger, historical.

"I'm sorry about last week," he said. "I knew you'd be upset, but they'd arranged to meet me and surprise me. Sandy's mother came to stay with Mike and Emily. I could hardly say no."

"It's all right," Prana said. The words came out of her, soft and soothing. What else could she say? Why be shrill now?

He reached his hands up under her shirt, around her back, and rested his face in her neck. He smelled like air, with a trace of the bitter scent of fixer still on him. He'd been in the darkroom.

"Let's sit," he said. "It's been quite a week."

She brought him a glass of wine, and he slipped off his shoes and stretched out on her sofa in a domestic posture, as if he would watch television, but she had no television.

She arranged herself across the room in a large leather armchair, knowing how she looked, knowing he was pleased to simply be here. She wanted to maintain her distance, to let him feel contrite a while longer.

"So how was New York?"

"It was fine, exhausting. Betsy wants to go to Columbia, but her mother is nervous about her living in the city. I end up mediating." He smiled wearily.

"What do you think?"

"What most men think—my daughter should be locked in a convent, out of harm's way."

"I'd think, after being married to you, your wife would be less worried about a daughter moving to New York."

"It's the opposite, I'd have to say." He looked at the stacks of books on the floor. "What are you doing?"

"Sorting out my books."

"You're the quietest intellectual I know."

She smiled, knowing he meant it as a compliment. Stephan was dismissive of people who liked to hear themselves talk, especially academics who theorized about photography. He was often asked to speak at universities, which he found vaguely amusing.

"Can I ask you a question?"

Stephan looked up, his expression wary.

"Why did you stop taking certain kinds of pictures? I don't want the answer you give to everyone else. What made you stop going to war zones?"

He sighed. "Prana, it's complicated."

"I really want to know," Prana said. She made her voice hard. "It's a fair question. It's not asking so much."

He looked over at her. She saw him seeing her curled in the chair. His daughter Betsy had been eight when he and Prana met; now she was thinking about colleges. He set his wineglass on the floor next to him.

"In Vietnam, we felt like were doing something important. It sounds trite, but it's true. No war had been recorded like that. And photographers like Burrows, and Huet and Potter and Shimamoto, literally gave their lives. It wouldn't have occurred to me to quit. But over the years, I saw so much devastation—the scope of it all is something a photograph never really captures. When I think of how many pictures I took of children crying over their dead mothers, sisters, brothers, it's sickening really." He shook his head.

"Each of my kids was conceived while I was home from a trip, and then I'd go off somewhere else, and leave Sandy pregnant, and then with little ones; and here's the truth, which sounds so *little*. I'm not even sure if I can make this make sense."

Stephan sat up and looked at her, as if he wanted to make sure that she understood. "I was in Nicaragua. I was shot in the leg, and I didn't know how badly I was hurt, but I knew I was bleeding like shit, and I thought I was going to die there, and it occurred to me that all those pictures I'd taken, all of them, the message behind them, at some level was: This is not how the world is supposed to be. I felt like I was sending those pictures back here. You have to remember that the press corps wasn't just Americans. The pictures we took went everywhere, but I felt like I came from this huge, rich country, and that people would see these images and be moved to do something, *anything,* to relieve that kind of suffering. And suddenly, as I was stuck there, bleeding, it all seemed wrong to me: I had a wife and three children who were living in a nice place, living in a world I wanted for them, and I wasn't *there* for it. I was off covering another insane war, off in the blood and muck and shit-filled water, and it suddenly just seemed wrong to be there, rather than here. And I knew I hadn't provided for them properly. Not really. I'm not just talking about money, but there was a huge amount of unfinished business. I was so young when I went to Vietnam. I was always planning to come home, and more than ten years after the war, I was still showing up in hell. And so, finally, I came home."

It had all come out of him in a rush. Stephan picked up his wineglass.

She bent to take a sip of wine, knowing that what she was thinking, she would never say. She wanted to ask him: *Would you think of me, would you think of me at a moment like that?* She looked up.

"Prana, you're not my responsibility," Stephan said.

She looked at him mute, then shook her head. "I wasn't

thinking that," she said. She felt hot, embarrassed, as if she'd been slapped.

"You were," Stephan said. "Don't you think I know?"

He bent his head and ran his hands through his hair. He was silent, and for a moment, Prana was afraid he was going to cry. "I should go," he said. "I'll call you later."

He slipped on his shoes, grabbed his jacket, and kissed her on the forehead before walking out the door.

Prana crossed the room to open a window, then moved to the couch, lying in the space where Stephan had been. She felt the warmth of his body, like an aura around her. Lighting a cigarette, she felt comforted by the ritual of it, the smell of sulfur, the drawing in, the little rush. She breathed out. It was time for this to be over.

LATER THAT EVENING, Prana headed over to Joe's. She had her keys in her hand when the phone rang, and she glanced at the Caller ID. Pagan. She waited for her sister's voice to come over the machine. "Hi, just calling to check in. I don't really have any news, but I wanted to see how you were doing." Prana hesitated, then closed the door behind her.

Joe handed her the pipe. He had warned her they shouldn't do this too often. With a slow series of breaths, everything she planned to tell him seemed inconsequential; she saw everything for how it was.

"Listen, Prana, I have to tell you—"

She heard seriousness in his tone, the beginning of an instruction, and made a motion with her hand, *No don't, not now, don't spoil the high.*

Joe sat back, put his hands behind his head, and looked

out the window. The blinds were drawn; it was night, but the orange light of the city sky seeped through the blinds. Prana studied the striated light. Night never truly became night in a city, it never grew fully dark. This seemed enormously sad.

"Prana, you know I can't believe I'm saying this, because I've kept plenty of women waiting in my day, but you really should quit this guy and get on with it. Shit, he's my age, isn't he? I mean, *get on with it*. You met him when you were a kid practically."

Prana nodded.

"You ever finish school?"

"High school."

"College?"

Prana shook her head.

"It's not really about school, but you need to find your own gig. Anyone could see you're not happy."

Prana started to laugh, a fissure breaking open inside her. She laughed so hard it scared her. It was like being tickled too much or having the wind knocked out of her, but now it was as if she were laughing to death. Joe sitting there with a crack pipe in his hand, telling her to finish her education. Oh, oh. She laughed so hard she had to lie down. She couldn't catch her breath.

eleven

AS A CHILD ZEKE LEARNED THAT, WHEN GROWN-UPS ASKED her name, the question was merely reflexive. Adults asked children their names as a polite pretense, to set an example: *This is how one behaves*. It annoyed her that they were unprepared to retain a real answer. When she told people her name, they usually looked puzzled and asked her to repeat it. "Zhikr, rhymes with speaker," she would say flatly, and then turn her attention to something else. Their expressions and responses followed a predictable pattern: the small, puzzled "oh" of their mouths, the unspoken shift of gears, reorienting themselves to ask: Who is this girl? She sensed the tacit judgments about her parents. Zhikr was named for a Sufi ceremony and her name meant "remembrance." The ceremony was an invocation, repeated many times: *La'illaha il'Allahu,* "There is no reality but God, there is only God," but for her, the idea of spiritual remembrance became fused with trying to remember her father, whose death she couldn't quite recall, although she had been right there. She could almost remember him picking her up and holding her, sun shining on the blond hairs of his forearms, sun in his beard, the sweaty salt smell of him.

Even as a toddler, she'd been a tomboy. By the time she was twelve, everybody, including her teachers, called her Zeke. For most people, acknowledging her almost masculine diffidence was easier than trying to understand the implications of her name. Through most of her adolescence, Zeke wore a baggy pair of overalls; her concession to dressing up was a pair of white painter pants. At seventeen, she had grown tall and leggy, lovely in a lean, athletic way; and when she wasn't at school, she spent most of her time working at a stable in Briarcliff. Her green eyes were narrow, as if perpetually squinting into the sun, and her dark blond hair, which she usually cut herself, fell into her eyes. Her mother once said she resembled her father, but her parents had been unconcerned with bourgeois things like cameras and photo albums, so there were few images of those early years. She felt cheated that she couldn't really remember her father; her early childhood was lost in a mist, impossible to retrieve. For Zeke, *remembrance* didn't mean "God," it meant "father," that early time before everything went awry.

The days were getting shorter, and although she usually liked autumn, the warm brightness against the shortened days seemed sad, a little ominous, this year. She tried to throw the feeling off, immersing herself in physical details around her: the soft weight of her old cotton clothes, the chill of early morning, her chores at the barn, the changeability of each day. When she drove to work, a precipitous fog settled in the valleys, but there was the feeling of impending movement: mist rising off the ponds, geese in flight, and by early afternoon the air was bright and clear.

TONIGHT THERE WAS an open house at the girls' school. The first time Marcie asked her to go, they'd been seeing each other a few months, and Marcie asked tentatively, as if asking her out on a date. She gazed at Zeke with those huge gray eyes, her irises like moth wings under glass, and Zeke understood that, for all Marcie's bluster and drama, this was where Marcie was vulnerable, this was the equivalent of asking her to move in.

To the outside world, Marcie was defiant. She declared Zeke her partner, and Zeke started going to Eleanor's and Amy's school plays and soccer games. If anyone questioned Zeke's co-parent status, Marcie practically dared them to step into the politically correct ring and go a few rounds with her. Zeke had never quite settled into the implied domesticity of this role, so each time Marcie told her about a school event and asked her to come, Zeke felt flattered and pleased. She started to report her school forays to Pagan, who asked a thousand questions about full-day and half-day kindergarten, how Amy handled the bus, and how Marcie liked the girls' teachers. Reconnaissance, Zeke called it. Tommy had made noises about Catholic school for Maud, and Pagan was gathering ammunition.

Driving into Marcie's neighborhood, Zeke noticed that some of the neighbors had decorated their houses for Halloween. Her mother had never been craftsy in that way, but Zeke remembered a rhythm to the fall, when each holiday was a marker of imminent pleasure. Halloween, with its abundance of candy, powdered doughnuts and sweet cider, seemed like opening day.

Marcie's house was filled with the smell of baking. Zeke hung up her coat and felt her shoulders relax, as if the smells of fruit and cinnamon could settle her. Marcie was a good cook, and last fall she had done a lot of baking: apple pie, pumpkin pie, blueberry cobbler. Zeke and the girls had filled themselves with the tart sweetness of the season. Zeke walked into the kitchen.

"Pumpkin pie, pumpkin pie," Amy chanted.

"We have to wait until it cools. We'll have some when we get home."

Marcie reached for Zeke and kissed her. "Your hands are cold!"

Marcie was dressed in tight-fitting black slacks and a red sweater that showed off her dark hair and high colors. Zeke wondered who she was showing off for, then figured it didn't have to be someone specific. Marcie liked to be admired, though she tried not to show it. For all her talk and dramatic gestures, Marcie was adept at analyzing a scene before her without revealing what she thought. Zeke had observed that people tried to impress Marcie, and she courted admiration by fixing her attention on a person as if he or she were the only thing that mattered. Under Marcie's gaze, her subjects either wilted or blossomed.

"Mom, can we go to my class first?" Eleanor asked.

"Sure," Marcie said, putting her hand on Eleanor's hair.

"No, me first!" Amy protested.

"We'll go to both of your rooms, back and forth," Marcie

said. "It'll be a party. Mardi Gras." She smiled indulgently and looked at Zeke over their heads.

AT NIGHT, THE school seemed unfamiliar. Rectangles of light fell on the lawn, and crowds streamed in and out of the brightly lit building. The atmosphere was festive with Halloween decorations pasted in the halls. In Amy's room, the class had made displays for different fall festivals: Octoberfest, Halloween, the Day of the Dead. One table, with a bright red tablecloth, looked like an altar decorated with bright paper flowers, cookies, plastic skulls and skeletons.

Marcie flashed a smile at Amy's teacher, a round-faced woman wearing pumpkin earrings, who was speaking to a small group of parents in front of her.

Zeke leaned over to Marcie, "Don't you think the Day of the Dead is kind of morbid for kids?"

Marcie looked at the table. "It's supposed to be a celebration, I think. It's actually less creepy than Halloween."

Walking toward them, Amy's teacher overheard her. "You're absolutely right, it *is* a time for celebration. You're Amy's mother, aren't you?"

"Yes, I am." Marcie gave the teacher her most winning smile. "This is my partner, Zeke." And with this introduction, Marcie seemed to draw them into an intimate circle, as if showering something magic on the teacher, obliterating her denim skirt and sturdy shoes.

"Amy loves school this year. She's really enjoying your class," Marcie said. The teacher smiled, looking almost embarrassed to be so pleased, and then the aide came up and asked her to meet another parent. When the teacher excused herself, Marcie looked around the room. Amy was giggling with some friends. Eleanor had wandered off. "They work so hard here," Marcie said. She gazed wistfully at the little cubbies with bright name tags.

Zeke felt something in her relax. Marcie was back to her old self. Of course she would be bitchy again, it was part of her humor, but Marcie knew how to appreciate people. It was one of the qualities that made her a good administrator. When Zeke met her, Marcie was starting a nurse appreciation program. Each month, the winning nurse and a friend could have dinner for two at a nice restaurant in town. Marcie had solicited funds from local businesses herself. It was a small thing, but the nurses seemed to like it. Marcie had also, and she was very proud of this, insisted on more flexible scheduling for the nursing and clerical staff, and over the past few years, she proved that giving people more control over their schedules actually saved the hospital money in loss time and sick time.

The little altar with its tiny skeletons and paper flowers unsettled Zeke. She wondered about her mother; she knew she wasn't dead, but the open-endedness of it all was strange. She thought of her father; he had never seen her childhood classrooms—she barely remembered them herself. She shivered unexpectedly. She couldn't think about him in this carnival atmosphere. Her childhood was another world.

"I think Eleanor went to her classroom," Zeke said. "I don't see her in here."

THEY FOUND ELEANOR in her own classroom, writing on the board with colored chalk. Zeke had met her teacher before, an austere woman with very short hair who seemed to relax only around children. Marcie strolled in, gave her a wide smile, then walked over to the board to see what Eleanor was doing.

"Hi, Zeke."

Zeke was startled to hear a man's voice addressing her, and she turned around to see Bert. He was dressed in khaki pants and a sport shirt. She had never seen him in anything except a work coverall, and she felt unexpectedly pleased to see him. He looked comfortable and happy, as if he was at a party.

"Do you have a kid in this class?" Zeke asked.

"Cecily." He nodded toward a slender girl standing on a chair. Her arms were open, gesturing, as if she were about to give a speech. The teacher walked over and asked her to get down, and Bert looked on, his expression slightly amused. "Kim, my quiet one, is over there." He pointed to a fair-haired little girl sitting in a chair, looking at a book.

Amy came up and tugged at Zeke. "I want to go back to my room. Becky's there, and I forgot my Print Journal."

Zeke put her hand on Amy's head, and almost reflexively smoothed her hair, as if to slow her down, so she and Bert could finish talking.

"This is Amy. She and Eleanor are Marcie's daughters." Zeke tipped her chin toward Marcie, who was talking to a group of Eleanor's friends. As if on cue, Marcie bent down to write something low on the board. Showing off her ass, Zeke thought. She wanted to deflect his attention and turned to Amy.

"Amy, this is the vet who takes care of our animals at the farm."

"Hi." She blinked at him for a moment, then said to Zeke. "*Pleeease* can we go back to my room? We're supposed to bring our journals home tonight."

"Go ask your mom," Zeke said, and made a shooing

motion with her hands. "I have no idea what a 'Print Journal' is," she murmured to Bert.

"Any word from your mother?"

Zeke was surprised that he would so easily pick up where they had left off. "None," she said.

Amy returned and tugged at Zeke's hand. "She says yes."

Bert smiled as if he knew a joke he had to keep to himself.

BACK IN THE first-grade room, Amy wanted Zeke to review everything in detail. She showed Zeke her cubby, her drawer, her Print Journal. Zeke perched next to her on a tiny chair, and Amy opened her stapled-together book. She showed Zeke her printing, how they practiced waves and loops, the beginning of cursive. The wobbly letters were practiced so carefully. Zeke surveyed the lines of whorls and swirls; she had forgotten about practicing penmanship. Amy's hand was the only reminder of her baby chubbiness, and Zeke ooohed and ahhed, thinking it was all so much easier than it had been, even two years ago, when there was more explaining to do. Amy asked fewer hard questions now. She mainly required an audience, and Zeke found that being an audience required less energy than explaining the world to a four-year-old.

"We should get back to the other room and show this to your mom and Eleanor," Zeke said.

"Did Eleanor do a Print Journal?" Amy asked, slipping her hand into Zeke's.

"I don't know," Zeke answered.

Amy led her back to Eleanor's classroom where Zeke noticed, across the room, Marcie talking to Bert. She was standing close to him, or closer than Zeke would have expected. Although Bert wasn't especially tall, Marcie gave the impression that she was looking up at him. "Look, a volcano!" Amy said, and tugged Zeke over to see a mottled papier-mâché model.

Marcie looked fascinated by something Bert was saying, and Zeke recognized her catching him in the glare of her attention. What was she saying? Her wide mouth moved so easily between humor and moodiness. Zeke felt oddly off balance.

Marcie turned as Zeke approached. "We were just talking about you," Marcie said, reaching for her arm as if to claim her.

The teacher clapped her hands to get everyone's attention.

"We've been talking about Hawaii for the past few weeks." She said the final "i" with a little hesitation, like a hiccup, "And in conjunction with that, our class has been working on science experiments. We're exploring some of the basic properties of acids and bases and, of course, volcanoes have been a very popular project. Let's have all our students come up here." She raised her arms, and the children, poking each other and giggling, moved up to the front of the room.

Zeke stood with Marcie and Bert in the back with the adults. The maps on the walls, the Day of the Dead, everything seemed to remind her of her mother. But of course she wasn't dead. Bert held his younger daughter's hand and watched the teacher. They listened to her explanations for volcanic explosions.

OUTSIDE, THEIR BREATH made cloudy funnels in the night air. Amy whispered "ghosts, ghosts, ghosts," as they made their way to the car. They slowly drove out of the lot with Amy chanting "pumpkin pie, pumpkin pie."

"So your vet seems nice. I didn't know you were friendly."

"We had dinner a week or two ago."

Marcie hit the brakes too suddenly as they came into a stop-light. "You never mentioned it," she said.

"It was the night we had your wrist stitched up."

Marcie was quiet.

"Cecily's in my class," Eleanor said. "He came and gave a slide talk one day. He used to work at the Bronx Zoo."

"Did he?" said Marcie. "He must know a lot."

They turned onto Marcie's street. Jack-o'-lanterns lined the porches like aged sentries, unsure of what they were guarding.

twelve

PAGAN HAD NEVER CARED FOR MARCIE, ALTHOUGH SHE couldn't say exactly why. Witty and quick, Marcie was full of entertaining stories, but her humor often had an edge of truth, and Pagan sometimes felt afraid of what she might say, especially in front of her own girls.

When Zeke and Marcie first met, Zeke's questions about parenting were casual, as if she were trying to get up to speed, and Pagan liked it that she and Zeke had a common ground for conversation. But recently, Zeke's questions were more pointed; she seemed to second-guess Marcie, asking what Pagan thought about this or that. Pagan was flattered that Zeke would even think about using her as a sounding board; she couldn't remember Zeke asking her advice about anything before.

Zeke didn't seem worried about the girls growing up with two mothers, but lately she seemed concerned with things that surprised Pagan. Pagan had always thought that Zeke paid more attention to animals than to people, but she had to admit that, in this case, she was wrong. For instance, Zeke worried that Eleanor didn't get enough exercise. She was afraid that Marcie, who was a killer tennis player, and vain about her figure, set too high a standard. Amy still sucked her thumb at night, and Zeke was worried about her teeth. Last week, Zeke had called to ask Pagan's advice about Halloween costumes.

"Convince one of them to be a banshee," Pagan said.

Zeke cracked up on the other end of the phone.

Pagan laughed too. When they were kids, at Halloween, Zeke had never been a princess. She was a pirate, a skeleton, a hobo, and one year, a banshee. No one knew where she had learned the word, but Zeke howled through the house, and whenever someone told her to be quiet, she said: "I can't. I have to scream like a banshee."

Pagan gathered up the improvised pieces of Maud's costume: ballet slippers, pink tights, a gold cardboard crown. Sometimes Pagan wondered, although she would never say it to Zeke, if Zeke was attracted to women partly because it was a stay against being left by a man. Zeke would say this was ridiculous, but Pagan knew it bothered her that she couldn't remember their father, whose death had been a kind of leaving. And Zeke claimed she didn't remember Marco's abandonment, but Pagan knew she did.

When Zeke was little, someone had given her a plastic hammer with an orange head and a pink handle. Hollow and dented, it was impossible to lose because of its bright colors. Marco and

Zeke developed a little game. He would pretend to hold an imaginary nail for Zeke to hammer. *"Tap, tap, tap,"* he would say. And on the third tap, Zeke would hammer his finger. Marco would howl, hop up and down, spin around as if he'd been terribly injured. Zeke laughed and laughed, "Do it again!" *Tap, tap, tap,* and she would reach over and catch Marco's finger, at which point he would go through his cartoonlike convulsions.

"Stop," her mother protested, laughing. "You're teaching her to hit."

"Oh, she knows it's a game," Marco said.

But after he left, Zeke would wander around the cabin, forlorn, saying *"tap tap tap?"* Her tone was tentative, as if she had misremembered a magic formula. Off and on, she'd done it for days, walking around with that ugly plastic hammer, until one day, when Prana was playing in her high chair, Zeke went *"tap tap TAP!"* and smacked one of Prana's fingers. Prana shrieked, and her mother moved across the room, snatching the hammer from Zeke.

"No more Marco! No more *tap, tap, tap!*"

Zeke, usually stubborn or truculent when crossed, pitched an absolute screaming fit. Pagan remembered thinking, even then, that she'd never seen Zeke so upset. Her mother picked up Prana and carried her outside to comfort her, leaving Zeke hollering in the kitchen.

Pagan sighed. Of course this didn't account for Zeke's diffidence, that her girlfriends all tended to be feminine, that Zeke always seemed to keep the upper hand. Marcie was rare, dramatic. She made Pagan think of an exotic bird, or a plant that required a great deal of sun and light, choking out all the other plants around it.

•   •   •

THE FIRST TIME they met, Zeke had brought Marcie and her daughters to Pagan and Tommy's for dinner. After dinner, washing up, Marcie looked at her and said, "Well, Zeke told me you weren't a wild woman, but it's not every day you meet someone named Pagan."

Pagan tried to smile. She often felt that she disappointed people. She had failed to live up to her name.

"I get that a lot," Pagan said.

Marcie's eyes went wide. "Of course you must. That's silly of me. I was nervous about meeting you. I get the sense that Zeke doesn't always bring her girlfriends home." Marcie wiped her hands on a dish towel nervously. Her apologetic stance was disarming.

"No, she doesn't." Pagan smiled. "Only the ones she thinks are worth keeping." She said it lightly, to set Marcie at ease.

Later, after they'd left, she realized this was true. Zeke introduced them only to women she was serious about. One minute, Marcie had seemed intrusive and, in the next, she'd made Pagan feel she was terribly vulnerable, as if Pagan had been allowed a glimpse of her insecurity about Zeke. Maybe Marcie wasn't so tough after all.

THESE KIND OF conversations were the reason she usually introduced herself as Peg. Her name was like a gift of exotic clothes that she didn't feel bold enough to wear. As a child, she felt self-conscious, but in the weepy rages of preadolescence, she resented the unusual nature of her name because she felt betrayed.

At the beginning of every school year, the class list revealed her as Pagan, and she had to contend with whispers from the girls, boys asking if her father was a biker or what. In middle school, she had silenced a taunting eighth-grader by saying her father was a Black Panther. She didn't know what a Black Panther was, but it sounded dangerous, and the boy had left her alone, banging his hand down the row of lockers as he walked away.

When she got off the bus, she stomped into the house and threw her backpack on the floor. Her mother was sitting at the dining room table, going over a contract.

"I hate my name! I hate it! Why did you do this to us?"

Her mother looked up, surprised.

"What happened?"

"What happens every year? People make fun of me. You named us for *you*, what *you* believed in. Now I'm stuck with this stupid name!"

Her mother took off her reading glasses, set down her pen, and turned to face Pagan.

"I didn't name you for me. I didn't want you to be—" and her mother stopped, searching for the right word, "constricted. I know you don't really remember my parents, but they were so self-righteous! So disapproving. Every single night at dinner, my mother would sit at the table and talk about what person in our neighborhood hadn't behaved quite right. Who didn't mow their lawn, who had a messy garage, whose car was too showy, who didn't bring this or that to the church bake sale." Her mother stopped and shook her head. "They wasted their lives over nothing, nothing!" She turned away from Pagan and faced the window; her voice sounded muffled. "If you don't like your name, change it. I wanted you to have license to do whatever you wanted. I didn't want you to grow up to be some pathetic woman who spent her time thinking about what shade of beige carpet to buy. My God," and her mother turned back to her, quickly wiping under her eyes. "My mother once complained that our neighbors had chosen geraniums that were too loud, *garish* was the word she used. For flowers!"

Pagan couldn't quite absorb what her mother was saying. "Is that why we never see them?" she asked.

"There's nothing to see them for," her mother said quietly. "I probably shouldn't say these things, come here." And Pagan walked to her mother, still seated at the table. Her mother reached for her and leaned her head against Pagan's chest, as if listening to her heart. Pagan smoothed her mother's hair, and looked out at the leaves, thick and sheltering, dividing them from the neighbor's yard.

thirteen

PRANA'S WORK SCHEDULE, WITH DEADLINES SET MONTHS before the holidays arrived, made her feel out of step with the rest of world. Halloween shoots were done in June, Thanksgiving in July, Christmas in August. When the actual holiday arrived, Prana often had an odd feeling of déjà vu combined with a sense that the holiday must have passed months ago.

Walking home from work, seeing children in their costumes, Prana realized tonight was Halloween. She was supposed to go to an opening at a friend's gallery. A little girl in a sweater and tights, cat whiskers drawn on her face, skipped next to her mother on the sidewalk. Prana remembered dressing up as a hippie during her freshman year at college. The tie-dyed shirt and string head band weren't hard to find. Bell bottoms took a bit more work. She carried a friend's guitar, and with her long hair parted in the middle, people kept saying "Flower Power" or "Woodstock" to her. Prana thought of her mother.

Halloween, with the arrival of cold weather, had always seemed like a doorway to the holidays, but her mother had never been one to fuss over the holiday season. They didn't have many traditions. As a child, Prana simply accepted this, but as she grew older, she suspected her mother didn't want to call attention to the absence of fathers in their lives. At Thanksgiving, her mother invited people from her office who were on their own, friends whose marriages were fizzling, and their house was filled with people, good food and wine, and felt like a day-long party. These days, when Prana thought about her mother's open houses, their holidays seemed especially sweet. Many of her friends had mothers who became tightly wound or totally unraveled: mothers who went crazy with Christmas preparations, who came unglued when something disturbed their party plans, mothers who became manic with lights and crèche ornaments, mothers who became totally depressed and told their kids to microwave TV dinners, mothers who took to their beds with Valium. Her mother had not done any of these things. Marco leaving must have been the last straw, but her mother didn't retreat into details, she retreated into her daughters.

One year, when Prana was small, they went to Vermont at Christmas, where a friend of her mother's had a large house. It had taken a long time to get there, and Prana remembered driving in the dark, the swirl of snow against their headlights. They had hot chocolate with marshmallows when they arrived. The next day, in the dazzling sun, she tried to learn to snowplow, but the tips of her skis kept crossing one another while Zeke flew past her down the hill. Another year, when Zeke was in college and doing some naturalist work out in Baja California, she said she couldn't come home for Christmas. She was miles from even the closest town and could leave the site only for a few days, so their mother had flown everyone to San Diego to meet her.

To Prana, the idea of Christmas in California seemed exotic. She was a senior in high school then, still living at home. Pagan was out of college and had her own apartment. Her mother started a flurry of arrangements, as if spending Christmas together had become an important mission. She said it would be less expensive for her and Prana to drive to Pagan's, leave their car there, and then all of them would take a car service to the airport. To Prana, these plans seemed luxurious: having a man put their bags in the trunk of an expensive car, arriving at JFK, and then, finally, landing in a sunny world of palm trees and cactus. She was entranced by the warm climate, by the unfamiliar flowers blooming around her, as if Christmas were happening only on the East Coast and they had left it behind.

On Christmas Day, they ate at a Mexican restaurant. Her mother ordered a margarita for Prana, and the unfamiliar blend of salt and lime and tequila was delicious. She felt blurred and happy, sitting in the sunny room with her mother and sisters. Prana was amazed to see her mother giggling, and with her flushed cheeks, her air of pleasure and lightness, Prana could imagine her as Marco's girlfriend, a young woman who existed not for her daughters, but in a private connection to someone else.

As a child, Prana felt as if they were all in a little boat by themselves. Her mother paddled through still waters as she and her sisters trailed their hands outside the boat, fingers rippling the surface. Her mother was the center from which they all issued, the arbiter in all important decisions. She had cut herself off from her own family, seemingly without regret. She had a sister who was an accountant somewhere in Ohio, a brother who had died in Vietnam. She rarely discussed her parents. Every year at Christmas, the girls received bulky holiday sweaters from a department store in Columbus. The sweaters, bright red and green, were undeniably ugly, but their mother always insisted on thank-you notes, her insistence tinged with defiance, as if sending an unspoken message: *See, I can raise children with proper manners.* On Christmas Day, sitting at the restaurant, Zeke made a joke about their annual sweaters, and her mother picked up a tortilla chip, and said, "God, those sweaters were so damn ugly!" They burst out laughing at her unexpected bluntness, laughed until they wept, and when Prana caught her breath, she looked around the table at her sisters and her mother; she felt happy and included.

After a few days, Zeke had to return to her project, and the rest of them flew back to New York. The cold was biting, but exciting, and Prana felt as if she carried a small circle of warmth inside her. Her mother had arranged for the inverse of their departure, and a driver met them at the airport and took them back to Pagan's apartment, which was just north of the city. Pagan had her own brass-plated mailbox in the foyer, her own dishes from Pier One, and Prana admired her independence. They lingered at her apartment for a while, separating their luggage and various souvenirs. Then Prana and her mother drove back home together.

PRANA DIDN'T FEEL like going to the opening at Jorge's gallery, but he would be disappointed if she didn't come. Stephan was invited, but he would most likely be home, seeing to his children, taking his younger daughter trick-or-treating. Mostly, he didn't care for openings, being forced to make polite comments. He mainly went as an excuse to see Prana, and they would circle each other, making small talk, pretending to be acquaintances. Afterward they would meet at her apartment.

She showered, got dressed to go out, poured herself a glass of wine. She hadn't actually spoken to Stephan since he'd left her apartment the other night. He didn't know about her mother's disappearance. Of course her mother and sisters were shadow cutouts to him, unreal, so her mother's disappearance was merely an absence on absence.

She called Joe, but there was no answer. It was better he wasn't home, she told herself. She'd been going over there too often. She breathed in and could almost taste the metallic rush of smoke.

THE OPENING WAS packed, loud with the clatter of talk. People in costumes dotted the crowd: a dragon with green face paint, a knight, a jack of spades. The photos were overwhelmed by all the people, which was too bad, some of the pictures looked interesting, but it was hard to see them without room to stand back. She liked to simply be quiet and look, let the image do the work.

Jorge saw her come in and made his way across the room. He was dressed like a bullfighter, wearing white satin breeches and a closely cut coat. Prana thought he looked like Spanish royalty, his black hair pulled back in a pony tail. He kissed her on both cheeks. "Everyone loves Eli's work," he said. "But you didn't put on a costume." His tone was accusing.

She raised one eyebrow and turned away, surveying the crowd.

"Oh, but you look lovely darling." Then he leaned over. "Stephan just got here and that bitch from the Corcoran is circling."

Prana looked over his shoulder. She had seen the woman before. She was dressed as a flapper in a beaded dress, her hair a smooth black cap, her mouth like a gash. Something about the woman reminded her of Marcie. She was standing in a little group with Stephan and a girl wearing chunky black glasses, clearly a student. Prana could hear the girl mouthing a long-sounding title, "The Work of Art in the Age of Mechanical Reproduction," rolling it quickly as if she had practiced the string of syllables. Her expression was serious. She said something about Benjamin. The flapper waved her cigarette holder. *Ben-ya-meen*, she tightened it with her red mouth, laughing, as if the girl's ignorance were the funniest thing she'd heard all day.

"I need to mingle," Jorge said.

Prana put her hand on his shoulder, as if getting ready to dance. She made him a shield, allowing her to see without being seen.

"Just a minute," she whispered in his ear.

"A photograph is always a metaphor," the flapper said.

She must be a professor, full of words, clever, and Prana saw the twist of Stephan's mouth, the wrinkles she loved at the corners of his eyes. The woman was interesting to him. She disdained what others admired.

"These pictures," she said, waving her cigarette holder. "They aim low and hit." Her lipsticked mouth blood red and clear. Sharp, she was sharp, and Prana felt herself blurry and vague, her borders ill-defined.

She had another glass of wine, and left without speaking to Stephan. He would call. It was a short walk back to her apartment, and in the clear night, the children in by now, she blew cold air out of her mouth and wondered if her mother knew about Stephan. Sometimes, Prana imagined that she knew.

More than a year ago, sitting in her mother's living room, Prana asked, almost idly, about business. Her mother said she had just found a wonderful house for a couple, but she guessed they were unhappy. She said that unhappy couples often bought new houses, as if the project of a new home would rejuvenate their marriage. Her mother had gazed at her, and Prana sensed she was waiting for her to say something. But what would she say? She wasn't afraid of her mother's judgment, only that her mother would voice what Prana knew to be the truth.

Her life was hinged on someone who was gone for months at a time, who came back to her when he could, who claimed she was his touchstone, his muse, his love, and the sad thing was that she believed him. Not sad because it was false, but because it was true. What seemed most pathetic to Prana was that, when she was younger, it had all seemed romantic, but now she was starting to understand what a terrible cliché it all was. Once, she had imagined that she and Stephan were exceptional and rare, but now she knew that wasn't true at all—they were one of the oldest stories in the world, and there was something humiliating about having imagined they were different. She has had other boyfriends, other lovers. Once, she and Stephan broke off for a while, and she started seeing someone else, but he turned out to be a terrible mistake. Each time she and Stephan were together, she thought that he was worth anything, the whole world. She knew she couldn't simply eliminate this idea; she needed something to supplant him: not a man, or another person, something larger.

Prana lit a cigarette. She told herself that one day she would quit smoking, break up with Stephan, take a trip to Europe, shoot pictures herself. But she was turning twenty-eight, and it had occurred to her that perhaps there was no new leaf, nothing she could radically change. She had tried to quit smoking. Stephan was a different matter; it was hard to split up with someone she wasn't truly with. It was like trying to eradicate a belief or an idea, someone who lingered because he was present even in his absence.

She pulled an ashtray toward her. The vessel on her table seemed the only warm thing in her apartment. She wished she could tell her sisters about Stephan, explain all that she had been thinking. She wished they would include her, although in what, she didn't know. With her mother's disappearance, the gap between her and her sisters seemed larger. They might simply float apart.

fourteen

PAGAN COULD STILL REMEMBER THE PRECISE MOMENT SHE had fallen in love with Tommy, or perhaps it was the moment when she knew she would fall into something beyond sex, beyond a diverting and thrilling complication in her life, into something larger. It had happened in those early weeks of knowing each other, sometime after they'd started sleeping together, when each of her senses seemed distinct and heightened, and ordinary objects around her—a coffee cup, a familiar piece of clothing—seemed to stand out in relief. As she moved through her tasks at work: reports and projections, analyses and charts, she felt a strange combination of being more preoccupied and more present than she had ever felt in her life. They were still new with each other, assembling their own versions of each other's histories, but they didn't quite know how to be together yet. One Sunday, after brunch with some friends, she and Tommy had gone back to his apartment and spent most of the afternoon in bed. When he got up to use the bathroom, Pagan idly, naked, got up to look at the photos on his dresser. They were all family pictures. Tommy with various groupings of his siblings, glasses raised at clamorous occasions: graduations, birthday parties, his sisters' weddings, the whole buoyant Irish-looking brood of them. She saw a folded slip of vanilla-colored paper tucked under a small box, and almost without thinking, she picked it up.

> *Lord, I know not what I ought to ask of Thee; Thou only*
> *knowest what I need . . . . I simply present myself before*
> *Thee, I open my heart to Thee. Behold my needs which I*
> *know not myself. Smite, or heal; depress me, or raise me up;*
> *I adore all Thy purposes without knowing them; I am silent;*
> *I offer myself in sacrifice; I yield myself to Thee; I would*
> *have no other desire than to accomplish Thy Will. Teach me*
> *to pray. Pray Thyself in me. Amen.*
> —*François Fénelon, 1651–1715*
> *French Archbishop of Cambray*

It was written in Tommy's hand, a slightly younger, more open version, but she recognized it. He had copied it himself. She was stunned by the humility of the prayer, the presumed activity of God. *Pray Thyself in me.* The expression of such devotion was so unexpected, so interior, that she was startled. He had grown up Catholic, but she had not expected this.

Pagan didn't believe in anything herself, but she resisted the idea that her lack of belief had anything to do with her name.

Her mother hadn't named her as a negative, *against* religion, so much as *for* something else—something dark and wild, unstructured, the worship of nature rather than organized religion. Pagan hadn't lived up to her name. She wished she were wilder, more adventurous, but she protected herself in ways her mother had not imagined necessary. Pagan thought of religion as something people turned to when life got difficult. The sense of community and common belief made life easier to bear. She didn't think there was anything wrong with this. If God was smoke and mirrors, the opium of the people, it didn't really matter. Whatever helped. Tommy walked back into the room and saw her standing at the dresser with the piece of paper in her hand. He flushed a deep red.

"You really believe, don't you?" she asked softly.

He took the paper from her hand, as if it were something small and delicate, a piece of eggshell, and set it back on the dresser. In memory, Pagan felt the exactness of that moment ripple out through time. If he had denied the import of the scrap of paper, she would never have completely trusted him. If he had become embarrassingly pious, or clicked over into the mode she thought of as Christian Cruise Control—straight ahead, black and white, the righteous and the damned—she would have thrown on her clothes and never looked back. But it was his silent acknowledgment, and then the fact that it was clearly too personal.

"I copied that a long time ago," he said, and she heard in his voice, not apology, but something else, and later she would wonder if it was a kind of premonition, knowing he hadn't been tested.

He took her hand, pulled her away from the dresser, and they lay down on the rumpled bed.

"But you don't go to church every Sunday, do you?"

"Mass? No, not anymore. Sometimes I go with my parents. I have a brother who was a priest."

"You're kidding."

"No, he's the oldest. He's . . ." Pagan watched him do the invisible math in his head. "Thirteen years older than me."

"Why did he leave? Did he stop believing?"

"No. He just thought the Church was screwed up on too many important issues. He said he had to leave because he didn't represent what the Catholic Church believed. And then there was the whole celibacy thing."

"What about it?"

"He said he wouldn't be able to keep his vows. I think he was falling in love. He's been living with a woman named Kate for years now."

"I've never met anyone who had a priest in the family." Pagan felt awkward after she said it, as if her surprise implied that Tommy's brother was a mere curiosity.

"I admire my brother," Tommy said. "He really lives according to what he believes."

"So with all this heavy-duty Catholic background, I'm surprised you believe in birth control." Pagan couldn't help teasing him.

"Some things are simply meant to be enjoyed," Tommy said, and pressed her down against the bed.

fifteen

ZEKE SURVEYED THE LOAD OF NEW BEDDING. SHE WAS GOING to try straw for a change. Someone had called the other day about buying manure, and he wanted to know what she used for bedding. He was growing organic portobello and shiitake mushrooms, and Zeke told him to come and take what he wanted, amused that someone had actually proposed to pay her for shit. With all the animals, Zeke had more than they needed for their own small garden, which was mostly finished now. The university administration would be thrilled if the farm could generate some income.

She supervised a variety of small-scale environmental projects: learning to compost; organic gardening 101. Groups of kids came from nearby schools to pet the goats, watch the sheep being shorn. Continuing Education used the cottage as a place to teach jewelry making, soap and candlemaking, batik. Zeke liked the unclassifiable nature of the place, although university paperwork constantly required her to defend the farm's existence and expenses in terms of community service.

She walked out into the south pasture. She wanted to make sure the sheep were safely corralled. Last Halloween, some frat boys, drunk she supposed, had spray painted some of the sheep. She had talked to the administration, who claimed the boys were contrite, but Zeke didn't imagine they were truly remorseful. She went over to the frat house to have a little talk with them. A group of boys, tapping a keg, looked surprised to see her. Since she wasn't a student, they couldn't figure out what she was doing, standing with her hands in her pockets, looking at them with disdain. She had not minced words about exactly where she'd like to put their cans of paint, suggesting that perhaps they'd spray painted the sheep because they'd found it too hard to get hold of the sheep for themselves. There were a few sniggers, but mostly the boys seemed too embarrassed to laugh. There was no trouble with the animals after that. Zeke had observed, even then, that Marcie's style was starting to rub off on her.

Zeke walked into the cottage, and sat down at her desk to do some paperwork, when Pagan called.

"Can I come up tomorrow and get the key to look around Mom's house? I was thinking about poking around Shady Grove too, maybe going to her office."

Zeke was quiet for a moment, then said, "You know, it'll look strange that we don't know where she is."

Pagan didn't answer, and Zeke could imagine her mentally reshuffling her plans.

"You're right," Pagan said, and then as if to change the subject, "How's Marcie?"

"Fine," Zeke said. "It's Amy's seventh birthday. We're going out to dinner. I've got to slip out this afternoon and pick up her present."

MARCIE HADN'T SETTLED on where they would eat that night, and at the end of the day, when Zeke called her house and got no answer, she felt suddenly anxious. They should be home now. Where would they be? Zeke felt a tightness in her stomach.

Half an hour later, when there was still no answer, she drove to Marcie's telling herself not to worry, take a deep breath, calm down. She pulled up to the curb and saw Marcie's Audi backed halfway into the garage, a gash on the front right side, the fender crumpled. Zeke reached for Amy's present, but its bright wrapping and curly ribbons seemed out of place, and she left it in the car. When Marcie opened her front door, Zeke could see from her expression that she had forgotten their plans.

"What happened?" Zeke asked.

"We had a little fender bender." Marcie leaned forward and kissed her on the cheek. "I'm so sorry we forgot about dinner. We can go in a little while. I've had a ridiculous afternoon on the phone. We're waiting for the insurance adjuster."

Zeke looked over her shoulder at the girls, and from the blanched, chastened looks on their faces, Zeke knew Marcie had told them to keep their mouths shut. Amy was clutching a ratty doll Zeke hadn't seen in a year.

"Happy birthday, sweetheart," she bent down to hug Amy, who clung to her for a moment, but remained quiet. Zeke asked Marcie to come outside.

Marcie looked as if she were going on a job interview: fresh makeup, a dash of perfume that Zeke didn't like. Zeke walked her away from the front door, down the path toward the garage.

"You were drinking." Zeke felt herself shaking.

"All I had was a glass of wine," Marcie said. She waved it off as if Zeke's concern were trifling. Zeke watched her mouth, lipsticked to seem more suburban and femme. "The other driver was going much too fast. The police even said so."

Zeke guessed the police had looked at Marcie's sleek, sporty clothes, the girls in the car, and had been too stupid to give her a Breathalizer test in the middle of the day. So here was Marcie, revising the story to suit herself only a few hours later. Zeke felt blood pounding in her temples. Marcie's ability to talk a good game drove her crazy. She always sounded plausible. She could take a kernel of truth and spin it into something else entirely. The more Marcie talked, the sicker Zeke felt, because she knew that as Marcie spoke, she became enamored of her own version.

They were standing at the edge of the garage and, almost to steady herself, Zeke put her hand on a rake tipped against Marcie's garage wall. It was an old rake, with short, iron tines and a thick wooden handle, and as Marcie continued to talk, protesting that it was only one glass of wine, it wasn't her fault, Zeke suddenly couldn't stand the ridiculous self-serving stories Marcie made up about herself. Poor Marcie, who played the victim when it was convenient, who had everything her way and made it everyone else's fault. Zeke lifted the rake high in the air and stepped forward, feeling the heft of it. She wished it were a gavel; she wanted to get Marcie's attention, make her stop her self-righteous ranting, and raising it high, Zeke let gravity bring the heavy rake down hard, the metal tines cracking the windshield of Marcie's car.

"I don't want you driving this car until you get yourself sober. I'll take you to court. I'll have the girls taken away from you," Zeke yelled.

Marcie looked over her shoulder. Eleanor stood in the back doorway to the garage; her expression was terrified as she took in Zeke holding the rake, the opacity of shattered glass. Zeke felt a hot, searing regret. She stepped toward Eleanor, who ran back into the house.

"I can't believe you!" Marcie hissed, looking toward the neighbor's yard. "What the hell are you doing?"

"Marcie, I've had it. Do something. Go to AA, check into rehab, I don't care, but this is it!"

"You're damn right, this is it."

"I'm just going in to say good night to the girls."

"No you're not," Marcie said. "Get out of here."

Zeke stepped away from the car and walked down the driveway. She looked back to see Eleanor and Amy peeking through the front storm door. She lifted her hand, as if to say "I'll be back in a minute." Eleanor looked out, unmoving behind the glass.

t w o

one

IT HAD BEEN TWO WEEKS SINCE THE AMNIO, AND PAGAN didn't want to sit around the house, waiting for the results. When Maud started pulling Tupperware out of the cupboard for the second time that morning, Pagan felt suddenly suffocated by the idea of going to the local park one more time. "Push me, push me, push me," Maud would call, kicking her legs back and forth. Pagan dialed Zeke, to make sure she'd be at the farm when they arrived.

"I still don't think Mom would want you asking around town," Zeke said.

"She had to know we'd be curious."

"What are you going to do?" Zeke asked. "Play Nancy Drew with Maud?"

Pagan laughed. Once, when she was about nine, checking out a stack of mysteries, the local librarian sniffed and declared the books weren't worth the paper they were written on. Pagan felt as if she'd been slapped. Standing at the counter, she clutched her library card and focused on the tight grain of the shining blond wood. It had never occurred to her that someone could disdain something that gave her so much pleasure. Zeke, standing at Pagan's shoulder, murmured "Cow" under her breath, just loud enough for the librarian to hear. The woman looked back and forth between them, not sure which sister had spoken. In spite of her humiliation, Pagan was thrilled that Zeke had taken her side.

Pagan gathered herself to get out the door. Even for the forty-minute drive up to Briarcliff, there were Pull-Ups to put on, snacks to pack, Tippy Cups to rinse and fill, a change of clothes for spills and accidents, important toys for distraction, kiddie tapes for the car—a last resort, because Pagan thought she might lose her mind if she had to listen to any more *Wee Sing* tapes. As they drove, Pagan smiled at Maud in the rear-view mirror. She would love being a big sister. Her eyes were starting to close, her head drooping against the side of the car seat. Of course she would fall asleep just as they were getting close to the farm.

As soon as Pagan stopped the car, Maud woke from her dozing and realized where she was.

"Horsie?" She waved her hands in the air. "Auntie Zeke?"

"Yes, Auntie Zeke."

Pagan got out of the car and stretched. She smelled pine and sun, fallen leaves, the Hudson in the distance. Briarcliff seemed like the country to her now. Zeke came out of the cottage, the screen door banging behind her. She looked puffy around the eyes and leaned into the car to get Maud out of her car seat.

"How do you get these damn things undone?" she asked.

"Damn tings!" Maud smiled.

Pagan sighed. "Thanks, Zeke."

"Sorry, I forget she's a little minah bird."

"Damn tings! Damn tings!"

"Okay, enough now," Zeke said. "Let's go see the ponies."

They walked over to a paddock where a large gray horse and two shaggy ponies pulled at tufts of grass.

"Are you okay?" Pagan asked.

Zeke made a gesture of dismissal with her hand and shook her head.

"What happened to the sick pony?" Pagan asked.

"That's him." Zeke pointed to Ebenezer.

Maud was fascinated by the horses, but when they came to the fence, she was frightened by their big-lipped snuffling for carrots. She crowded Pagan's legs, and Pagan reached forward, patting the horse's head.

"See, just be gentle," Pagan said. She looked over at Zeke, who seemed tired, and Pagan realized she'd been hoping for some revelation, something Zeke wouldn't say on the phone.

"What are you planning to do?" Zeke asked.

"I'm not sure," Pagan said. "I can't go to her office. You're right, it'll look strange that we don't know where she is."

Zeke nodded and looked out over the paddock.

"I was thinking of going into town, to see if she has a safe deposit box."

"I doubt they're allowed to give out information like that."

Pagan blew out of her mouth in exasperation. "Do you think I shouldn't bother?"

"I didn't say that." Zeke reached over the fence and pulled a burr out of Ebenezer's mane.

"Have you talked to Prana?" Pagan asked.

"She doesn't call me," Zeke said, and flicked a bug off the fence.

Pagan nodded. Zeke didn't exactly invite confidences, but Pagan felt this way too. It was hard to say when this distance had crept up on them. Their sister never initiated a phone conversation, rarely seemed to be home. Pagan left messages, and Prana called back at odd intervals.

"What do you think's going on with her?" Pagan asked.

"Beyond Mom being gone?"

"She seems . . . unconnected."

"Man trouble," Zeke said.

"How do you know?"

Zeke shrugged.

"Why wouldn't she tell us?"

"He's a senator, a Russian spy, he's on the House Ways and Means Committee, who the hell knows?"

Pagan remembered coming home from her freshman year at college, and realizing that Prana wasn't a kid anymore. Slender and ethereal, she suddenly seemed enigmatic. Prana was named after her mother's time in an ashram. Her name meant "breath," a life force, and like air she seemed both insubstantial and necessary. Of all of them, she looked most like their mother. Her straight brown hair was long and fine, parted in the middle. Her mysteriousness coincided with the onset of adolescence, as if something large and silent had bloomed inside her; but her silent blooming didn't manifest itself outwardly, so she bore a sense of potential that was undefined, like water underground.

When it was time to leave, Maud didn't want to go.

"More horsie! Goat! Goat!"

"We'll be back, sweetheart." Pagan put out her hand, but Maud dropped to the ground. Pagan picked her up, brushed her hair out of her face, then hauled her, unwilling, to the car. Maud started to sob. Pagan turned to Zeke after getting her buckled in.

"It's the little things, you know? Sometimes just getting from one place to the next is such a hassle."

"How are you feeling?"

"Okay, better than last time." Pagan sighed. "I should be getting the amnio results soon. We're really curious about whether it's a boy or a girl."

PAGAN HAD ALREADY called the real estate firm where her mother worked, posing as a potential customer, but the receptionist merely said her mother was away. Pagan didn't press her; she imagined it would seem suspicious. Shady Grove was a small community, and unless she was discrete, her inquiries would be noticed.

As a child, Pagan hadn't realized that Shady Grove was a privileged place to grow up. Families bought large colonials set back from the street on one-acre plots, or modern houses of wood and glass perched in the sapling woods. The town was not made up of neighborhoods, although children might play together in certain suburbs or subdivisions. The elementary schools were spread out among its rolling suburban distances, but there was one middle school and one high school so that, by the time she reached high school, she understood her place in the social structure of the town.

It wasn't that everyone knew each other, but rather people knew of each other. A critically famous movie actor moved to town when Pagan was in high school, and the town had been abuzz for a while, but he had been gracious and friendly, and people had grown used to his presence. The woman who'd written

My Side of the Mountain lived in Shady Grove. There were other
types, the minorly famous, her mother called them: an eccentric
writer of children's books, a few techno-whizzes at IBM. There
was Carl Schulman, the violinist, whose wife was the principal at
the high school. He used to teach at Juilliard, but now mainly
composed and played experimental music. Although he occasionally taught violin here in town and Pagan had briefly and disas-
trously taken lessons with him herself, people mainly knew about
him because of his wife's job. The principals, assistant principals,
notorious teachers—everyone knew who their spouses and kids
were. Everyone knew if they divorced or found themselves in
legal trouble. Pagan remembered thinking that Schulman and his
wife didn't match. His bearing was quiet, but imposing. He was
from eastern Europe, or somewhere she imagined as rich and
dark and full; his wife seemed antiseptic and formal.

She pulled into the parking lot at the top of King Street;
some of the smaller stores had changed, but the Grand Union
was still there. Across the road was Mullane's, the bar they all
congregated in as soon as they could drink. She got Maud out
of the car seat and led her into the bank. A young woman, who
didn't look old enough to have a grown-up job, greeted her.

"Hi, I'm wondering if you can help me," Pagan said. "My
mother is out of the country, and when I stopped at her house, I
found some jewelry missing. I'm trying to find out if she'd put
anything in her safe deposit box recently." Pagan knew she was
talking too fast; her lie sounded rehearsed.

"I'm sorry, but we don't have safe deposit boxes here. Even
if we did, we certainly couldn't give you that information." The
girl pinched her eyebrows together in disapproval. "You could
try the bank at the bottom of the hill."

Pagan resisted the urge to say something snotty. She took

Maud's hand and led her out of the bank. Outside, Maud pulled
her toward a gift shop window.

"Did you know I used to go into this store when I was little?"

Maud shook her head and stared at a toy carousel on dis-
play. It turned slowly in the window, the toy horses moving up
and down.

"I used to love the glass animals they kept on the back
shelf," Pagan said. As she spoke, she started to guide Maud
toward the car, as if there were other magical things to see.

The town of Shady Grove was mostly comprised of quaint
shops in old houses. At the turn of King Street, an antiques store
occupied a large home with uncharacteristically southern pil-
lars. There was the local music store, where her mother had
bought violin strings, sheet music, and other music parapherna-
lia for them. At the bottom of the hill, Pagan passed the real
estate firm where her mother worked.

There was so much she had half-forgotten or never recognized in Shady Grove. She supposed it was the self-absorption
of adolescence, but other people in town had seemed like back-
drops on a set. When their neighbor, a gentle, bearlike man, left
his wife and moved in with the high school French teacher, it
had been a real scandal, but Pagan never would have said anything to his kids, who she played with almost every day. Saying
something would have broken down a necessary wall and
brought a distant drama into the foreground of her life.

She parked behind the bank and wondered if her vague
story would work. One of her sisters, it must have been Prana,
had played with the daughters of the president. She remembered
Mr. Reynolds as a stern, balding man.

When she walked in and asked for Mr. Reynolds, the teller
nodded toward a large, glassed-in office.

"You can just knock on the door. It's open," she said.

Maud was fascinated by a large cardboard cutout of a dog digging up a bone, an ad for not burying your investments. Pagan tapped on his office door.

"Excuse me? I'm not sure you'd remember me. I'm Pagan Williams. Prana's older sister."

"Please come in." He stood up and extended his hand with the formal bearing of someone accustomed to dealing with the public. "I haven't seen you in years. Is this your little girl?"

"Yes, this is Maud." Maud promptly hid behind her legs. "Of course she's not shy most of the time."

He laughed. "I've got grandchildren myself now. Three of them. Gail has two boys and Margaret has a little girl. What can I do for you, Pagan?"

"Well, my mother is out of the country and not really accessible by phone. My sister stopped to check on the house, and there's some jewelry missing. I'm not asking to look in her safe deposit box, but I wondered if she'd been in recently. We want to make sure nothing was stolen."

Mr. Reynolds frowned. "We can't check on the contents of the boxes or verify any transactions, but your mother was in, well, let's see . . . maybe a month or so ago. I remember seeing her go into the vault. She didn't tell me she was taking a trip."

Pagan forced a smile. "I'm assuming she put things there for safekeeping. She probably didn't want to leave jewelry in a closed-up house."

"That's always wise. Where is your mother traveling?"

Pagan tried to think of somewhere where there weren't lots of phones, somewhere not too improbable.

Maud reached for a pencil-filled cup on his desk.

"Oh Maud, no!" Pagan reached to steady the cup.

"Wanna pencil!" Maud stuck her lower lip out.

"I know sweetie, but we have crayons in the car."

"Pencil!"

She took Maud's hand. "Oh, she's really moving around a lot."

Mr. Reynolds nodded.

PAGAN'S HEART THUMPED as she strapped Maud into her car seat and gave her a kiss. An imminent tantrum had never been so useful. She turned up the road toward her mother's house and pointed to the duck pond.

"See that big tree by the pond, Maud? Every year they make it into a huge Christmas tree."

Maud rubbed a crayon on the harness of her car seat, and Pagan drove on.

WHEN SHE PULLED into her mother's driveway, Pagan noticed a woman sitting on the front steps of the house next door. She was watching a little boy ride a Big Wheel in the driveway. An older couple had lived in the house for years. They had no children. Pagan wondered if the house had been sold. Clearly, her mother hadn't gotten the listing, because she would have mentioned it if she were responsible for finding a buyer for the house next door. She got Maud out of the car, straightened up, then waved. The woman, hesitant, waved back. Pagan wondered how to casually pump her for information. She took Maud by the hand and walked over.

"I thought I'd say hello. Have you just moved in?" Pagan asked.

The woman smiled. "You have to excuse me. I don't have my contacts in, so when you waved, I was thinking 'Do I know her? Am I supposed to?' Yes, we're new. My name is Anne—this is Matthew."

"Big Wheel," Maud said, and smiled winningly.

Matthew ignored her and made car noises with his mouth.

"There you have it," Anne said, "the relationship between the sexes."

Pagan laughed. "I'm Pagan Williams."

"Do your parents live next door?"

Pagan started for a minute. Had this woman seen her mother with someone, or was it simply an innocent question?

"No, just my mother. She's away, and I wanted to check on the house."

WHEN SHE AND Maud went inside, Pagan considered the woman's question. How could she ask a stranger: "Did you see my mother with someone?" On the other hand, two parents was the usual thing to assume. It would have been awkward for the woman to ask "Does your mother or father live here?"

Inside, Pagan saw it was just as Zeke had described it. The orderliness was eerie. There was sheet music on the piano, and Pagan glanced at it. Could it be left over from Prana? It looked difficult. There was something indecipherable scrawled across the top margin in pencil. She walked into her mother's office. Pagan had never seen her desk without mounds of papers to be filed. She opened a wide desk drawer: pencils, paper clips, staples. Recent household bills, all paid. In the smaller top drawer she found stacks of business cards held with rubber bands. Maud pressed her face against the window.

"Outside," she said.

"In a few minutes, sweetie."

Her mother's computer was a dark empty blank. Pagan plugged it in, and as it booted up, she took Maud's hand and went upstairs.

In the jewelry box she found only inexpensive jewelry and trinkets: a long feather earring, a silver bracelet with tiger's eye, locks of hair saved in tiny boxes. Her mother hadn't labeled them because their owners were clear: Pagan's dark curls, Zeke's sun-bleached hair, Prana's light brown strands. All so different. The fact that Prana's father was not theirs was inconsequential. They were their mother's daughters and felt this in a tribal way. Their mother had circled them around her, used them as protection, not exposing them to arrows or danger, but building the facade, and then the reality, of a normal suburban life.

Pagan reached for a red yarn necklace with a construction paper heart. The yarn had once threaded macaroni, and she remembered thinking it was truly beautiful, but the pasta must have cracked and fallen off, because now there was only the yarn and a picture of herself pasted to the heart. She remembered the dress and the little red shoes; she must have been six or seven years old. Pagan stared at the mass of curls around her tiny face. She was serious even then. Her father had died. Marco had left. She was the only one who remembered. Pagan put the picture down, went to her mother's night table and opened the drawer. She felt vaguely guilty, as if her mother might walk in on her.

The unexpected quiet startled her, and she ran to the landing to see Maud poised to jump from halfway up the staircase.

"Maud, wait!" Pagan ran down the steps. "Let's see if the computer is on."

She didn't know how to get into the MLS system, but that

wasn't what she was looking for. She tried her mother's e-mail, but after a few tries realized she'd never guess her password. Zeke once said Marcie had all kinds of questionable computer skills, that if Marcie had been a lonely teenager, she would have been a notorious hacker. Pagan wished she were here now. She clicked on DOCUMENTS and scrolled down the list. They were arranged in alphabetical order, mostly by last names that meant nothing to her. She thought for a moment, then changed the settings to see the files by date.

Will, Eisenberg, McCormick, Bettelheim. Pagan felt a rush of anxiety, hoping that "Will" was a person's name. She clicked on the document and it blinked up on the screen. There it was, her mother's will. Revised just before her mother left. It was a template from a program, with highlighted spaces her mother had filled in.

Pagan scanned the legal-sounding language. She was named as the executor. Why? Because she was oldest? Because her mother assumed Tommy would know how to handle this? Cursoring through it, she could only discern what she might have expected. The house was left to all of them. Everything to be divided three ways. The thing that made her tremble was the date. October 12. She told herself that making a will before taking a big trip wasn't an unusual a thing to do. It was a legal formality, nothing suggested a final note. She closed the file. There were no other documents created on that day.

Pagan left the house and carefully locked the door behind her. She wouldn't mention it to Zeke, not yet. Tommy would reassure her, tell her it was routine. She certainly didn't need to give Prana anything to worry about.

Maud started to fuss, and Pagan reached for the crackers, handing them back to her, one at a time, as she drove. Zeke had always seemed the most likely to take off—although she wouldn't have been so mysterious about it. When Zeke was younger, she said she was going to live in Australia or Alaska. They all thought she would do it. No one seemed to have a claim on her. When she was in high school, one of the most sought-after seniors had a crush on her, and Zeke, not really out, even to herself, went around with him; she actually seemed to like him. She did what she pleased, wasn't a joiner; she used to say she was in love with the Marlboro Man. After a few years of college, no one was surprised when Zeke announced she had a girlfriend, but Pagan had always suspected it wasn't quite that simple, that what Zeke needed wasn't necessarily a man or a woman, but someone who would not be intimidated by her.

When Pagan got back to the farm, she lifted Maud out of the car. She thought how simple life would be if it were safe to leave a child alone in a car for five minutes. Of course she wouldn't, not for a second. They found Zeke inside the cottage.

"Hey there." Zeke reached for Maud who cuddled into her neck. "Find anything?"

"Not really." Thinking of the will, Pagan felt herself flush. "She does have a safe deposit box at Yorkville Bank. Mr. Reynolds—remember him? He said she visited it before she left, but, of course, there's no way of knowing what she did there."

Zeke looked out the window, as if she were considering something.

"There's one other thing," Pagan said. "Someone new moved into the house next door. I stopped to say hello because the woman was outside with her kid. She asked me if my parents lived at the house. Parents. I didn't know how to ask if she had seen Mom with someone. It would sound strange."

"*Parents* would be the natural thing to ask though," Zeke said.

'That's what I thought."

Maud started to wriggle in Zeke's arms. "Horsie down, horsie down."

"Oh sweetie," Pagan said. "It's time for your nap. As soon as I start the car you'll fall asleep."

"No." Maud started to wail.

"Come on now, help your Auntie Zeke." Zeke carried her out toward the car.

"Damn tings, Damn tings, Damn, damn!"

"Enough now," Pagan said.

Zeke settled Maud into her car seat, and Pagan stood still, suddenly tired, grateful for the help. As Zeke straightened up, she waved to Maud through the car window, then stuck out her tongue. Maud laughed.

"I'm hardly feeling festive," Pagan said. "But I guess we have to think about Thanksgiving. We can't really plan on Mom being back, you know?"

"I'll keep you posted if I hear anything," Zeke said.

BY THE TIME Pagan reached the main road, Maud had fallen asleep. She turned the classical music station on low and let the music soothe her as she wound down the parkway. It wasn't rush hour yet, and she was going against traffic. She glanced at her watch. Sometimes she could move Maud from the car to her bed, and she would finish out her nap and give Pagan a few extra minutes of peace.

As Pagan carried her into the house, the phone rang. She

gently laid Maud on the living room carpet, still in her coat, and ran for the phone.

"This is Paul Michaelson, calling from the hospital."

"Do you have some good news for me?"

"No, Pagan, I'm sorry, but I'm afraid we do not."

Pagan sat down, suddenly out of breath. "Is the baby Down syndrome?"

"No, I'm afraid it's more serious than that."

Oh, it couldn't be. After last time, this couldn't be right. Hearing the man's calm, concerned tone, Pagan felt something worse, more frightening and clinical, crashing in on her. A heavy sound, like water, rushed in her ears.

"What is it?"

"I'm sorry to tell you this, but the baby has a genetic abnormality called trisomy eighteen. Instead of a problem with the twenty-first chromosome, which results in Down syndrome, the eighteenth chromosome has an extra fragment, and I'm afraid it's a severe condition. The fetus usually dies in utero. Sometimes the baby will live through delivery, but there is about a ninety-five percent chance that the baby will die within the first year."

Pagan felt herself starting to cry. It couldn't be. After last time, it just couldn't. She heard Maud's thin wailing in the other room. Cranky at being woken in mid-nap, she would start bawling.

"But the baby is alive right now?"

"Yes, it is, although it's quite small. I know this is very difficult to hear, but the boys usually die somewhere between the fifth and seventh month. The girls are often a bit stronger, and sometimes live through delivery."

"Which is it?"

"It's a boy."

Pagan thought of Tommy then. Maud wobbled into the kitchen tugging at her coat, wailing.

"What are the baby's chances if it lives?"

"Well, the chances for survival are slim, but unfortunately, even if the child survives, he will be severely retarded. Most of these children are blind, with multiple physical defects."

A whirring sound filled her ears. "Can you hold on?" She spoke into the receiver, not waiting for an answer. She pulled Maud toward her and unzipped her fleecy jacket. Outside the back door, Pagan heard a step, then a key in the lock; it must be Tommy, home from work early. Tears ran down into her mouth as she held the phone under her chin, trying to get Maud out of her coat. She looked up at Tommy and turned to the phone.

"I'm afraid I can't quite—" and she felt her voice start to break. "I'm afraid I can't quite absorb this. I had no idea. My husband just came in. Can you talk to him?"

She handed Tommy the phone.

two

PRANA LAY ON HER MOTHER'S BED, WATCHING HER PUT ON A dark green velvet dress. Her mother examined herself in the mirror, her hair falling down her back, catching on the thick material. She held up an ornate jeweled brooch. Prana looked at the mottled array of stones and thought how ugly it was.

"Were you expecting your father to send you that?" Prana asked.

"I didn't expect anything," her mother said.

"What happened? With them, I mean."

Her mother continued to face the mirror, but she looked at Prana in the reflection. She hesitated, holding the brooch against her dress.

"After Pagan and Zeke's father died, my parents offered to take them while I went back to school."

"Take them?"

"Raise them. Keep them. They said—"

"What?"

"My mother said the accident never would have happened to someone with a real job. She said the way we lived was . . . 'hippie navel gazing' was what she called it."

"So what did you do?"

Her mother twisted her hair into a long coil, raised her arms, and wrapped it onto her head. "I took the girls and left." She reached for a hairpin on her dresser, bowing her head as she pushed the slender pins into the knot she had fashioned. She picked her head up. She looked formal and elegant, but when she swallowed, her eyes became bright, and she reached for a Q-tip and ran it quickly under each eye. Prana picked up a thick gold chain. The gold was almost rose colored. She ran her fingernails along the links.

"What about Marco?"

"Well, you can imagine what my parents would have thought about him."

"Not that," Prana said. "What happened with him?"

Her mother sat down on the bed and looked at her. The fine lines around her eyes were apparent when she smiled. She was beautiful, Prana thought, she had always been beautiful. And sitting before her mother, who gazed at her with such approval and affection, Prana guessed that her grandmother had been unlovely. Perhaps she had been jealous of her daughter's beauty.

"I met Marco about two years after Pagan and Zeke's father died. I was barely getting by in those days." She shook her head, as if wondering how she had managed. "I worked at a bookstore, cooked at an ashram for a while, but Marco had a plan. He always had a plan." Her mother smiled, and Prana looked for some hint of sarcasm, but saw none. "He had some friends who worked on an apple farm in Somers. Marco said he could pick apples in the fall. Maybe I could make apple butter, apple bread; we would do something else in the off-season. So we gathered ourselves up, put everything we owned into a VW bus, and I got pregnant with you." Her mother was smiling widely now, but she must have seen the doubt in Prana's face. "You know, I'd been sad for a long time, and it might seem shallow to say this, but Marco was *fun,* he was full of possibility."

"But what happened then? Why did he leave?" Prana tried to keep the desperation out of her voice.

Her mother pushed a strand of hair from Prana's face.

"Come on now, think about Marco." Her mother's voice was indulgent. "Can you imagine him doing real physical labor? He was thrilled with you, but he wasn't the family type."

Prana wanted to protest—if he was so thrilled, how could he leave? She didn't ask the question, because she knew there was no answer that would make her feel any better. He had left, and his leaving spoke for itself. Her mother pulled her close and murmured that Prana was a gift, a blessing. Prana let herself be held, enclosed in her mother's emerald softness, thinking it was utterly transparent, the way her mother selected what was real.

three

IN THE PAST, WHEN ZEKE SPLIT UP WITH SOMEONE, SHE FELT relieved to regain her solitary status. She might briefly feel sad, but then quickly felt distant, as if the daily world were something she could visit or retreat from. She had thought of this as a strength, but now it seemed dangerous that her connection to other people so easily became tenuous. The lives of people around her seemed like a kaleidoscope design—interconnected and changeable—one turn of the wrist and the pieces would still be connected, still have the same colors, but form a different pattern. Her detachment was like a recurring dream. Mostly, she didn't think about it, but on arriving, the distant place was suddenly familiar. She couldn't get back to that place now. She didn't know whether she and Marcie were truly split up. Ordinarily, this would have been a waiting game, and Zeke would have busied herself with other things, waiting for Marcie to make the next move. But Eleanor and Amy changed everything. Amy's birthday present, with its bright paper and purple ribbons, still sat in the back of her car.

Zeke sighed and looked around the inside of the carriage house. The brown paneling, which she had vowed to take down, was still up; the bookshelves were mostly empty. She had moved here shortly before she met Marcie and had never taken the time to fix the place up for herself. She had not taken the time to do a number of things. Preoccupied with the drama of Marcie, Zeke hadn't noticed anything unusual about her mother, although her mother didn't often confide in her. It was as if, due to Zeke's reticence, her mother felt it was her job to know Zeke, and so she had been thoughtful in little things as a way of having access to Zeke's inner life.

Last month, her mother had given her a book about Lillian Hellman. Although Zeke's interest in the famous owners of the farm across the street was part of her childhood, a curiosity she hadn't talked about much, she was touched that her mother had remembered, but also—and this was so like her mother—her mother had not given her a child's version of her interest, but an adult version. The book was written by a young woman who worked for Hellman one summer, and she wrote about her admiration and disillusionment. Zeke found it eerie that, in many ways, the central character in the book was not Hellman, but the writer's mother, who kept a terrible secret after the death of her husband. Zeke hoped her mother wasn't trying to tell her something.

Her mother's gift surprised her because Prana was the

reader in the family. Prana was always preoccupied with some
book none of them had read, as if she existed in two worlds at
once. When she was younger, she read the usual children's
books, but as she got older, in high school, she seemed to accumulate an odd stash of books on vaguely Eastern, mystical
themes: *Be Here Now, The Doors of Perception, Stalking the
Wild Pendulum.* Last year, at Christmas, her mother had given
Prana a gift certificate to the Yes! bookstore in Washington, and
Prana had been thrilled.

Zeke had never been interested in the mystical or metaphys-
ical. She liked information that could be put to practical use.
Her subscription to *Organic Gardening* came to the farm. *Fine
Homebuilding* came here to the carriage house. She liked to
browse through it, and think about what she might build for
herself.

ON SUNDAY MORNING Zeke bought the *New York Times.* She
didn't usually bother with the paper; the arty stuff bored her, and
the news confirmed her cynicism. Shaking the paper open, she
found today was no exception. The front page story was about a
doctor who'd been killed by a sniper. The doctor worked at a
family planning clinic in Buffalo, and some lunatic lurking in the
trees had taken aim at his living room window. There he was
with his family, home from synagogue—shot in his own living
room. Christ, what a world. Bad enough that those crazies
harassed people at clinics, threatened doctors and their families.
Now this. Zeke set down the paper and saw dust motes floating
in the sun, tiny particles of light, spirit babies.

Her freshman year at college, Zeke's roommate had

explained, very seriously, why she wanted a large family: all those spirit babies lined up, waiting to be born. Zeke remembered watching her berry-sweet mouth and thinking the girl had no idea what she was talking about.

Living in a dorm had been strange. So many girls rebelling against their upbringings, while Zeke herself didn't have anything to push against. She felt sorry for the straight girls, that their sexual experimentation could have such serious consequences. A girl down the hall, a very pious, fundamentalist type, had gotten pregnant her freshman year. Apparently, she hadn't been able to deal with it until she was into her second trimester. Zeke heard the induction or abortion, or whatever they called it, was really horrific. They hooked her up to something in the hospital and let her sweat it out alone in that sterile environment. Of course the girl had chosen that, wanting punishment, she supposed. She was plain, and very near-sighted, with large blue eyes swimming behind her lenses.

Zeke shook herself, put the paper down, and swung her legs from the couch to the floor. Her slightly bony knees, visible through her thinning jeans, pleased her. Would Marcie ever call? The silence seemed foreboding. When the phone did ring, she was startled by the sound.

"Prana?"

"You sound surprised."

I am, Zeke wanted to say, but didn't.

"I've been calling Pagan all weekend, but there's no answer." Prana's voice sounded strained, as if she were holding her anxiety in check.

"She's fine. I saw her Friday. She went into Shady Grove, playing detective."

Prana was quiet. They easily fell out of rhythm with each other.

"I'm kind of messed up," Prana said. "I've got to get out of Washington for a while."

"Are you okay?" Zeke asked.

"I imagine."

Zeke waited for her to say more, but Prana had slipped away, back into herself.

"You could come up here, stay at the house," Zeke said.

"I'll let you know," Prana said.

Zeke hung up the phone feeling awkward. If Prana wanted to talk, she called their mother or Pagan. Usually Zeke didn't feel slighted by this, it was a matter of temperament more than anything, but on the rare occasions when Prana did call, Zeke felt as if she had failed her in a way she didn't completely understand.

Zeke got up, unsettled by Prana's words, "I'm kind of messed up." Occasionally Prana would admit some vague but overwhelming drama. Then, honored by this rare confidence, you were supposed to follow her, tentatively, into the cave of her silence with a flickering candle, while Prana, a cipher, a ghost, escaped or blew out the light. It was irritating, especially because she never seemed to reveal what she was thinking. As a kid she hadn't been like that. She was always bouncing around, her fine hair flying behind her, beside herself with excitement about this or that. She anticipated seeing Marco at Christmas for weeks. But in that nether region before Prana became a teenager, talking to her became like playing that game Operation. One false move, one touch to exposed metal, and a buzzer went off: Prana stopped talking.

Zeke decided to head over to Birch Hill. When she wanted

to get away, she called the stable owner to ask if any horses needed to get out. As a teenager, Zeke had exercised horses and taught riding lessons there. Charlie would always give her something to ride.

THE STABLE YARD was busy with riders setting out on the trails. Birch Hill was across the road from the Rockefeller Estate, which had miles and miles of bridle paths stretching from Briarcliff through Pocantico, almost to the Hudson River. The weekend people waited in the yard, sleek in their boots and breeches, tugging on their leather gloves. Those who rode every day wore hunt caps and jeans, down vests over their sweaters. Zeke liked the bustle of the place, the idea that, beyond a few changes in fashion, something about the scene of horses and riders setting out had been constant for ages. Grooms led horses, hooves polished with oil, up to the mounting block.

Zeke pulled her saddle out of the car. Charlie stood near the stable door, surveying his yard. A thick stone wall divided two large riding rings. The barns were set back, terraced on a hillside. Charlie grinned as she walked up.

"Lark hasn't been out for a few days—if you're feeling brave. Mrs. Wittingham didn't make it up here Friday."

"So you've been saving her for me, Charlie? Want to see me get dumped?" Zeke laughed.

Charlie ran a good barn, which required more than most people knew, and he didn't try to mix, socially, with the owners, which was why they believed him to be straightforward. Zeke knew that many owners, despite their sleek cars and diamond earrings, had lives built on quicksand: marriages with elaborate prenup agreements, high-paying jobs that depended on keeping a large client, while Charlie, who had owned the stable for almost thirty years, had the confidence of landed wealth.

She walked into the barn and the smell of grain and wood shavings, Murphy Oil Soap and leather, washed over her. At Lark's stall, she slid back the metal bolt, swung open the door, and put out her hand.

The mare snuffled and came forward, clearly restless. She was a smallish bay thoroughbred with a little quarter horse to her, you could see it in her rump. Zeke had seen her in the ring. She was quick, not really skittish, but fit. She should have been out every day, especially in this weather. In summer, even the nervous horses were quiet in the heat, but in autumn, when the wind picked up, the cold made them want to run.

Zeke slipped a halter up, over her ears, and led her into the aisle. She clipped her to the cross ties and reached for a brush. It wasn't much work to clean her up; the grooms did a good job here. Zeke remembered when most of them had arrived. There were three small apartments upstairs, so she knew the history of when they'd been occupied, by whom, and how those histories had become intertwined. She brushed the mare briskly and pulled a few woodshavings from her tail. Placing her saddle up near the mare's withers, she slid it back into place.

When she led Lark out into the courtyard, Leon was coming in from the ring, talking to one of the pony kids. Although Charlie owned the stable, Leon was a fixture at Birch Hill, the person everyone turned to for advice. Zeke guessed he was in his sixties, but he appeared much younger. He coached the kids until they outgrew ponies, trained a few owners who weren't on the fast track. He would occasionally go to horse shows with them, where they always did well under his quiet tutelage, but he wasn't interested in returning to the show circuit. When the pony kids got older, if they became more ambitious, and their parents had money, he encouraged them to train at the show stable down the road.

The parents loved Leon because he possessed a quiet authority they did not. All the pony kids cleaned and saddled their own ponies, cooled them out when they were done riding, bathed their ponies in the warm weather. It was unheard of for a child to hand a pony over to a groom. If Leon noticed a kid hanging around, looking as if she had nothing to do, he would gently suggest that she clean her saddle and bridle, and it would only happen once that a kid might say, "My bridle is clean." Leon would smile and say, "Well, take it apart, darling, and make it really clean." He didn't allow anyone to hang around the stable and gossip. Although Leon was too polite to show his amusement, Zeke had once seen him smile slightly when someone new to the barn referred to him as African American. In the white and moneyed world of horses, he had been anomalous for so long that he was accepted. He always wore a button-down shirt, khaki pants and tweed cap, a tie on the weekends. On cool days, he wore a clean navy windbreaker. Years ago, he had worked as a groom at Boulder Brook Hunt Club, but Charlie had brought him up to Birch Hill to give riding lessons, which parents paid for handsomely. It had been a highly strategic move, and one of the things that led Zeke to think Charlie was more shrewd than he seemed.

"Zeke! Haven't seen you in a while."

"Been keeping pretty busy, Leon."

"Want a leg up? Or are those legs of yours still long enough to get you up from the ground?"

"I'll take a leg."

Leon put his hand beneath her shin and tossed her up. The mare danced away and Zeke leaned forward in the saddle.

There was a cackle from the riding ring. A girl astride a chestnut horse was smoking a cigarette, her arm languid by her side. A young man, who Zeke guessed to be her boyfriend, or at least her audience, was watching. She looked to be about seventeen, and wore a pair of tightly fitted chaps. Her hair was pulled back, her profile sleek in the cool air. Leon grimaced. He didn't allow smoking in the ring.

"Who's the new kid?" Zeke asked.

"That's Angela Barron's daughter. She's been living with her dad, but I guess she's living with her mom now."

"She belongs at the barn down the road," Zeke said.

"That's right." Leon nodded. "I think she's got her eye on her mother's new horse. Big rangy horse. Lovely. But he's too green for her. Or she's too green for him."

"Do you coach her?" Zeke asked.

"Me? Oh no. I wouldn't get into that." He rubbed a spot above his right ear, as if rubbing away a worry. "The munchkins are doing good though. Remember little Karen? She's turned into a real jock. You should see her."

"You raise 'em right, Leon."

"I try." He tipped his hat toward Zeke. "You keep her trotting for a couple miles. She needs to come back here good and tired."

She smiled at his instruction, both of them knowing it wasn't necessary.

BIRCH HILL WAS separated from the Rockefeller Estate by a busy two-lane road that opened into four lanes just beyond the stable. Local drivers sometimes stopped when they saw a horse and rider waiting, but trucks couldn't stop easily, and getting across the road could be difficult, especially on a nervous horse. Occasionally a driver would blow his horn, thinking it was funny, but it set the horses off, dancing and trying to run at the edge of traffic. She patted Lark on the neck to distract her as she skittered on the shoulder, and then, when there was a break in the traffic, Zeke relaxed her hands, squeezed her legs, and they moved across the tarmac.

On the other side, the trails were wide, elegant pathways made of banked dirt and cinder. The opening mile was a slow, gradual rise, the path lined by sumac turned crimson, an ascent moving away from the road and houses, up a brushy sapling hill, and then the path became winding, like a fairy-book path, through the woods. Zeke softened her hands on the reins and the mare picked up a trot. Zeke rode through the forest, crossing streams covered by small bridges, the railings made of wood to blend with the natural landscape, the bridge boards covered with loamy dirt.

The afternoon was cool and bright. As they trotted along, she thought about her mother, wondered where she was, and what she was doing then. She wouldn't abandon them completely. Of course *abandon* was a silly word, they were grown, but she had thought of her mother as central, a point to move outward from. She was starting to realize that perhaps this was selfish, perhaps she had taken her mother for granted. Her mother had been a fixed and constant presence, and she had watched them grow and become themselves without many of the constraints her friends had felt. Growing up, Zeke felt their mother watched them with a certain detachment, as if she had scattered seeds without labels and was curious to see what they would become.

What would their lives have been like if her father hadn't died? They wouldn't have ended up in Westchester, Zeke was sure of that. They would have stayed in Oregon, had a house in the woods. She might have had brothers. Her mother would have remained a hippie-type mom who drove a Subaru wagon and wore clogs with wool leggings. Zeke smiled at the idea; this alternate fate seemed only a faint possibility now. Of course, if her father hadn't died, there would be no Prana. Or at least not in the way she was now. As a child, Prana had been a wide-eyed little girl with Marco's fine-boned features, but as she grew older, the resemblance to her mother became more clear. They were both slender, although Prana was taller; both had the same high forehead and large eyes, but their mother was more grounded, enduring. Prana was like an unstable vapor. She was the artist her mother had not become. Zeke felt surprised at this thought, then corrected herself. Prana wasn't an artist—she was merely artistic.

Zeke thought of Prana's call that morning. What was bothering her? Zeke knew better than to say it, but she thought Prana's problem was that she hadn't found a focus yet. She needed to start *doing* whatever she was going to do. Prana had a drive that she didn't like to admit to, and without the proper channel for it, she was messing herself up. Zeke thought it was strange that, although she knew little about the specifics of Prana's life—it was hard to picture Prana at her job for instance—she imagined she was accurate about Prana's emotional tenor. Even Prana's silences seemed ominous these days. Zeke slowed Lark to walk, the mare's hooves loud in the dry leaves. She couldn't say these things to Prana. She might have said them to her mother. This triangulation was foolish, but without their mother, it was hard to know how to be with each other. It seemed they had no glue except habit.

●   ●   ●

A MILE OR two in, at the top of a field, two rows of black oaks lined the trail. The trees must have been planted a hundred years ago, and the decorous, overarching columns made a grand approach. She let the mare into a canter. Lark had a bouncy, springing gait, and Zeke got up in a half-seat as the mare picked up speed. She wished she had a talented horse to work with. The horses at the university were retired donations, athletes long past their prime. She gave a few lessons on them each week, but she'd never have the money to buy or keep the kind of horse she wanted for herself.

She cantered around a turn that opened onto an apple orchard set high on a hill. In spring, an acre of pink-white blossoms topped the hill, and in autumn the bees were dizzy with fallen fruit. She paused at a crossroads. To her left, the path cut into a rocky outcrop. To the right, down the hill, she could pass through a tunnel, under the road to Pocantico, and come out at the start of the hunt course. The fences were tempting, but it was foolish to jump big fences on a horse she didn't know, especially since she was alone. She could take another path down to Swan Lake, an irregular oval-shaped lake with a wide track all around it. One side had a long straightaway she used to race on with her friends. She chose the path around the lake.

She was gone for several hours, but it felt much longer. By the time she headed in, the sumac leaves were purple in the fading light. It was easier to get back across the road when the mare was tired.

As she turned into the driveway she saw the same girl she'd seen on her way out, this time on a large, dark thoroughbred, leggy-looking and coltish; he must be only four or five.

"Set it up!" The girl called, and the young man raised the rail on a jump at the end of the ring.

Zeke pulled up to watch, knowing that if Leon saw this, he would be annoyed. No one was supposed to jump without an instructor in the ring, and it was clear from how the young man fumbled with the cups on the standards that he didn't know what he was doing. The girl nudged the horse into a canter, and rose into a half-seat. The horse was hot, fast moving, his stride uneven. They came around the turn, and the girl pointed him at the jump. One stride away, she pushed her shoulders forward, and the horse dug in, threw up his head, and skidded to a stop. The horse's neck hit her in the face, and the front rail clattered down. She grimaced, took the crop in one hand, the reins in the other, and faced the horse toward the fence. Swinging her hand from side to side, she yanked on the horse's mouth, beating him behind her leg with the crop. His mouth gaped, his tongue swooped, lathering the bit. Zeke rode up to the fence.

"You dropped your shoulders before leaving the ground. If you get ahead of the motion, of course he's going to stop."

The girl looked at Zeke as if she were speaking a foreign language. She flushed a deep red.

"He's a quitter," the girl said, clenching the crop in her fist. "It's a habit I'm going to break."

"Don't get ahead of the motion then," Zeke said.

The girl shot her a nasty look, then turned away from the jump and picked up a canter. She did stay back this time, trying to find the horse's stride, and as she approached the jump, in the last three strides before it, she sat back and dug with her seat and the horse snorted and made a huge ungainly leap over the fence. Zeke shook her head. The girl kept going, down toward the end of the ring and Zeke saw her head for a small wall, a practice jump about three feet high that the pony kids sat on when they watched each other ride. The wall wasn't high so much as solid—a plywood rectangle painted to look like a gray stone wall. Unlike a rail fence, it didn't knock down. Zeke saw the horse flatten around the turn, and the girl set her mouth and dug with her seat. Her elbows were rigid, her hands stiff. Zeke watched them canter up to the wall and, just as the horse was leaving the ground, the girl shot her shoulders forward. Zeke couldn't see exactly what happened next, but the horse must have panicked and put his legs down. She heard the cracking of boards and saw the horse's front hooves go down through the wall, down to his knees in the wood. He reared back, trying to get himself out, but his front legs were caught inside. The wall slid in the dirt as he reared up again, his haunches straining, and Zeke prayed the plywood would give. The girl started to slide, but hung on, grabbing for his mane. She couldn't get a grip with the crop in her hand, and he went up again, pulling back, and the girl let herself go, landing against the standard. Even without her weight, the horse was caught: eyes rolling white, lunging back, his haunches pulling taut. It kept going and going, like something replayed in slow motion, the horse sunk in splintered wood to his knees, trying to extricate his legs from the wooden block.

Zeke jumped down off Lark and yelled at the young man frozen there.

"Run, get Leon. Quick!"

The girl got to her feet, holding her upper arm. The horse reared up, he was going to go over backward, and Zeke heard the crack of breaking wood and finally he went over, one slender bloodied leg, then another, pulling out of the broken fence. He rolled awkwardly on his hind end and slowly got up, snorting and shaking, his front legs bleeding. He started to run, but Zeke saw him sway wildly, limping behind. She wanted to get to him and calm him, but didn't want to tie Lark to the outside fence. If she got loose she could run into the road.

Charlie came running out of his house as Leon came jogging out of the barn.

"What happened?" Charlie shouted, but his question floated into the air as he got to the fence and, not wanting to spook the horse, climbed over it slowly.

Leon didn't even need to ask.

The horse stood at the far end of the ring. Charlie walked over to the girl, who immediately started sobbing in huge open-mouthed cries. Leon walked across the ring and reached for the horse who snorted, but did not move.

Leon patted him on the neck and picked up the broken reins, knotting them so the horse wouldn't step on them, yank on his own mouth, and scare himself further. He slid the stirrup irons up, tucking in the straps while talking to the horse, trying to settle him. When he tried to lead him forward, the horse wouldn't move. He made a clucking sound and pulled on the reins. The horse stood still, the skin on his back twitching. Leon looked over at Zeke.

"I think he pulled his stifle," Zeke said. "He had a hard time getting his front legs out. When he got up, he was limping really badly behind."

A few of the grooms had gathered at the end of the ring. "Beep the vet." Leon called to them. "Tell him it's an emergency. And bring two blankets out here."

Charlie asked the girl if she could walk to the car. His tone was solicitous, but when he looked up, toward his jeep, his expression was flat and unrevealing. Zeke guessed his concern was a matter of diplomacy as much as anything else.

"I'll take Valerie to the emergency room," he said to Zeke. "I think she's broken her arm. Will you wait for the vet?"

Zeke nodded, feeling suddenly deflated, as if she'd come out of a shocking movie that had ended too abruptly. She called to Leon, "I'm going to put Lark away, but I'll come back and see if I can help you move him."

"Ask Dot to bring a bucket of warm water so we can wash the dirt out of these cuts. And if Cory can't find blankets, take them from Fonzie's box, he's big too, and the Taylors won't need them for a while yet."

Zeke nodded and went inside. She had walked Lark the last mile in, so the mare was almost cooled out. It was warm in the barn, and Zeke reached for a towel. The pony kids came running up.

"What happened, Zeke?"

"She was jumping without Leon or anyone watching her," Zeke said.

"You were watching, weren't you?"

"She wasn't listening to me." Zeke kept her tone even.

"Her mother is a nice lady, but she is going to be pissed." "Valerie wasn't supposed to be riding that horse." "You should see how she acts around here." "She pulled into the driveway going *real* fast yesterday." The chorus of tattling broke out, mostly, Zeke suspected, as a kind of release valve, because Leon didn't permit such conversation.

"Where's Dot? Someone go get her. Leon asked me to get something from her." Zeke dispersed the kids to their duties.

BY THE TIME Zeke put Lark away and went back to the ring, it was getting dark. Bert had arrived and given the horse a sedative.

"Let's try to get him into a stall," Bert said to Leon. "This won't make him fall asleep, but we don't want him stumbling either."

Leon stood to his left and pulled on the reins. The horse wouldn't move. Bert tapped him on the rump and the horse lurched forward, limping behind like a broken toy.

He looked over at Zeke. "Leon said you called it. He dislocated his stifle. He's going to be out of commission for a few months."

They moved slowly inside, then stopped in the aisle where Bert could look more closely at the horse's legs.

Leon and Bert both tended to the horse. Leon spoke in a low voice, trying to settle him, while Bert moved matter-of-factly around him, not startling when the horse flinched. He seemed to move through the world this way: acting essentially the same, as if he had arrived at a place in himself that he did not need to alter.

"Hate to say it, but there isn't enough skin here to stitch anything. The best I can do is to clean up his legs, put on some antibiotic cream, and bandage him, but if she's planning to show him, well . . ." Bert shook his head. "There's going to be scarring. In a conformation class it will show."

Leon tightened his mouth.

"How did this happen?"

"He's green. The girl is young," Leon said. "I'm going to move a horse, so we can use a stall up here."

Bert turned to put his equipment in his bag. Zeke felt awkward, hovering for a moment.

"Leon is the resident wise man, isn't he?"

Zeke was startled and looked at him closely. She nodded.

"I've got a green horse myself. I'm hoping I don't have an accident like this."

"Why would you?" Zeke asked.

He clipped his bag closed. "I bought a horse about a year ago that I really think can jump. I've got him over at Jay Stark's, across the river. Do you know Jay?"

"I know who he is."

"He had a blowup with the woman who used to ride for him. He's got some kid there now. I'm not sure she knows what she's doing. Anyway, I have to figure out what I'm going to do. Nice horse though. Athletic." He reached for a jar of antibiotic cream. "Want to take a ride tomorrow? I have calls in the morning, but I thought I'd head across the river in the afternoon."

Zeke composed her expression as if she were considering her schedule.

"Maybe you'd sit on him for me? Tell me what you think?"

"Sure," Zeke said. "I'd love to."

four

AFTER TOMMY TALKED TO THE GENETICS COUNSELOR, PAGAN asked to speak to him again. She motioned for Tommy to take Maud out of the room.

"I know everyone must ask this, but I can't help it." She took a deep breath, and felt the air slide out of her with a jagged shiver. "Is there any chance the lab could have made a mistake? Or labeled the wrong sample?"

"I'm sorry to say not." And she heard the concern in his voice; he sounded genuinely sorry. "You see, after the doctor takes the sample of the amniotic fluid, the lab divides it into three separate specimens, and they grow the cells in three concurrent trials. All of yours came up, definitively, with this condition. I know this is very hard to hear, but if there was even the smallest bit of gray area, I would tell you."

She stared at a scribbled drawing of Maud's, orange and pink, hung on the refrigerator. It seemed surreal in its brightness.

"This is a question I hate to ask, but—"and she took a deep breath. "Is it necessary to continue the pregnancy?"

"No, it is not," he said. "Did you and your husband discuss what you might do in a case like this?"

A case like this? Pagan didn't know what to say. She had never even imagined, not really. She remembered a Saturday morning when they were out doing errands; she had checked to make sure Maud was asleep in her car seat before posing her question. Sitting at a traffic light, she asked, *What would we do if the amnio came back with a problem?* The sky was gray behind a billboard advertisement for a lumber yard. She waited. Tommy said, *It would be an experience we were given, something we'd have to deal with. But no, I wouldn't choose to live with a Down syndrome kid, although I could if I had to.* She remembered feeling relieved. One summer, in college, he had worked at a camp for disabled kids, and she wasn't sure exactly where he stood.

Pagan tried to imagine carrying a child that would die inside her. The counselor waited.

"I really don't know if I can continue with the pregnancy. Of course, I have to talk to my husband, but . . ." She waited for some sign of disapproval.

"If you decide to terminate the pregnancy, we can take care of it here at the hospital. It's absolutely confidential." He paused for a moment, then said, "I'm happy to answer questions, but I'm not allowed to advise you about your decision. You do understand that, don't you?"

Pagan nodded into the phone.

•   •   •

AFTER PAGAN HUNG up, she sat down on the kitchen floor. She didn't want to move. She felt as if she had stepped into a world she was not supposed to be a part of, a world she had hoped to protect herself from. Last winter, after her miscarriage, she had assumed there was a problem with the baby—her body had corrected itself, these things happened for some reason. So this seemed weirdly disproportionate, out of line with what should be. She stood up and shook herself. If there was no large force governing things, then why should there be any sense to it at all? Was the world random, or was it not? Perhaps the whole idea of failure before success was a human pattern, a way that people constructed stories for themselves. Perhaps those were the stories people told themselves because they wanted happy endings.

SHE AND TOMMY were up half the night talking, and finally they spoke in fragments, as if handing shards of glass back and forth, testing the edges, making sure they were real. In the morning, she woke slowly, burdened by the phantom dialogue that had continued in her sleep. Tommy made oatmeal, clumsily, for Maud. He made tea for Pagan. She felt as if they were surrounded by a dense, but invisible fog.

"What do you want to do about Mike and Kate tonight?" he asked.

"I can't begin to think about cooking." Pagan slumped in her chair.

"It will be strange to cancel without saying why."

They had made dinner plans with Tommy's brother weeks ago, but if she had to go through this, she didn't want people to know. It would make everything seem too large, too public. Maud chirped in her chair, playing with her oatmeal. Pagan wished they could speak plainly without having to aim the conversation above her head.

"You want absolution, and your brother isn't even a priest anymore."

Tommy placed his palms on the table and looked down. He seemed to consider his hands as if they were wholly unfamiliar. "It's not confession. I don't think of him that way, he's my brother."

"You do think of him that way," Pagan said. "You want to be told it's all right."

Tommy set his chin and turned to wipe orange juice from Maud's cheek. She burbled and waved her spoon. "Oats, oats, oats."

The yellow curtains, the plants, everything seemed precarious, as if it could wither and blow away.

"We'll do whatever you want to do," Tommy said.

Pagan sat up, furious. "Don't put it on me! This is us!"

"I meant about dinner," Tommy said.

Maud was startled into silence. Pagan felt a terrible anger shaking her.

"Have them then! Take Maud to the store with you."

Tommy opened his mouth to protest the idea of taking Maud to a crowded grocery store on a Saturday morning. She shot him a nasty look, a look that implied, *What kind of hassle would it be if I didn't go through with this, imagine that?*

It seemed to take forever to get Maud fed and dressed, to find her shoes and hat and coat, but as soon as Pagan closed the door behind them, she felt panicked, as if they could be in an accident, as if something random and terrible might happen.

She sank down in an armchair and put her head in her hands. She wanted to weep, but she had cried herself out. She had never gotten used to his family. They were a clan, their own world within a world. Of all Tommy's siblings, Pagan liked Mike the most, but it frightened her that he would disagree with them on this, that he would divide Tommy from her, and how could she withstand that?

WHEN MIKE AND Kate arrived that evening, Pagan watched them as if they were emissaries from another world. Kate, wearing a bright blue overcoat, looked festive and happy. Mike walked in the door, handed Tommy a bottle of wine, and rubbed his hands together. "Where's the lady of the house? Where's Maud?" He shouted and called, swiveling his head as if he couldn't see her. Maud laughed and shrieked, "Here I am! Here I am!" jumping up and down.

Mike was smaller than Tommy, his face wizened, his copper-colored hair threaded with gray. Tommy said he'd once had a considerable temper, but Pagan found this hard to imagine. He had a sense of humor about ordinary things: odd newspaper headlines, old ladies in his neighborhood, fast food. He wore a collarless shirt, worn at the neck and cuffs, patched jeans, and a corduroy jacket that was clean, but looked as if it were a thrift shop find from twenty years ago. He clapped Tommy on the shoulder and gave Pagan a hug. He smelled of soap and pipe tobacco.

Kate settled herself next to Mike on the couch; she slipped off her shoes and tucked her brightly stockinged feet under a long skirt. Her face was youthful, her hair silvery and thick, worn in a loose braid down her back. Her colorful clothes and slight overbite made Pagan think of a parrot with bright plumage. It was hard to imagine she had once been a nun.

Tommy was making pasta for dinner, and Pagan gave him the run of the kitchen, allowing the impression that he was indulging his pregnant wife. She was careful to keep any allusions to difficulty out of the conversation and instead asked questions about their various projects. Mike worked with at-risk teenagers in Yonkers. Kate had been a midwife in Mexico for years, and now worked as a nurse and Spanish-speaking liaison at a community clinic. She also worked with unwed mothers, helping them finish high school. As they talked about their clients, the difficulties of funding their projects, Pagan thought how small her own world was. They had causes, epochs, it seemed they had many lives. Pagan had one life, threaded with passages that had been ordinary until now.

One by one, Maud hauled out all her toys for Mike and Kate's inspection. Mike kept handing various toys back to her, then encouraging her to run upstairs and bring something else back. He grinned at Pagan as Maud's chubby legs carried her in and out of the room, and Pagan thought how Tommy must have felt this enveloping warmth, this sense of constancy and belonging all through his growing up. The conversation floated along comfortably through dinner until Tommy took Maud upstairs to bed. Pagan and Kate cleared the table, and Kate started to run water in the sink.

"Kate, leave those. I'll put them in the dishwasher later," Pagan said.

"How about I just rinse them off?" Kate said, which she proceeded to do quickly, as Pagan and Mike moved to the living room.

Pagan heard Tommy upstairs, getting Maud changed,

calmly persisting through her various resistances. She had been waiting for him to come downstairs and start explaining, and suddenly the whole idea seemed so awkward and staged that she couldn't wait any longer.

Kate came back into the living room, wiping her hands on a dishcloth, and Pagan began by addressing her as Tommy came down the stairs.

"We have some really bad news, I'm afraid."

Kate looked up. Mike set down his glass of wine and looked at her carefully.

"We haven't told anyone this, but we got the amnio results back, and they're not good. The baby will probably die inside me."

Kate let out a breath. "Oh dear," she said. "Do you know what the problem is?"

"It's a genetic problem called trisomy eighteen."

Mike looked over at Kate. Tommy walked into the room and, sensing what Pagan had set in motion, stood in the middle of the floor.

"I gather that's not good," Mike said.

"I think we're going to 'terminate the pregnancy' as they say," Pagan continued. "But Tom and I have been talking. I think he feels guilty about it."

"I don't feel guilty, it's just—" Tommy turned a furious red, caught off guard.

"Tom, you do, just admit it."

He flushed and looked over at Kate.

"Have you ever delivered a child like that?"

They all looked at her. Kate nodded. It was as if she were an oracle, someone to deliver a pronouncement because she had seen to the horizon.

"A child like that has no quality of life," Kate said simply. "Some might argue, but I have to tell you—especially since you seem to have decided—it's a real mess."

Tommy sat down next to Pagan. He was still angry, but Kate's declaration seemed to settle him.

"I'm so sorry," Mike said. "I obviously don't have the medical background that Kate does, but you're sure about the tests?"

Tommy nodded, then said, "I don't want you to tell the girls, especially Sheila and Eileen. I don't need their opinions, which aren't informed, and Pagan certainly doesn't. We'll just say she had another miscarriage."

Mike nodded, and said to Tommy, "There won't be any problem about finding someone to do it, will there?"

"No, I don't think so."

Pagan sensed a weight behind the question. "What?" she asked.

"Pagan, if there's anything we can do, baby-sit for Maud, or anything else, you must let us know," Kate said.

"I will," Pagan said.

They sat there awkwardly, as if the evening were over, although it was still early.

"So on top of this," Kate ventured, "Mike told me that your mother has taken a trip somewhere."

"Yes, a trip, if that's what it is."

"How long has she been gone?"

"Almost a month now."

"Are you worried?"

Pagan looked over at Tommy, thinking of her mother's will. "Worried in the sense that it's completely out of character. But it's clear that she really prepared and then took off."

"I bet she'll be back for the holidays," Kate said.

"I don't know," Pagan said. "I keep expecting to get a postcard, but nothing."

"It's everything at once," Kate said.

"Yes," Pagan echoed. "Everything at once."

LATER THAT NIGHT, lying in bed Pagan said, "I don't want you to tell anyone else."

"I won't."

"I wish you'd talk to me."

"I do, Pagan." His voice was tired and exasperated. "There's not much more to say."

Pagan knew that his restraint was for her now, that there was much to say, but it would only hurt more, *our son, our son, our son,* like a child in a tiny boat floating out to sea.

five

THE TELEVISION FLASHED AN IMAGE OF CHOPPY SEA WATER. The anchorman announced that tiny fragments of the space shuttle had been recovered. Bits of metal and bone could finally be identified. Zeke was sitting with her mother in the living room when the image of Christa McAuliffe, her dark hair and wide smile, flickered on the screen.

"It reminds me of your father," her mother said.

"Why?" Zeke was startled.

"The unexpectedness of it, I suppose. It seems like awful things happen just when you're actually happy."

Zeke looked down at her mother's hands. She wore a ring of twined gold bands on her right hand; her slightly reddened knuckles had whorls like tree knots. Zeke weighed what her mother had said. It was a morbid way to look at things, but it seemed unkind to say so.

"Don't you think it's just the contrast? Life is regular, ordinary, and then something terrible happens and it seems like everything before was happier?"

Her mother tried to smile. "That's the kind of thing your father would have said."

Zeke started to chew on her thumbnail, then put her hand in her lap. "I know what happened, but I still don't see how it's possible." She held her breath lightly, as if movement might startle her mother away from the story.

"We were living in Oregon then, outside Eugene." Her mother's voice sounded far away, as if she were beginning a fairy tale. "Your father was taking classes at the university, and working as a carpenter. Some friends had taken a job out in the country: propping up an old farmhouse and building a new foundation under it. They'd done this type of work before, but it was going slowly, and they asked your father to come out and give them a hand." Her mother paused, and Zeke was afraid she was going to cry, or retreat into herself and leave the story untold. "He said he couldn't. It was getting toward the end of the semester, and he had a paper to write for an anthropology class. But his friends asked again, and your father was like that— always willing to give someone a hand—so he finally said he'd give them one weekend. We'd all go together on a Saturday."

"I packed a picnic, and the girlfriends of the two other men brought food too, and we sat on a blanket far back from the house." Her mother sighed and twisted her mouth in a half-smile. "I remember thinking it was good that the owners were fixing the house up rather than pulling it down, because it was a beautiful setting: open fields, the house surrounded by huge old trees. I kept you girls back from the house because I didn't want you stumbling on rusty nails or cutting yourselves on old wire." She reported this detail with a wry laugh, seemingly at herself, the idea that she had worried so over the wrong thing. "You know, I remember it so clearly. I wish I didn't. The men were under the house, looking at part of the new foundation. I was kneeling over you, changing your diaper, and telling Pagan not to pull apart a worm, when I heard a loud crack and I grabbed for Pagan because I thought someone was hunting. But then there was a huge sound, like thunder, and the ground actually shook. I thought it was an earthquake. I looked up and saw this haze of dust—the house had caved in." Her mother stopped, as if she could see it. "It's so odd how strange details stick in your mind. I remember I had a diaper pin in my mouth. The front of the house was lopsided, like someone who'd had a stroke."

Zeke didn't want to imagine her mother in the following half hour. What had they done? Had they had tried to get the men out? No one had cell phones in those days. Who went for help? What had her mother done with her and Pagan?

"You know, when the shuttle first blew up, a lot of people didn't think it was real—they'd seen so many things on television that were stunts or trick photography, but when that house came down on your father—" She shook her head. "I felt the earth shake and saw that house; God, it was a huge house, tilted and sunk, and all in a second I knew what had happened. I didn't have a moment of imagining it wasn't real."

In the smooth planes of her mother's face there was no palpable sign of trauma, but the accident had sobered her, made her afraid to be what she had been. Anyone would say her mother was still a beautiful woman, but Zeke thought of her as opaline, an aspect once fiery and bright had been muted. When

Zeke imagined her before the accident—young and hopeful, playing music, married to a man she loved—it was like staring at a rippling image underwater. The other two men had been killed too. No one ever understood exactly what had happened, what had cracked or slipped or given way.

SIX

WHEN PRANA WALKED INTO HER APARTMENT, LATE ON SUNDAY afternoon, and saw the red, blinking light on her machine, she felt a startled flush of hope, but the message was from Pagan, whose voice was low and private sounding. Prana felt a hot flush of fear. She touched the speed dial and heard the ribbon of tones unwind itself.

"Did you hear from Mom?" Prana asked.

Pagan sighed. "I wish."

All weekend, Prana had a felt a vague anxiety, as if something was shifting below the surface of things.

"There's a problem with the amnio," Pagan began. Prana heard the sound of a toy clattering on the floor, babbling in the background, Maud must have walked into the room. Pagan's voice changed, became brighter. "Maud, go back inside with Daddy."

"What happened?"

"The baby's got this rare chromosomal thing. It's going to die, probably inside me."

Prana felt the room grow still around her.

"I thought I'd gotten through the bad stuff." Pagan made a snorting sound that sounded like a choked laugh. "Can you come up and stay with Maud while I'm at the hospital? Tommy will be with me, and I don't want to leave her at the sitter's all day."

"Of course," Prana said. "Are you all right? You're sounding very practical."

Pagan didn't reply for a moment, and Prana was afraid she had offended her.

"I feel like shit, but what can I do?"

"Is there any chance the baby could live?"

"Hardly any. You know when you go to a festival or something, and you see a bunch of kids in wheelchairs who are really out of it—sunken eyes, banging their heads, wearing helmets and moaning and stuff?"

Prana waited, knowing her reply wasn't necessary.

"Well, if it lived, this child would never even be that good. We'd basically have to set up a hospital room in the house."

Prana felt as if the sky had cracked open. Pagan's news seemed to supersede everything else.

"They're not going to give you any problem about it at the hospital, are they?"

"Why does everyone keep asking me that?"

Prana looked at the *Washington Post* on her table. Tommy must be shielding her from the news of that doctor being shot.

"How is Tommy taking this?"

"Not too well. It's . . . a boy." Pagan's voice broke.

"I'll take the train up tomorrow," Prana said.

WHEN SHE HUNG up the phone, Prana felt disoriented. This sort of thing didn't happen to Pagan, who seemed eternally capable. She rarely needed help, but when she did, she had the means to pay for it. Zeke called her Quick Draw McGraw, fastest check-book in the East. It occurred to Prana that they didn't usually call on each other for help the way some families did. For instance, she wouldn't have asked her sisters to help her move or paint her apartment. Pagan's husband, Tommy, had a huge family, and it seemed they were always helping each other—building a garage, wallpapering a room, watching one another's kids.

Pagan always planned for the unseen. She would consider the future and think of three solutions to a potential problem, where Prana hadn't considered any difficulty at all. Pagan's looking ahead made Prana feel dreamy and inadequate, mostly because all that strategizing seemed to work. Pagan had done well in school, finished college, gotten a good job, eventually quit that job to become a stay-at-home mother, and did even that well—not in an overdone, cloying sense. Pagan had always been ahead of her—not just in years, but in accomplishment.

Prana walked to her bedroom, trying to think of what she should do next. Like their mother, Pagan was resilient, prag-matic, she would do what had to be done. Eventually, she would be all right. Prana looked around the small room and felt, in the midst of her sadness, an odd buoyancy. She had been asked to come up and help. She felt oddly proud, like a child praised for an ordinary drawing. It was just baby-sitting, but Pagan had asked her instead of Zeke. Of course, Zeke would do whatever Pagan asked, but it was a family joke that Zeke handled most problems with a Swiss army knife, duct tape, and take-out pizza.

Prana reached for her cell phone. She would cancel her next job. She already had the props; someone else would have to do the shoot. She punched in the familiar numbers and explained she had a family emergency. When she turned off the phone, she felt lighter.

What should she should pack? Warm clothes, something to read on the train. She didn't want magazines; the bright images made her think about work. Looking at her shelves, she picked up a book she had bought a long time ago, a book she had bought in defiance of Stephan.

One day last spring, she had wanted to be out in the world with him, to feel as if they were real, among others, and they went to browse in the stores around Dupont Circle. She loved idling in bookstores, the possibility of discovery. When she read a book she particularly admired, she felt the writer represented something beyond the book itself, a particular distillation of a larger world, and through reading the work, she touched that distillation and understood its larger implications.

She stopped in front of the photography section, and Stephan paused behind her. She felt him wanting to lean forward, to rest his face in her hair, but he was still. In the past months, when she asked him about photography, he spoke to her as he would a serious student. He seemed to sense that her interest was not a tribute to him, but an interest that had been overshadowed. As his daughter started to consider different colleges, he must have known, although they had never discussed it, that Prana had dropped out of school partly to be with him.

Stephan glanced at the shelves, touched her gently on the arm, then went off to another part of the store. Prana sat, picking through the books. She liked unusual close-ups that you had to stare at for a moment to understand what they were, obscure images, images that forced you to look and look again.

She picked up a book without a dust jacket and thought, when she first opened it, that it had been shelved in the wrong place. More text than pictures. The photographs sprinkled through it were older photos, an unusual mix. Opening to the first page, she was drawn by the writer's voice: confiding and intimate, he seemed to address her personally. He wrote about a photograph he had found, a picture of Napoleon's younger brother. The writer was amazed when he imagined what Napoleon's younger brother must have seen.

> Sometimes I would mention this amazement, but since no one seemed to share it, nor even to understand it, (life consists of these little touches of solitude), I forgot about it.

Life consists of these little touches of solitude. Yes, exactly. She felt this constantly: what mattered to her did not matter to others. She ran her fingers over the pages. The table of contents had poetic titles for its short chapters. She liked the fragments, the mosaic of prose.

Stephan wandered back to her. He was careful to be casual in public. His wife and children were at the beach in Delaware; he was following them tomorrow, but he had once pointed out that school friends of his daughters might see them. One never knew.

"What did you find?" he asked.

She held up the book.

"Lots of mumbo-jumbo," he said.

"What do you mean?" She couldn't keep the petulance out of her voice.

"Barthes. Lots of blathering about photography as Art."

"It seems interesting."

"Those who can't do, write."

She cradled the book to her, and walked to the counter. This wouldn't spoil the mood of the day. She needed some difference from him, some way of distinguishing herself, the way they vanished into each other so easily.

Prana hadn't picked up the book in a while. She loved the intimate voice, but didn't really understand what Barthes was saying. She felt she was missing some commonly understood element, or that she simply wasn't smart enough to grasp it. Later, a friend would tell her, "It's theory, philosophy, you're not meant to read it and *get it* all in a swoop like that." And Prana felt stung, knowing that, once again, she had underestimated herself before giving herself a chance to understand.

She set the book in her suitcase. For weeks she had felt burnt out: too little sleep, too much partying with Joe. She felt a kind of distance from everything. Pagan's call made the world come back to her.

Then she remembered. The book was about Barthes' mother. His mother was dead. Prana felt a stabbing sensation in her stomach. Her mother wasn't dead. She would have felt it, would have known. She flipped through the pages, looking for something she had read before. Barthes had written about his search for a photograph that captured his mother.

To say, confronted with a certain photograph, "That's *almost* the way she was!" was more distressing than to say,

confronted with another, "That's not the way she was at all."
The *almost:* love's dreadful regime . . .

"The *almost:* love's dreadful regime . . ." she whispered. She almost knew her mother. She almost had Stephan. Really she didn't have either of them at all.

s e v e n

ON MONDAY MORNING, WHEN ZEKE GOT UP AND BEGAN TO dress, she felt the way she did in springtime: restless to get outside, to go somewhere unfamiliar, a feeling of potential in the air. It was nothing special, she reminded herself, just going across the river to look at a horse.

When Pagan called last night and gave her the news about the baby, her voice had the shaken intonations of a person coping with disaster. Zeke knew better than to say what she really thought: *thank God you had the amnio*. To her mind, Pagan was avoiding a tragedy, but when she thought about the doctor who'd been shot upstate, Zeke felt a cool tinge of fear, like alcohol wiped across her skin.

On Mondays, she did the morning chores herself. She liked

to make sure the students had taken care of things properly over the weekend. In the courtyard, the rooster strutted in front of her and pecked at a stray piece of corn frozen in the dirt. His yellow eyes seemed doll-like, artificial. Zeke liked to joke that she'd make a meal out of him, snapping the lunging whip in his direction. The sheep huddled in their shed, but when she carried a bucket of pellets out to their trough, they trotted toward her. Under their grubby wool, it was hard to tell if they'd put on enough weight; she'd have to ask Bert to check them. As she pulled the hose from the barn and filled the outdoor troughs, she wondered again about Marcie. She didn't want to separate the girls from Marcie or turn them over to their father, who lived in Las Vegas and wasn't the least bit interested in his children.

She fed and watered the horses, cleaned the stalls, working quickly. With a long-tined pitchfork, she removed the manure and wet straw, pitched it all into a wheelbarrow, and wheeled it out of the barn. When she was done, she went to the tack room for the toolbox. An Appaloosa named Mr. T had started to crib on the top of his stall. She measured the top of the partition, then let the tape measure snap back into place.

Out in the courtyard, she laid a plank across two sawhorses and picked up a saw. In the rhythm of physical work, she thought about her father. She felt cheated she couldn't really remember him. Her memories were reconstructed from the few pictures they had. When she tried to remember him fully: the way he moved, the sound of his voice, she could almost summon the feeling of being held against a flannel shirt, the tickle of his beard, the movement of his chest when he laughed, but the feeling was elusive. It was as if she couldn't stand back far enough to see him. Zeke pulled a carpenter's pencil out of her pants. She wished she had her father's tools. She would have liked to hold what he had held.

Mr T was out in the field, and she carried the board into his stall. Cribbing was a strange habit: the horse version of smoking. A horse would grab hold of a board with his top teeth and suck in air. One horse would see another do it and learn to do it himself. You could put a strap around a horse's neck, loose enough to let the horse breathe, tight enough to prevent him from bending his neck and sucking in air, but she hated how it looked, as if the horse were being strangled. This was better. She set the plank in place, resting it on top of the lower board, which was rutted with scallop-shaped teeth marks. Starting on the right side, she drove the 16d nails into place. Five hard strokes. When she finished on one side, she moved to the other, ending with the post in between. When she was done, she felt satisfied. Maybe she should be a carpenter. She heard the crunch of gravel in the courtyard and tugged on the board. It held tight. Bert walked into the barn and tipped his chin toward Zeke's work.

"Cribbing?"

"Yeah."

"That should take care of it."

He carried a cup of coffee from the local diner in Pleasantville. He drank the ordinary coffee appreciatively, smacking his lips as if it were perfect and rare.

She carried the toolbox into the tack room. When she came out of the barn, the day felt overwhelmingly bright and clear.

"So they let you out of here for the afternoon?" he asked.

"The kids or the animals?"

She got into his car, pushing aside a clipboard and papers. They drove slowly through campus. It felt strange to be the passenger.

"Shame about that horse yesterday," he said.

"Yeah, that girl's mother is going to be pissed."

He took the turnoff toward Pocantico. The road cut through the hills Zeke had ridden yesterday; the hunt course looked small in the distance.

"Ever been there?" He pointed to a little chapel on the town green. "They have a stained-glass window that's supposed to be the last piece of art Matisse ever designed."

Zeke had no idea what to do with this piece of information. "I have a sister who's the artistic type," she said.

"I get it from the kids. They came here on a class trip."

Zeke felt deflated, thinking of Eleanor. She'd never mentioned it.

"It was interesting to meet Marcie the other night," Bert said.

Zeke thought of Marcie gazing up at him. "Yes, Marcie's hard to miss," she said. Outside the car, the trees were thick and leafless. "We split up, at least I think we did. But we ended on bad terms and she won't let me see the girls."

"So you two were serious."

"Like a heart attack." The road narrowed coming out of the forest, then edged a lake, or two lakes really, divided by a thin strip of land. The road ran along this narrow division, and coming around the turn, it looked as if you would drive into the water. Zeke had always liked the illusion. "I think Marcie is one of those keeping-it-all-together alcoholics. I didn't realize it in the beginning. And I still don't know whether she let down her guard or started getting worse, but it finally got to be too much. I told her she had to go to AA. I thought she'd do it."

"She has to want it for herself."

"You sound like you know."

"I do."

They drove up the hill and into Tarrytown. She could see the silver span of the Tappan Zee. From the bridge, on a clear day, you could see the George Washington Bridge to the south. To the north, the forested, mountainous banks rose above the water, all the way up to Cold Spring and Bear Mountain. He steered them toward the Tappan Zee. The steel was white in the sunlight. The Hudson spread wide and ancient before her.

ON THE OTHER side of the river, they turned off the freeway and drove for ten or fifteen miles. Bert turned into a long driveway, a grassy pasture bordering one side. At the end of the drive, there was a large riding ring. The jumps were set high. The barn was deserted.

Zeke pulled her saddle out of the car and followed Bert into the barn. The aisles were swept, blankets hung neatly on poles outside stall doors. Tack trunks rested in front of large box stalls. Bert walked down a shadowed aisle.

He reached for a halter outside a stall and went in, murmuring to the horse. Zeke found the light switch and turned it on as he led a dark bay horse, well over sixteen hands, into the aisle.

"Oh, wow, he's a nice looking horse," Zeke said. "How old is he?"

"He's six."

"He looks like a thoroughbred mixed with something else," Zeke said.

"Hanoverian, Trakehner maybe."

"Gives him some bone."

"It does. I see so many lame thoroughbreds. I like them to have a little cold blood. The substance helps."

He picked up a brush and started going over the horse. A teenage girl with braces came up from the end of the aisle.

"Hey there," he called. "Is Jay around?"

"He was here this morning."

"Wendy still gone?"

The girl looked uncomfortable and chewed on the inside of her cheek.

"She was pretty mad when she left. She . . ." the girl trailed off, and Zeke looked up from tightening the girth to see why.

The outline of a young woman appeared at the end of the aisle. She was hard to see against the sunlight. As she moved closer, Zeke saw she was short and stocky, with a child's round cheeks and open face. Something about her made Zeke think she'd been a cute kid, but hadn't lived up to her sense of promise. She wore boots and breeches, which only accentuated how short-legged she was.

"How's he doing Lisa?"

"Really well. I had him out yesterday, doing some work on the flat."

"I was going to have Zeke sit on him, but maybe you could warm him up, so we could see him go."

"Sure. I'll go get his bridle." She hurried off.

ZEKE DIDN'T MIND Lisa warming him up; it was nice to watch him move. He was a big, rangy horse. His mane, neatly pulled, bobbed in the breeze. As they picked up a trot, Zeke tipped her head to the side and watched them move around the ring. He needed more muscle. He carried his head too high, pulling against the martingale.

Lisa bobbed up and down on his back. She had a decent seat, soft enough hands, but she was too small for him.

"Can we tighten up the martingale a bit?" Zeke called. Lisa stopped and Zeke bent down to tighten the strap that ran from his nose band, down between his front legs to the girth. "See if that helps."

Lisa picked up a trot again. Zeke waited for him to soften and drop down onto the bit, but he didn't relax in quite the way she'd like to see.

"He needs work on the flat," Zeke said quietly to Bert. "Needs to get his hind end under him and get muscled up."

He nodded.

"Put him into a smaller circle," Zeke called out. "Keep him in the bottom third of the ring."

Lisa nodded and turned, blowing out of her mouth with the exertion of trying to keep him in a smaller circle.

"She's not quite tall enough to really force him to get his legs underneath him," Zeke murmured. "Seems like a nice kid though, capable enough."

Lisa brought him back to a trot, then circled the other way.

She was aware of Bert standing next to her, leaning forward on the fence. He was only a few inches taller than she was, but efficient in his movements. She could imagine him boxing; she didn't know why. Underlying competitiveness perhaps. He watched his horse move around the ring as if he were weighing a question.

"Why don't you ride him yourself?" Zeke asked.

"I don't do jumpers."

"You must ride."

"Played polo in college."

"Polo!" she snorted. "I didn't know real people did that."

"Most don't. The horses belonged to the university."

Zeke shook her head.

"It was great," he grinned. "You'd like the speed—I can tell."

Zeke met his eyes, held his gaze a second too long.

"Let's see him over a fence," she called out. "I'll set up something on this side."

Zeke took the high bar down from the first jump and made a crossrail. She paced off the distance to the second jump and made a little oxer.

"Take him down through here. It's an easy three strides," she called.

Lisa trotted toward the crossrail. The horse hopped over it and easily covered the next three strides, up and over the oxer.

"Hardly had to pick up his knees," Zeke said. "Can I set it up?"

Lisa nodded.

Zeke went to the second jump and set the second bar higher than the first. She moved the two standards farther apart. Lisa trotted up to the crossrail and cantered down to the oxer, and again, they easily cleared it.

"What else have you taken him over?"

"I haven't jumped him that much. He still needs the work on the flat."

Zeke nodded and surveyed the ring. "Let me make this a vertical, then come down this side again, around the turn, and take a long approach up to the gate."

She made the first jump a straight bar, and raised the oxer again.

Lisa cantered down the side. The distance was tighter now

that the first jump was substantial. He got a little close to the oxer, but cleared it easily. She came around the turn for the long approach. This was harder to ride—not to get anxious, not to get ahead of the motion. Zeke had set the gate a bit high, and she chewed her lip as Lisa came toward it. Three strides away, Zeke knew she wouldn't find a spot to leave the ground: she was going to tighten up, chip in, and sure enough, she buried the horse at the jump. Zeke waited for the horse to quit, which would have been the natural thing to do. But unbelievably, he chipped in a short stride, then rocked back on his hind end and picked himself up, snapping his knees and rounding his back, up and over the jump. He didn't touch the rail at all.

Lisa came jolting down, falling onto his neck, red in the face. "Oh, I made an awful move," she said.

"But damn, it shows you something!" Zeke turned to Bert. "That horse can really jump."

He looked pleased. "Yes," he said. "It looks like he can."

Zeke wanted to try him herself before they left. She trotted him in a circle and felt how much work he needed. She closed her right leg against his side, but he didn't bend; he felt like stone. She started working him in figure eights, trying to get him to soften and relax.

"He's better to the left," Lisa called out.

Zeke turned him in a circle to the left, and kept working him at a slow trot. She halted him by dropping her seat in the saddle, letting her seatbones push him up, onto the bit, then asked him to walk forward, squeezing lightly, softening her hands. She asked him to halt again, and repeated this several times, until she could feel his steps becoming more balanced, his hind end underneath him. She picked up a canter and made a few small circles, taking her time, getting a rhythm.

She turned him toward the two jumps she'd set up for Lisa and he moved toward them steadily, eager. She cantered down to the first jump, met it evenly, and held him steady down to the second.

"He's barely using himself," Zeke called out, "Set 'em up!" Bert walked across the ring, and raised the first jump six inches. "Raise the back of the oxer too," Zeke said.

She came at the two jumps again, keeping his stride short so he could lengthen if he needed to. Again, they met the first jump evenly and she could feel him in the air, using his knees, and between jumps she checked him a little so he wouldn't run up under the second one. An easy three strides and she felt them rise into the air, his back rounding to cover the width, and landing, he hit the ground with an even stride.

"You should have seen him over the oxer." Lisa's face was red with excitement.

Zeke grinned. She told Bert to spread the oxer a bit, and set the front up a notch, so it would be square. Riding down the fences again, she felt him using himself in the air. He landed on the wrong lead, and she made a small, tight circle, getting him to change, then headed for the gate. She counted with her breath, didn't let herself hurry, that was the whole trick, not to look too early. She closed her eyes for a moment, felt his stride as he tugged at the reins, then felt what she needed, a long three strides, and softened her hands, let him move forward up to the gate. When he landed, he snorted and shook his head.

Zeke let him walk, reins loose, her heart beating fast. She was sweating and felt the wind through her shirt. She walked the horse over to where Lisa and Bert were standing. Bert clapped him on the neck.

"I like what I see, but we have to go on to the next place. Lisa said she'd put him away for us."

Zeke hopped down and unfastened the girth. Looping it into the stirrup iron, she pulled the saddle from his back.

"Nice to meet you," Lisa said, looking up at her.

"Nice to meet you too." Zeke grinned. Lisa reminded her of the pony kids.

When they got into the car, Zeke waited until they were out of the driveway before she spoke. "She's a nice kid," Zeke said. "I don't see her being reckless with your horse."

"You're right, not reckless, but she doesn't fit him."

Zeke wanted to be diplomatic. Lisa couldn't help being dumpy. "There are short-legged jumper riders who can make a horse go." Then she shook her head. "Ever seen Corky Lawson, over in Bedford?"

"He's an ass."

Zeke was surprised. He was right, but his vehemence told her that there must be more to the story.

"Well, style isn't everything," Zeke said. "Did you ever see Harry DeLeyer ride?"

"He was unbelievable."

"He sure was." Zeke smiled to herself. DeLeyer was an old-fashioned legend. He broke every equitation rule in the book, flailed around on top of a horse, elbows out, legs swinging; he was almost comic. His horses went great though.

They stopped at a bagel store in a strip mall, and Bert bought a dozen bagels of various kinds, some of which Zeke guessed were his daughters' choices. They ordered sandwiches for themselves, and sat down at a table.

"So what's 'Zeke' short for?"

"Zhikr."

"You're named for a Sufi ceremony?"

Zeke stared at him.

"Don't look so surprised," he laughed. "Some friends of mine spend a fair amount of time at the Message of the Abode."

"I'm not up on the New Age scene."

"You got your name before the New Age became 'new'."

"That's right. Back when they were poor and called themselves hippies."

"Do you have brothers and sisters?

"Two sisters—Pagan and Prana."

"So your mother is a spiritual seeker."

"Well, she was, maybe. Or it was in the air in those days, all that Eastern stuff, and then the shit hit the fan. I don't think she could quite keep it up."

"What do you mean?"

"My father died when Pagan and I were really small."

"What happened?"

"A house fell on him."

"Whew." He blew out of his mouth and looked as if he would ask for clarification, then decided not to. "That's awful. How old was your mother?"

Zeke paused to do the math in her head. "Twenty-two or twenty-three."

"So what happened?"

"Well, I was too little to really know what was going on, but she ended up in Shady Grove, got a job as a secretary at a real estate firm. I guess she couldn't pay the bills on a secretary's salary, so she learned to be a realtor herself."

"She sells houses to people?"

"That's what they do." She didn't feel like thinking about the irony of it now.

He took a bite of bagel and was quiet for a moment, looking out over the cars in the parking lot. "So what do you think? Where has she gone?"

"I don't know." Zeke set down her bagel and looked at him. He was tanned from spending so much time outside, but the skin under his eyes was pale and papery, as if he'd stayed up late, reading or talking. He seemed to absorb surprising news without being thrown by it, and she found this quality reassuring.

"When I think about it, I kind of hit a wall," Zeke said. "My sister Pagan gets all up in her head, imagining a thousand things, most of them catastrophic. But that's how she is about everything. I figure that my mother's a grown-up. She has her reasons. I mean, we take it for granted there's stuff we don't tell our parents. We spare them certain things. So I don't know why Pagan gets her shorts in a knot about my mother not telling us everything."

He smiled at her vehemence. "What about your other sister? How's she taking this?"

Zeke thought of Prana calling the other morning. "She's kind of a lost soul. Although you wouldn't think it to meet her. She's . . ." Zeke searched for the word. "Posh. Sophisticated in a way. She lives in D.C., but she keeps to herself. I mean, she talks to us, but I usually find out she's coming up to New York through my mother. And now, with my mother gone, I think she feels, I don't know, out of the loop." Zeke felt tired. It was all too much to think about.

"So your sisters don't know any more than you do?"

"No, I don't think so. But the weird thing is that we keep hoping the others will come up with something. Thanksgiving should be interesting."

He took a bite of his sandwich, considering. "Well, let me know."

She heard his implication, that it wasn't merely a matter of curiosity, but concern.

"Ready to stop at one more barn before we head back across the river?"

"Yes," she said.

eight

PRANA FELT SHE HAD TO MAKE A BREAK IN THINGS. FIRST, SHE had to stop smoking with Joe. She had started to anticipate the rush, to taste the metallic smoke before she lit up, and she knew this was not a good sign. And she always felt like hell the day after, not merely hungover, but brittle, like a delicate shell. She could barely eat. But here in Washington everything was so readily available—Joe, Stephan—she was always making private resolutions, but didn't take action. She kept hoping things would fix themselves.

Prana wished she could start over. She should have told her mother about Stephan from the beginning, risked her disapproval. She wanted to rest her head in her mother's lap and be comforted. She would call her now if she could. What would she say? I'm leaving my lover? I've made a terrible mistake? She wanted, unreasonably, something to blame her sadness on. When she was little, tired and frustrated, she would sometimes call out: "Zeke's being mean to me!" But her mother would shush her and take her up for a nap, or give her something to eat. Zeke was never mean, that was the problem. It was her diffidence, even then, that upset Prana. For as long as she could remember, Prana wished she could be like Zeke, who simply did what she wanted, who didn't define herself for anyone. Instead of feeling the need to set people at ease, Zeke seemed almost happy to keep people off balance. Let them wonder. Let them guess. Even now, she slept with women, slept with men. She never bothered to explain.

Prana remembered a winter day, back in high school, when she had come home from school early. Her mother was showing houses, and a friend had given her a ride. She walked into the empty house, and Zeke and a senior boy, one whom Prana secretly admired, came down from Zeke's room. The boy looked sleepy and disheveled. Zeke barely batted an eyelash. She'd looked at Prana coolly, evenly, as if to say *This is between us. Right?*

This silence, gestures half understood, marked the distance between them. The beautiful young man standing at Zeke's shoulder would not be explained. Nothing was explained. Her mother was like this too: she didn't offer anything up. When Prana asked questions about Marco, about Pagan and Zeke's father, she only got part of the story. It was like looking at a moonrise in daytime: through the filmy white, she could almost see the part of the moon that wasn't visible.

Prana walked up the stairway as Zeke and the boy went

down. Sometimes she hated Zeke. She flopped down on her bed, tears welling up in her throat; she swallowed them down. Her head felt heavy and hot. She didn't hate Zeke, it was something else, something more. Their father had loved them. Marco had left. She knew it was a terrible thing to feel, but sometimes she envied her sisters because their father had died. At least he had left them unwillingly.

PRANA TOOK HER calendar down from the wall and set it on the table. She had canceled an upcoming job right after Pagan called, but she'd already finished most of the Christmas shoots. She looked at her checkbook, then reached into a desk drawer and pulled out some financial statements. She studied the most recent one carefully. She had saved a fair amount of money. It was something that most people, even her sisters, wouldn't have guessed. She had started saving so she could travel with Stephan and had been surprised to watch her small investments accumulate. She didn't own a car, didn't live expensively. Most people thought that, because she shopped for her job, she enjoyed material things, but aside from a few nice items, she bought very little.

She got out a calculator and set it on the table, trying to figure what she needed to live on for the next two months. She totaled the figures, added a little, and totaled again. Gathering her hair in her hands, she lifted it off her neck. She decided that, after staying at Pagan's, she would stay at her mother's for a few weeks. Why not? She could have some quiet, go into the city, she would wait for her mother to come home. She picked up a pen and started to make a list: forward mail, change the message on her machine . . . she paused. There really wasn't much she had to do. Or actually one large thing. She looked around her apartment, then dialed Stephan's home phone.

"I'm coming to your house. I need to talk to you, and then I'm going to leave."

"Prana, don't. Everyone's out, but they'll be back in a little while."

"I don't care. You can say I'm writing an article or something."

"Prana—"

She hung up. When the phone rang a moment later, she turned it off and reached for her long leather coat. The weight of it made her feel armored. She checked her wallet and hailed a cab, giving Stephan's address.

She had never been to his house. Once, she had seen pictures of his library in a magazine article: a large room filled with prints and photos, mementos of foreign places, shelves and shelves of books. She imagined a large, bright kitchen, a narrow hall, a quiet living room in shadow. She had seen it in her mind a thousand times.

Along Macomb Street, the houses were old and spacious, built for large families at the turn of the century. From the cab, she saw leaded glass in entrance hall windows and imagined the interiors had oak floors, wood trim, and high ceilings, the trappings of gentility. She leaned forward to give the cabbie the house number.

"I'm going to be in there for ten minutes. I want you to wait for me here."

The cabbie looked back at her doubtfully.

"I really mean it. I'm not going to stiff you. Here." She

thrust twenty dollars at him. "I'll be right back. I'm going to be really pissed if I come out and you're gone."

She got out of the cab and slammed the door.

Stephan, looking rumpled and astonished, met her at the front door. "Prana, this is not a good time. Everyone will be back in a few minutes."

"I can't help it. We've been on your schedule for years now."

He pushed the door open, and she came inside. He touched her arm and led her to a darkened library at the back of the house.

"It's time to stop," she said. She gazed at the familiar lines of his face, his wrinkled shirt, his eyes red as if he'd been sleeping. She thought how much they were a part of each other. "I mean it this time. You can't just call me two months from now when you're feeling sad. I can't do this any longer."

He stared at her, silent, as if he understood everything.

"You're tired of this too," she said.

"Prana, I'm not tired of you."

She felt furious at his abdication, that he would let her go so easily. "Everyone is moving forward in their lives but me," she said.

He opened his hands. His open palms, the gesture of helplessness, infuriated her. She understood now. He wanted his wife and family more than he wanted her. They represented something real to him, while she did not.

"Prana, you're acting as if I should have pushed you in some direction, but I couldn't. I shouldn't. You're an adult now."

She felt suddenly pathetic, ashamed, a hot fear moving over her. The whole time they'd been together, he had been waiting for her to grow up. She had grown in years but hadn't done anything with herself. She walked over to a wall of books and ran her fingers along the spines.

You're an adult now thudded in her ears, as if she'd outgrown being attractive or appealing, as if she'd been lovable only when she was a child. She wanted to upset him without speaking, to hurt him back for the fact that he was willing to let her go so easily. She could feel him across the room, waiting for her to speak, and she imagined he felt panicked because his wife would pull up in her car any minute. His wife and children would come into the house and sense the thickness here, even if Prana did not make a scene. She felt meanly pleased that, through having her here, in his family home, he would have to live more closely with his lie. She looked at his books and, almost idly, to provoke him with her slowness, she picked up a slender hardback from the shelf.

The book was covered in faded red cloth. She rested the spine in her palm, and the book's vanilla-colored pages fell open easily. She glanced down. They were poems; she couldn't tell what they were about.

"Do you like these?" she asked.

"I don't remember."

The margins were marked with penciled notes, written in a boy's cramped hand. She looked at the title. *Harmonium.* It seemed wrong to write in such a nice book.

"I want this," she said.

"Take it."

She snapped the book shut, and it made a soft sound, the weight of thick paper.

"Please, don't call me," she said, and turned toward the door. She wanted him to touch her, to stop her, to make her wait, but he simply stood still, watching her go. She walked down the hall, through the house, past the shining kitchen, her eyes streaming with tears. The house seemed immaterial to her, but it had been real to him all along.

Outside, she noticed his neighbor looking out her window, probably wondering why a cab was parked in front of the house. Prana glared at her, then got into the cab and gave the cabbie her address.

Settling back in the seat, she felt the beginning of a terrible headache, the one she always got from trying not to cry. She looked down at the book in her hand. Why had she taken it? She threw it on the floor.

n i n e

PAGAN WRAPPED A HEAVY RED SWEATER TIGHTLY AROUND her as she sat on the back steps. Maud wanted to dig a hole in the backyard and rather than say no, Pagan had given her a thick wooden spoon, which was too dull to be a good tool. Maud crouched in the grass, damp leaves stuck to her bottom, and studied something moving in the dirt. Pagan wished she could just go to the hospital and have everything be over with. She didn't let herself imagine what would happen there, only getting to the other side of it. A seeping anger spread through her, and she wrapped her arms around her knees. Her mother should be here. She should have sensed something was wrong. Pagan reached for her mug of tea. At least it had caffeine—everything she had been so careful of—none of it mattered now.

She took a sip of the hot, dark tea, and looked out over the yard. The previous owners had liked to garden, but Pagan had been pregnant for most of the time they'd lived here and didn't have the energy to weed, or prune, or grow anything except the child inside her. Her mother had given her a large metal watering can, which Maud loved to lug around the yard. In the shaded back corner, a large outcrop of rock had flowering plants growing in the cracks of soil. Maud dumped the accumulated rainwater on the gray stone in front of her, and standing in the wet grass, she giggled at how the water returned to her. Pagan felt a deep and bitter pleasure at watching her, and wondered if this was how her mother had felt after their father died: every detail seemed bright and sharp.

They were living in Oregon then. Pagan remembered playing outside in her bare feet, the overwhelming green. She didn't remember the accident itself, but she remembered her mother kneeling and sobbing in the grass. Her mother's face, contorted with grief, had frightened her. Several years later, her mother met Marco, and Pagan's impression was that her youngest sister had somehow appeared like magic.

Even then Marco had seemed flimsy, like a boy paper doll, easily torn. He seemed most real, most animated, when he was talking about the future. She remembered Marco explaining they were going on a big trip, driving across the country to upstate New York where he had a job with some friends. He had shown her a big map, told her about apple trees and farms. Her mother seemed happy. On the long drive, Pagan traced the colored states on the map, then traced the horizon with her fingertip. She was disappointed it didn't have the same colors.

She didn't remember Marco's leaving, but she did remember just after: her mother sitting at the table in their cabin upstate.

Her mother had called it the kitchen table, but now, when Pagan pictured the plasticized top and spindly metal legs, she realized it was actually a card table. Her mother was folding a letter.

"Can I read that?" Pagan asked.

"No."

"Why?"

"It's a letter from Marco."

Pagan stared at her Cheerios melting in milk. She was tired of being told what she could and couldn't do. She *could* read, she *did* know how, and she kicked her foot, and a leg of the table skidded out, and the milk and cereal and everything on the table crashed to the floor. Zeke laughed. Prana wailed in her makeshift high chair. Milk and Cheerios flowed over the planks. Her mother put her hands over her face and sobbed.

"I'm sorry, I'm sorry," Pagan cried. She crouched to pick up the dishes, then sliced her finger on a broken bowl. She turned around, looking for a dish towel. She couldn't find one. Wherever she walked, bright drops of blood splattered in the milk. She felt caught in an invisible snare, crying, her head buzzing. Wherever she turned seemed wrong. Whatever she did made more of a mess. Her mother reached for her, wrapped a cloth around her hand, and cried.

After Marco left, her mother moved them to Shady Grove. Pagan remembered looking at a map while her mother explained that Marco lived in the city now, in Greenwich Village. When she asked how long it took to get there, her mother said it took an hour on the train. Pagan didn't think an hour was very far away, but by then she understood that she shouldn't ask about it anymore.

In the fifties and early sixties, before their arrival, Shady

Grove had been a quietly privileged, sleepy little place. The sixties passed through the town in a diluted form—mostly reflected in the teenagers' music and clothing, some discreet drug use, but the conservative and successful tenor of the town had not changed. By the early seventies, a large number of well-to-do families were buying homes there. Of course Pagan had not been conscious of any of this at the time. She remembered taking the bus to the white-brick elementary school. She remembered getting up in the middle of the night for a glass of water and seeing her mother studying for her real estate exam at the kitchen table.

Her mother had quickly learned that the wives decided on the homes. Most husbands commuted into the city; others drove the wooded suburban roads to Ossining or Armonk where IBM's manicured lawns spread like golf courses around sleek buildings of glass and steel. For many couples, buying a home in Westchester represented a financial and social arrival, a belief that they were moving over the threshold into a sunnier life. Even as a receptionist, her mother had observed that Westchester wives were put off by feather earrings and sandals, which might suggest flakiness or an inability to get the contract right, and so her mother made certain changes—beige pants substituted for a flowing skirt, a sleek turtleneck instead of something more revealing.

SHE HELD THE empty mug in her hands and wondered if her mother had transformed herself once again. It didn't seem likely, there was no need for it now, but over the years, Pagan had noticed that being a realtor required a verbal chameleon-like quality. At home, her mother answered the phone in a carefully neutral tone, which allowed her to slip into the casual intimacy of talking to a friend, or the formality of talking to a client, without an obvious change of gears. When she spoke to clients, her mother's voice became more definite, sympathetic without sounding indulgent. She consistently gave the appearance of interest and sincerity, and Pagan simply thought of this as a professional demeanor. It wasn't a mask—it was merely manners.

But now that her mother's disappearance called everything into question, Pagan went over things she hadn't thought about in years, gathered them up to find a pattern.

When she was a teenager, she would sometimes meet her mother at the office to catch a ride home after school. This usually involved a certain amount of waiting around while her mother filled out counteroffers and amendments, fielded phone calls from anxious buyers and sellers. Pagan noticed that when a client brought up a topic in conversation: country clubs, the public schools, politics, or window treatments, her mother sometimes echoed a phrase with her own inflection, drawing the person out. If a client expressed an interest in gardening, her mother could talk about borders and rock gardens, annuals and perennials, but if a client wasn't interested, or said she didn't have time to garden, her mother would nod sympathetically, and joke about the catalogs she accumulated, the seeds she bought that she never had time to plant. Once, driving home, Pagan had asked her mother about this; her mother had smiled and said that, when it came to buying expensive houses, which was emotionally as well as financially frightening, buyers often got cold feet. Instead of reminding them of the legality of their contracts, which only made them panicky or anxious, she said it was better to remind them of little things they'd liked about the place—the proximity of a certain elementary school, the built-in bookshelves, the screened porch, the Jacuzzi in the master bedroom. The small things she learned about clients often helped keep the deal together. Pagan remembered thinking it was a compliment that her mother revealed how she worked. These were the calculated skills of adulthood.

One of her mother's little courtesies, whenever she closed a deal, was to send a gift from White Flower Farm, an upscale nursery in Litchfield, Connecticut. Privately, her mother described the place as overly precious. She never bought from there herself. Through fall and winter, her mother received eccentric seed catalogs, some in plain black and white, stapled together, from out on the West Coast. The catalogs contained a lot of ranting about agribusiness and the environment. Sometimes, on winter evenings when Pagan was supposed to be doing homework, she would come downstairs and find her mother, feet up on the sofa, thumbing through her catalogs. She put Post-It notes on the pages, but she never seemed to order anything. Pagan thought of these seed catalogs as a remnant of her mother's original self, but of course she had changed, she had to. She imagined her mother had made certain exterior changes out of financial necessity, and then they became second nature, something she would have grown into anyway.

Maud came running up, her sweatpants muddy, leaves in her hair.

"Look!" she commanded, and she opened her chubby fist. A caterpillar curled in the palm of her hand.

"It's a woolly bear," Pagan said. "Don't squish it."

Maud gazed down at the fine black and orange bristles.

"It's a little scared right now," Pagan said. "Do you know what the colors mean?"

Maud poked the bristles with her finger.

"When the orange in the middle is long, it's supposed to be a long winter," Pagan said. Her tone was light, but with the words out of her mouth, she felt a sense of dread at the idea. "Come on," she said, "It's time to go in."

"What about the caterpillar?"

"Let's leave him out here to munch on some leaves."

"Where?"

"You can set him right here in the grass."

And for once Maud followed her without protest.

ten

ZEKE HAD NEVER EXACTLY FIGURED OUT HOW TO BE WITH men, not that she lost any sleep over this. When she was in college, there was the easy buffer of keeping things casual, and this spared her having to define herself for anyone, but after college, that borderless region seemed to evaporate, and people wanted to know what you were, or how you defined yourself. The idea of choosing one path irked her, especially since each seemed to come with a prescribed set of rules.

People imagined that being with women was freeing, as if she could finally be true to herself, but Zeke found it ironic that, in many ways, sleeping with women involved more rules than sleeping with men. A few years ago, she'd been dating a woman who lived in Massachusetts, and Zeke found the whole atmosphere claustrophobic—the ultra-careful language, the borrowed twelve-step terminology, the honoring of emotions and 'safe space.' She didn't want to process everything. There was a sense of overwhelming PC vigilance; it was taboo for a lesbian to shave her legs or wear makeup. If they went out to dinner with friends, and Zeke ordered a steak, some woman would be sure to have a fit and rant about the inhumane ways cows were killed, growth hormones, organic meat, on and on. Zeke understood the point. She just got tired of everything being politicized.

In some ways, men were easier. There was less talking about the relationship itself, which was a plus. She could eat meat, smoke a cigarette, shave her legs if she felt like it—although of course she never did—and a man would not feel entitled to comment. She had imagined, once, that being with women would be a relationship of equals, but that had turned out to be only half true. With Marcie there was always the subtle struggle to retain the upper hand.

IT WAS A lovely day, bright and clear, a day when things were bound to go smoothly. Zeke spent the first part of the morning cleaning up the tack room: sweeping up behind the galvanized metal garbage cans she used for feed bins, looking for feed scoops and a few tools that had gone missing. Bert made her nervous, interested, uncomfortable, because he didn't require her to fit neatly into any particular category. What would they be like together? She sensed he would take her exactly as she was. Of course there was the possibility she was misreading him; he knew about Marcie, but she thought of the way he looked at her, and knew that he liked the way she thought. He liked her capability. Zeke guessed that, if she cooled toward him, he would easily take the hint. But what if she didn't? She thought of Eleanor and Amy. It would confuse them if she started seeing a man.

Marcie had tried to prepare them for going out into the world with two mommies. Zeke couldn't remember exactly what had triggered the discussion, but Amy came home from kindergarten one day with a question about her friends' parents, and Marcie had explained how most families had a mother and a father, but how Zeke was really important to all of them, how they loved each other just like other parents did. Zeke remembered being amazed that Marcie could, off the top of her head, give them a matter-of-fact explanation, which didn't say too much, but included her so completely in their lives. As Marcie spoke, she reached for Zeke, putting her hand on Zeke's shoulder. She said that if the girls had any other questions, they should be sure to ask.

Zeke took a rag and wiped the cobwebs from a window. The problem was that Marcie couldn't be depended on. She could veer from marvelous to psychotic, all within an evening, and while Zeke could split up with her, the girls couldn't. She sighed and looked at the grimy rag. There was a core of something extraordinary in Marcie, but it was being corroded by her drinking. She thought of a middle-school science project where the teacher had left something hard and white sitting in Coca-Cola as a way of demonstrating how soda would rot your teeth.

After putting it off as long as she could, Zeke went back to the cottage to take care of some paperwork. She looked over the garden as she went in. She wasn't a true gardener; she had trouble remembering what she had tried from year to year—what had worked, what had failed, and why. The brussel sprouts were the only viable plant now. She loved their odd knobby stalks; they looked like a science fiction plant, a wild invention.

"Disappointed cabbages," her mother called them. She nudged a pumpkin with her boot, wondering if it was still okay. When she pushed it over, it was rotten underneath.

In the kitchen, odd dishes were piled in the sink, coffee spills puddled on the counter. She would have to talk to the students; she didn't want to clean up after them. Most of the students were likeable, but some were so preoccupied with their weekend activities that their brains didn't function past Wednesday. The young women seemed permanently addled from watching the Giants practice here in summer. Their fascination was a mystery to her, not because they were preoccupied with men, but because their whole attitude toward sex was a strange mixture of puritanism and verbal flippancy. *Just Do It.* Zeke's impression, from half-overheard conversations around the cottage, was that although they might be *having* sex, they actually knew little about it. They were like precocious children repeating three-syllable words without understanding their meanings. Most of the men didn't suffer from this pretense, and she liked them better for it, but the girls used their lovely bodies in place of words, as if their physical willingness might articulate what they could not, and what these young women failed to see, as far as she could surmise, was that they articulated nothing, they knew nothing about truly connecting with another human being, nothing about eroticism. She carried a cup of tea to her desk, and was gazing out the window, when the phone rang.

"Is this Zeke Williams?" The woman's voice was official-sounding.

"Yes, it is."

"I'm calling from Emerson Middle School. You are listed on Eleanor Watson's forms as an emergency contact and—"

Zeke was out of her chair, "Is she okay?"

"She seems to be having stomach pains, and her mother is away on business. Eleanor says there's a housekeeper, but we don't get any answer at the house."

"I'll be right there." Zeke hung up the phone before the woman had time to finish.

She grabbed her keys and ran out the door, calling to one of the incoming students. "I've got to run, I'll be back." When she tried to start her car, it stalled. She sat back for a moment and took a breath. "Calm down," she ordered herself. "It's probably nothing." She started the car again, and forced herself to drive slowly through campus. She picked up speed on the main road, then turned down a side street, toward the middle school.

Zeke tapped on her steering wheel at a stoplight, *hurry up*. Marcie would never willingly get a housekeeper—housekeepers knew secrets. Would she have checked into rehab? Probably not. She pulled into the parking lot and swooped into the closest space. A thickset woman, wearing a sweater with turkeys marching across it, looked up at her, surprised, but Zeke ignored her and hurried into the main entrance. In daylight, the school was a foreign land. With a few questions, she found her way to the nurse's office.

She stepped in the door and felt suddenly out of place, smelling of horses and other animals. The antiseptic room was filled with DARE slogans and posters about AIDS. Did they teach kids about that so young? The nurse poked her head out from behind a curtain. Her cap of gray hair and pointed chin made her seem silvery and elfin.

"Are you Zeke? Why don't you come in here?"

Zeke stepped inside the curtain and saw Eleanor lying on the vinyl-covered bed, her brown hair spread out behind her. Her faintly pudgy, childlike body seemed solid and relaxed.

"Eleanor, are you okay?"

Eleanor wordlessly put up her arms to be hugged, and bending to her, Zeke recognized Marcie's scents: soap and lemon-smelling shampoo, mixed with a clean child smell that was different from Marcie's own dusky scent. Eleanor hugged her hard, then released her.

"My stomach hurts." Eleanor's tone was whining and plaintive, but she didn't seem frightened or upset. The nurse looked at Zeke over her glasses.

"Eleanor, I'd like to talk to your friend in private for a moment, all right?" The nurse gestured that they should step outside the curtain. Zeke wondered if she had ever met Marcie.

"She's come in every day this week complaining of stomach pains, and I've let her rest a while, then sent her back to class. But yesterday, she started saying it was worse, maybe we needed to call you." The nurse looked at Zeke carefully. "I have to tell you, I've taken her temp and all that. The stomach pains may be real, but yesterday I had the feeling I was being set up, you know? She's not a convincing liar. Is there trouble at home?"

Zeke hesitated. "Lots of changes going on," she said.

"I'm going to release her into your care. You'll have to go and sign out at the front office."

"Fine," Zeke said. She didn't want to blow Eleanor's story by saying too much.

Eleanor was quiet as she led the way down to the front office. Marcie hadn't thought to change Zeke's name on the contact card. Sly Marcie. It was unusual for her to make a mistake. Zeke put her arm over Eleanor's shoulder and followed her down the hall. She thought that, if Eleanor were pretending she'd hurt her foot, she would have limped on both legs.

Once they were outside, Eleanor gave a little skip.

"You look pretty good for someone in the early stages of appendicitis," Zeke said.

Eleanor looked down at the ground.

"You scared me to death, Eleanor. When they called me at the farm, I thought something terrible had happened." Zeke tried to sound serious; she didn't want to show she was pleased with Eleanor's ingenuity. "Your stomach doesn't really hurt that much, does it?"

"It does," Eleanor insisted.

Out in the sunlight, Zeke felt her fear go out of her. Eleanor walked quickly toward the parking lot, as if some school official might recall them. When Zeke caught up with her, a few drops of sweat dotted the crescents below Eleanor's eyes, and Zeke wanted to weep for this little detail, holy water, to touch the drops the way people did in church. Once, when they had all been together, she pointed this out to Marcie as Eleanor came running up from some exertion, then dashed off again. Zeke remembered saying it tenderly. "Look, she sweats below the eyes." But a few weeks later, when Marcie had been drinking, she snapped at Eleanor, "Look at you for Godsakes, you're tubby, you're sweating under your eyes." Eleanor flinched and wiped the back of her hand across her face. Zeke felt sickened that Marcie could take something particular and dear and turn it so unkindly.

"Mom went to some conference two days ago. She got this doofy Mabel housekeeper who said she had to go grocery shopping today. I remembered those cards Mom had to fill out when we started school, and I hoped if they really thought something was wrong, they'd call you."

"Is the housekeeper's name really Mabel?" Zeke was amused.

"Zeke! That's hardly the point." Eleanor's tone was adult

and stern. "I'm sorry I scared you, but I had to do *something*."
Her eyes filled with tears.

"Oh sweetheart," Zeke bent down to give her a hug and
Eleanor collapsed in her arms and began to sob. Zeke crouched
by the car, holding her for a long time, letting her cry herself out.
By the time she stood up, her legs felt prickly and undependable.

"Look," Zeke said. "We'll have a day together. We'll call
Mabel, or whatever her name is, and tell her you're with me so
she doesn't worry when you don't get off the bus, and then we'll
hang out at the farm, get something to eat, all that."

Eleanor stopped crying and dug in her backpack for a tissue. She leaned on Zeke as she blew her nose.

Driving back to the farm Zeke asked, "So what's going on
at home?"

"Mom is a pain. She's not drinking, but she's mad *all* the
time. Well, not all the time. She wakes up okay, but when she
comes home from work she's horrible and yells at us, and tells
us to wash the dishes and clean up and stay out of her hair. She
went to one of those triple A meetings you told her to go to."

"She did?" Zeke felt a flutter of hope.

"She hated it. She came home and said the people were a
bunch of pathetic losers who had no friends and who went to
these meetings *every single night!*"

Zeke could hear Marcie's inflections delivered in Eleanor's
child voice, but beside the familiar resonance, she was surprised
to hear Eleanor talking without censoring herself. In Marcie's
presence, her exuberance was easily squelched. Amy was still
too young to really know what was going on, but Eleanor
seemed to have known all along.

"I guess that some people don't take to it at first," Zeke
said. *Triple A.* She smiled in spite of herself.

"You wouldn't really try to take us away from our mother, would you?" Eleanor asked.

Zeke gripped the steering wheel and felt her face flush. "Oh Ellie, I'm sorry. No, I wouldn't." She felt a heaviness in the pit of her stomach, and concentrated on the traffic ahead of her. "I lost my temper. It was a terrible thing to say."

"It scared me when you smashed the windshield like that," Eleanor said.

Zeke chewed the inside of her cheek. What had she been thinking? That she and Marcie were the only two people in the world? It must have looked awful. How would it look to someone official? She could imagine the headline: *Lover Smashes Windshield with Rake*. It had been a stupid thing to do. The simple fact of it seemed violent.

"I'm really sorry. I shouldn't have done it, but your mother—" Zeke didn't want to talk Marcie down, but she wanted to protect Eleanor with some knowledge of how Marcie operated. "Your mother takes the smallest thing, and kind of twists it. It drives me crazy. I just wanted her to stop."

"You know it wasn't the right thing to do," Eleanor said in a lecturing tone.

Zeke smiled and touched her cheek. "I know. You're right," she said.

BY THE TIME they got back to the cottage, it was almost noon. Zeke didn't want to call the housekeeper. She wished she could just drop Eleanor off at the bus stop at the appropriate time so they could meet like this again. But that was silly. Who knew when Marcie would be leaving town on business again?

When Zeke dialed the number, a tired, laconic voice answered the phone. Zeke explained what had happened, simply saying that Eleanor's stomach seemed much better by now, and that she would have her back by supper, or early evening at the latest. The housekeeper seemed taken aback, but didn't protest.

"High five!" Zeke said.

Eleanor slapped her palm and grinned.

ZEKE LOOKED AT her calendar, trying to take stock of the day. Yolanda had a jewelry-making class in the cottage this afternoon. If Marcie wasn't so screwed up, this was exactly the kind of thing that Eleanor could do. She was young, but she could make something simple. Zeke was supposed to meet with some students who wanted to plant a garden next spring. Their botany professor was overseeing the project, but Zeke had to find space for them; they wanted to start seedlings inside this winter. She realized, suddenly, that she was starving.

"Hey Ellie, are you hungry?"

"I'm famished."

Zeke grinned. "Famished, huh? Did you leave your lunch at school?"

"I was supposed to buy today."

"Ugh. Cafeteria food. Plastic plates, mystery meat, scary gravy." Zeke made a face and Eleanor giggled wildly. Zeke felt overwhelmed, as if she couldn't contain this mixture of happiness and loss. Sometimes, it took so little to make them happy. When Marcie was in a conscientious mode, she fixed the girls' lunches, made healthy sandwiches, sent them to school with fruit juice, not just colored water. Marcie was like the little girl in the nursery rhyme: when she was good she was very, very good, and when she was bad she was horrid.

"Want to go to the deli and get a sandwich?"

"The place with good pickles?"

"Yeah, the place with the good pickles. We'll pick up food and bring it back, okay? I have to meet some students in a little while."

Eleanor gazed at her with such pleasure in her upturned face, that Zeke thought for a moment she might weep. She reached for her jacket, feeling in the pocket for her wallet.

They drove into Pleasantville and got sandwiches at the deli. It amused Zeke to watch Eleanor consider her options, how precise she was in her ordering, tipping her head back to see the man behind the counter.

"I'd like a rare roast beef sandwich on a kaiser roll, with cole slaw and Russian dressing please."

Zeke grinned and ordered a sandwich for herself, leaving her hand on Eleanor's shoulder, as if laying claim to something she had lost.

AFTER LUNCH IN Zeke's office, Eleanor looked around the room, then sat down at Zeke's desk.

"Is there anything special you feel like doing?" Zeke asked.

"I'd like you to read me a story," Eleanor said. "I have to write a book report for school."

Zeke tried not to show her surprise. Asking for a story was the type of request Amy would make. She thought of the night Marcie cut her wrist: Amy lying with her head in Marcie's lap, sucking her thumb. "A story? I can't imagine the kind of story I'd read would be much help with a book report."

"Our teacher is all big on local history. We're reading kid stories." Eleanor dug around in her backpack and pulled out a slender book. *Rip Van Winkle and the Legend of Sleepy Hollow.*

Zeke grinned. "I haven't read those in years."

"They seem like kid stories, but they have a lot of words."

Zeke sat in a student-made window seat and made room for Eleanor next to her. She opened up "The Legend of Sleepy Hollow." Zeke associated the headless horseman with ghost stories and high school football floats, but as she started reading, she felt a stunned sense of recognition. The landscape still evoked the same feeling.

In the bosom of one of those spacious coves which indent the eastern shore of the Hudson, at the broad expansion of the river denominated by the ancient Dutch navigators the Tappan Zee, and where they always prudently shortened sail and implored the protection of St. Nicholas when they crossed, there lies a small market-town or rural part, which by some is called Greensburg, but which is more generally and properly known by the name of Tarry Town. This name was given, we are told, in former days by the good housewives of the adjacent country from the inveterate propensity of their husbands to linger about the village tavern on market days. Be that as it may, I do not vouch for the fact, but merely advert to it for the sake of being precise and authentic. Not far from this village, perhaps about two miles, there is a little valley, or rather lap of land, among high hills, which is one of the quietest places in the whole world. A small brook glides through it, with just murmur enough to lull one to repose, and the occasional whistle of a quail or tapping of a woodpecker are almost the only sounds that ever break in upon the uniform tranquility.

"I don't understand what all the words mean," Eleanor said.

"I don't either, not all of them," Zeke said. "You're probably supposed to look them up."

"Look it up, look it up." Eleanor mimicked a schoolmarmish tone.

"I always felt like that too." Zeke smiled. "This sounds like the landscape here though."

"Not anymore," Eleanor said.

"I think it does," Zeke said. "If you came riding with me, out on the trails, you'd see what I mean."

I mention this peaceful spot with all possible laud, for it is in such little, retired Dutch valleys, found here and there embosomed in the great State of New York, that population, manners, and customs remain fixed, while the great torrent of migration and improvement, which is making such incessant changes in other parts of this restless country, sweeps by them unobserved. They are like those little nooks of still water which border a rapid stream, where we may see the straw and bubble riding quietly at anchor or slowly revolving in their mimic harbor, undisturbed by the rush of the passing current. Though many years have elapsed since I trod the drowsy shades of Sleepy Hollow, yet I question whether I should not still find the same trees and same families vegetating in its sheltered bosom.

"Lots of bosoms in this story," Eleanor giggled.

Zeke laughed. "I suppose so," she said. "All those sheltering hills."

They spent a long time reading. As they sat by the window, Zeke felt as if she were reading an old map, one with pictures of sea monsters drawn in the oceans. The jewelry-making class came into the next room, and she and Eleanor sat and listened companionably as the class rearranged the furniture and Yolanda explained their project. It grew quiet as they settled into work.

"Would you like to take a class like that here? If your mother would let you?"

Eleanor nodded.

Zeke was startled when she looked out the window and saw Bert's car pulling into the driveway. What was he doing here? His daughters got out of the car and headed toward the cottage. They came up onto the front porch, and Bert paused and knocked before stepping inside. He looked around the open doorway to see Zeke sitting with Eleanor, and Zeke felt as if she'd been caught in a private moment.

"Hi," he smiled. "You don't mind if the girls use the bathroom, do you?"

"Oh no, of course not."

The younger girl disappeared down the hallway. Eleanor gazed at Cecily, and Zeke felt for a moment that Eleanor was almost lordly in her lounging against Zeke.

"You're really good at gymnastics," Eleanor offered.

Cecily shrugged, and Zeke felt hurt at the way she brushed off Eleanor's compliment, although Eleanor seemed undisturbed.

"She can do every obstacle," Eleanor said, addressing all of them. "She can even climb the rope to the ceiling of the gym."

"It's not such a big deal," Cecily said, although she looked noticeably pleased.

"I'm not any good at gymnastics," Eleanor said. "The only thing I can do is the balance beam."

"Balancing is hard," Cecily said. Sensing that her encouragement was falling flat, she asked Eleanor, "Don't you think it's a joke how Miss Lynn blows that whistle for *everything?*"

"Yes." Eleanor grinned.

Bert looked over the girls' heads at Zeke and smiled.

eleven

PAGAN HAD NEVER GIVEN THE LOCAL HOSPITAL MUCH thought, but now, its chemistry and science, its gleaming indifference, represented a universe without belief. The randomness of the world was frightening. Bad egg, bad luck. And even though she didn't think of herself as a believer, she wondered if she had believed in something without knowing it. Her father's death was a sign, early on, that the world was a hard place, but she had thought of his death as a defining tragedy, a blow that wouldn't be repeated because it would be too cruel, but of course, troubles weren't meted out like that.

She wished her mother were here. Tommy had assured her that her mother's will, as Pagan described it, was a completely sraightforward, preparing-for-the-unexpected document. She thought of the note her mother had left. *I'll be with you in spirit*. What the hell did that mean?

She and Tommy were scheduled to meet with the genetics counselor. Weeks ago, she had resisted the first meeting, not wanting to look at the pictures of broken chromosomes that signaled a Down syndrome child. The genetics counselor was a soft-spoken, bearded man wearing earth-colored clothes. He explained how rare this was, that it was nothing they could have predicted, nothing Pagan had done.

"I have to tell you that some people choose to keep these babies, and occasionally they do live. I'm required to offer you some literature as well, but I should warn you that it's written by people who have chosen to dedicate their lives to caring for these children. Some people find the photographs very disturbing."

Pagan shook her head.

Tommy took the envelope, and Pagan stared at him in disbelief.

"I don't want to find those anywhere," she said.

"You won't," he said.

IT SEEMED ODD that the doctor who did the amniocentesis was going to do what they called "the procedure," but they had to talk to him too. She was reassured it was the same doctor, although he didn't give any sign he remembered her. She imagined he was being polite, not referring back to that more hopeful time.

He spoke about the various ways the procedure could be done and said there were mainly two choices. One was to induce labor, which could take an unspecified amount of time, a day or longer; the other was to give her general anesthesia, and he would do it as a surgery.

"My advice," he said, "is that you don't want to be awake for this."

Pagan nodded, too frightened to allow herself to get upset. She had to sign forms acknowledging the possibility of hemorrhaging, or a punctured uterus, and in the cool, rarified air, she started to sweat. More could go wrong. She had always imagined that, if Tommy or Maud needed surgery, she would question the doctor about every aspect of the anesthesia and operation. Now she didn't need to ask. She knew.

"We're going to do a small pre-op procedure," the doctor said. "I'm going to insert some small, I don't know what to call them, 'sticks' is the closest thing, into your cervix. It will help with the dilation. I'm afraid it's a bit uncomfortable, but it will make everything go more smoothly tomorrow."

She nodded again. The doctor said he would be back in a few minutes, and ushered Tommy out the door. Pagan got undressed and put on the flimsy gown.

When the doctor and nurse came back, Pagan tried to calm herself, but her chest felt tight. The hard speculum going inside always pinched. She breathed out while the doctor was talking, trying to reassure her, and Pagan tapped her fingers rapidly on the bone above her heart, her breasts flattened beneath the thin cloth gown, tapped her breastbone, telling herself *I'm okay, I'm okay, I'm okay, I'm okay, I'm okay* very quickly, as if she were counting, willing it to be all right. And with each sharp insertion, she repeated *I'm okay, I'm okay, I'm okay, I'm okay,* the words holding her together.

When they were done, she put on her soft, familiar clothes.

As she buttoned her blouse, an old cotton shirt with small lilac flowers, her clothes seemed a costume from a place she could not return to. The nurse gave her two prescriptions for the following day: a painkiller and something to thicken her blood.

THAT NIGHT, LYING in bed, she thought of the words the genetics counselor had used on the phone: *damaged, profoundly, severely.* She tried not to think of the baby as their son, although it would be until it died. She couldn't actually go through with having a child like that. She felt as if she'd ridden a bicycle into a concrete wall. It could happen. It *had* happened. And if there was a ninety-five percent chance that the child would die, then there was a small chance the child would live, and that was the truly frightening part. They would have a life defined by a child who would most likely be blind, shitting himself forever, never learn to talk or eat by himself. There would be thousands of dollars in medical bills. If Tommy were unhappy at work, he might never be able to change jobs because the child's whole life would be one huge preexisting condition. As far as she knew, there weren't even places such as institutions anymore, and even if there were, even if the child were unbearable to live with, how much worse to think of a child, even an oblivious one, living somewhere like an unwanted animal.

THE NEXT MORNING, Pagan woke early. Outside their bedroom window, the maples had lost most of their leaves and the stark outline of branches cut the deepening sky. She heard Maud downstairs, asking a string of high-pitched questions, and Prana answering in a low, calm voice. When Prana arrived last night, her hair twisted up on her head, Pagan had been startled—for a brief, almost hallucinatory moment, she thought Prana was her mother. She started to move down the hallway in a rush, but caught herself. Even in the dim light, she could see how thin Prana was. She didn't have their mother's roundness. When Pagan hugged her, she felt bony, all elbows and ribs; she smelled like cigarettes.

Pagan wished today was already over. When she went downstairs, Prana and Maud were playing with checkers, which Maud didn't really know how to play. "King me!" she crowed.

Prana put two checkers on top of one of Maud's, then looked up. "Do you want any breakfast?" she asked.

"I'm not allowed to eat anything," Pagan said.

Prana nodded and moved a checker on the board.

"Watch me play," Maud insisted.

Tommy came downstairs, and waved away Pagan's suggestions for breakfast. When the time came to leave, Pagan felt a teary thrumming in her throat. "Thanks for coming up to help," she whispered to Prana. She bent to kiss Maud good-bye.

IN THE ADMITTING office, Pagan sat down next to a receptionist who tapped her information into the computer. A small butterfly sign on her desk said something about Jesus and the Power of Love. Pagan tried not to fidget as the woman read her prognosis and procedure, but the woman was blandly pleasant and didn't comment. An old man wearing rainbow-colored suspenders, clearly a volunteer, led them to pre-op. Following him down the hall, Pagan looked over at Tommy. He had cut himself shaving and his skin looked drained under the fluorescent lights. The man led them to a private room, where a nurse made her take off all her jewelry, even her wedding ring and wedding band and, as Pagan pulled off her rings, she felt suddenly afraid that they were making a terrible bargain for their love, that this would undo them. The nurse held out a small plastic bag, but she turned to Tommy.

"I want my husband to hold these."

Tommy held out his hand, and she took off the first real present he had given her, a garnet pendant with three small diamonds. She placed the necklace in his hand, the chain making a small pool of gold, then set her engagement ring and wedding band on top. He closed them in his hand.

After she had undressed, and gotten into bed, the anesthesiologist came in. He was rotund Chinese man with a soft voice, and he explained that he would administer certain drugs, and that a nurse anesthetist would be in the operating room during the entire procedure. He told Pagan there would be a tube in her throat, which might be sore afterward, and that he would give her something for nausea. He handed her a little paper cup and Pagan drank obediently. He said there would be a little Valium in her drip and looked down at her file.

"Why are you doing this procedure?" His tone was merely curious.

"The baby has genetic problems. It's going to die." She spoke in a low voice.

He nodded and made a note.

"You will remember going into the OR, but after that, the next thing you'll be aware of is waking up. It's part of the anesthesia we use. It will feel as if you didn't even go out."

The nurses bustled around her. Tommy asked one of them where the bathroom was and she pointed down the hall.

"Will you be okay here for a few minutes?" he asked.

"Sure," she said. She couldn't feel the drugs. She didn't feel different at all, but she wondered why he needed to ask. He returned a few minutes later, as a nurse leaned over and spoke to her.

"I've never prepped anyone for this so late in a pregnancy." She had a pug nose and porcine cheeks. Her eyes seemed to glitter.

Pagan looked up. She felt muffled, as if snow had started to fall outside.

"Is there anything else you planned to say to my wife while I was out of the room?" Tommy's voice was loud and imposing. Pagan understood she'd been insulted, but felt the Valium in the drip taking the edge off everything.

"Why, no." The nurse looked surprised.

Tommy came over to the bed and started to take Pagan's hand, then saw the IV needle, and reached for her shoulder. He stood over her, as if to guard her, and looked out over the parking lot. When they came to wheel her into the operating room, the nurse told him he would have to wait outside.

Tommy leaned down and whispered in her ear. "I love you. I'll be right here, I'll be waiting."

Pagan nodded and suddenly felt that the calming drug had dissipated. What if they made a mistake with the anesthesia, what if something went wrong, what if she never woke up? She felt a panic rising into her throat. What about Maud? Who would take care of Maud? The nurse-anesthetist, a tall, ghost-like figure in scrubs and glasses, swooped in on Pagan as they wheeled her toward the operating room.

"Please, I'm a mother. I have to wake up from this."

"Honey, I'm going to take real good care of you. I guarantee it." Her voice was deep and booming. She sounded like a waitress in a country diner telling someone their eggs and toast would be right up. She wore a mask over her nose and mouth, and Pagan could only see her eyes, brown and clear behind her glasses.

"Do you promise?"

"Yes," the nurse said. "I'm going to be watching you every minute. This is going to be just fine."

Pagan tried to be reassured by her voice.

HER NEXT AWARENESS was of lying in a bed, blue curtains all around her. She wondered what had happened, then realized it was over. She must be in the recovery room. Outside the curtain, she heard the thin sound of a baby crying. She tried to shake her head, shake away the sound, but felt too tired. Gradually, she became more awake and realized it wasn't a dream. Behind the curtain next to her, a woman had a tiny baby. Pagan felt the sorrow of it rise up out of her. A baby, the woman had a baby and she did not. Pagan started to cry. She was too tired to sit up, and the tears leaked over her temples, into her hair. The curtain slid back, and a nurse came in and sat down next to her. She put her hand on Pagan's forehead and smoothed her hair; she held Pagan's hand and let her cry.

After a few minutes, the nurse said, "I'll be back, we'll get her moved," and she stepped out on her quiet shoes, pulling the curtain behind her. Pagan heard mumbling outside the curtain, and the faint rubber tread of a bed being wheeled away. The recovery room went quiet and Pagan drifted back to sleep.

She woke again later and remembered that first waking, the thin sound of the baby crying, the nurse stroking her forehead. Closing her eyes, a checkerboard pattern, blue and silver, swirled against the darkness of her lids. Squeezing harder, the pattern moved, distorted, and then she heard Tommy's step and opened her eyes. His expression was hesitant and sorrowful, the smudges of dark skin beneath his eyes almost purple. She would always remember him like this. His eyes were red-rimmed, not from crying but from fear, and he bent down over her and Pagan smelled his clean, familiar scent in the antiseptic room. She was afraid he would cry. She felt it building in him. She could not bear it if he did.

He sat down next to her and took her hand.

"I want to go home," Pagan said. "Will you ask the nurse if I can?"

When the nurse returned with her clothes, Pagan wondered if it was the same woman who had sat with her. Pagan stared at her as if to silently convey, *say nothing*. She sat up gingerly and Tommy held her shirt, guiding her arms into the sleeves. He buttoned it down the front, his large hands awkward with the buttons, and knelt on the floor to put on her shoes, tying them the way he did for Maud.

They helped her into a bathroom in the recovery room. When the door closed, she felt the quiet surround her. She had never needed those silver railings before, and she sat on the toilet, fully clothed, one hand on the cool metal. She was afraid to use the toilet, afraid her insides would fall out. She didn't know what to do. After a few minutes there was a knock on the door.

"Pagan, are you all right?" Tommy's voice was anxious.

"Yes," she said, but she could not move.

A few minutes later, a nurse came to the door.

"Do you need help with anything? Are you bleeding too much?"

"No, I'm fine," Pagan said.

The door was locked. She looked at the chrome handle. She could sit here for as long as she wanted. She wanted to sit here forever. She imagined Tommy on the other side of the heavy door. How tired he must be, how hurting. She got up unsteadily and moved to the door, opening it to the brightness.

The nurse had a wheelchair ready, and Pagan let herself down gently. It didn't hurt the way it did when she'd had Maud.

"Let's go home," Pagan said.

She wanted to tell him about her waking, about the baby crying and the nurse's kindness, but she couldn't form the words. Even if she could, it would only increase his burden. Tommy bent to kiss her, his lips as dry as paper.

three

one

ON THANKSGIVING MORNING, PRANA WOKE WITH A SENSE OF expectation. She hoped that she and her sisters gathering together might conjure their mother, as if each of them possessed an inconclusive puzzle piece, blue sky or water, that would fit together in some larger, unforeseen pattern. She wanted her mother to sense, from wherever she was, that things had gone awry and that they needed her.

She had offered to make Thanksgiving dinner, and she was surprised, and a bit flustered, when Pagan agreed. As Pagan started to feel better, Prana half-expected her to change her mind, take over in her usual capable way, but she didn't. Pagan moved around the house with small bursts of energy that quickly faded, leaving half-done chores in her wake. Prana found herself in the unfamiliar position of chiding her sister, telling her to sit down and relax.

Prana had decided against a traditional meal; it would only highlight her mother's absence. She wanted rich, buttery tastes cut with tartness: baked salmon, new potatoes with dill, spinach with pine nuts, fresh rolls. Tommy bought apple and lemon meringue pies. As she considered her menu, she had flipped through Pagan's cookbooks, wanting a recipe for lemon grass soup. Pagan's shelf looked as if it had been stocked by Tommy's sisters: Betty Crocker, *The Joy of Cooking,* an ancient Moose-wood cookbook with the cover torn off. Update, Prana thought. You need a new look.

Zeke showed up midmorning, smelling of horses and damp leaves, like a wind blown in from outside. Her jeans were mud-died along the bottom; she carried an armful of cattails.

"Do you want to borrow a pair of pants?" Pagan asked.

Zeke looked down at her splattered jeans. "Oh, I guess so," she said. "Maybe a pair of sweats? I don't think your pants are long enough." She waved a branch and called to Maud. "Mice on a stick! Mice on stick!"

Maud squealed. Pagan made a face. Tommy grinned for what seemed like the first time that week.

"Zeke, that's disgusting," Pagan said.

"Maud doesn't think so." Zeke beckoned to her. "Come on, I'm going to take off these muddy pants." Maud followed Zeke up the stairs. "And then," Zeke told her, "I feed the ponies big buckets of cranberry sauce, and they knock it on the ground, and roll all over in it, and get totally sticky! So the goats hose them off, but they can't turn off the water with their little goat hooves, so it makes a huge swimming hole out in the pasture—"

Prana smiled to herself. Zeke could go on like that for ages.

Maud was smart enough to be dubious about Zeke's stories, but her excitement spurred Zeke on to taller tales. Prana returned to the kitchen, and a short time later, Zeke appeared in a pair of Pagan's sweats. With a mock sneakiness staged purely for Maud, Zeke stole bites from whatever Prana was preparing, rattled the pots and pans, until Prana waved a spoon at her and told her to get out of the kitchen and leave her in peace.

Prana had never cooked a holiday meal by herself, and over the past week, the preparations had grown large in her mind. Sometimes, she felt annoyed with her mother for leaving her in this position, although she knew this was petty; her mother had spent a lifetime stepping in, doing what needed to be done. Her meal began to feel like a task in a fairy tale. If she could make a wonderful meal, rather than a pretty picture of one, it would break the spell and bring her mother back.

Months ago, she had done a Thanksgiving photo shoot. The art director, someone she didn't usually work with, told her he wanted a "Martha Stewart look," and inwardly she cringed, while outwardly she nodded coolly, thinking all she had to do was make a trip to K-mart. The banality of it depressed her. Today required something different; she had to make something real. She pulled two bags of spinach out of the refrigerator.

Pagan was in the living room, reading to Maud, and Tommy wandered into the kitchen.

"Can I help?"

It was on the tip of her tongue to make a crack about watching football, but she stopped. Tommy was less verbal than the men she knew; she couldn't sense his internal weather. On the day he brought Pagan home from the hospital, Prana felt as if he looked, not only tired, but actually older than when he had left that morning. After helping Pagan upstairs to bed, he sat on the couch with Maud for ages, and instead of putting her to bed at the usual time, he let her fall asleep on him. When he came downstairs in the mornings, his eyes were red-rimmed, and she couldn't tell whether it was allergies, or that fair Irish coloring, or whether he'd been crying. She didn't want to ask Pagan.

She gave him spinach to wash, then covered her dough with a warm cloth and set it on the stove to rise. They made small talk about the stock market, and she posed certain questions so she could only half-listen to his answers. Retrieving butter from the refrigerator, she looked at Maud's bright, oversize letters scrambled on the door. She and Tommy were like two magnets; they pushed off each other, weakly, instinctively, without being able to help it. Gently she told him to go inside, be with Pagan and Maud, she could finish by herself.

When the meal was ready, she called Zeke into the kitchen and asked her to help set things out. Prana had imagined it would be reassuring to have dinner with her sisters, but when they all took their seats, Prana felt how their gathering only emphasized her mother's absence. Tommy passed her a tulip-shaped glass, opalescent, lightly swirled with color. The wine sparkled in the late afternoon sun. She started to raise the stem in her fingers. She wanted a secret word to chant, a charm to bring her mother back. She lowered the glass, hoping no one noticed her half-made gesture. She took a sip of wine. She had tried so hard. What if her mother never came back? They would never know what had happened.

At the foot of the table, Prana counted the plates and serving spoons. Everyone was seated, expectant, and she began to serve. At the head, Tommy was quiet, brightening only for Maud. Prana handed Zeke a basket of rolls. Her mother had believed in something once. Had she gone off to find something to believe in again? What one believed seemed hopelessly relative. Faith was a matter of choice. All of them named for their mother's spiritual whims, all that came to nothing.

When they started eating, everyone agreed that Prana had done a wonderful job. "Didn't know you had it in you," Zeke teased. Maud asked for more salmon, demanding "pink, pink, pink!" Pagan kept saying how good everything tasted, what a luxury it was to have someone cook for her. Prana felt their mother's absence swirling around them.

AFTER DINNER, TOMMY took Maud to his parents to visit. He had told them Pagan had another miscarriage, and they understood she wanted rest. After the conversation that could be had in front of Maud, after the plates were cleared, the candles extinguished, Prana stacked the plates in the sink.

"I'm stuffed," Zeke said. "I'll help you with all this in a little while, okay?"

They moved into the living room and settled on the sofa and armchairs. Prana thought it felt much later than it was.

"How're you doing?" Zeke asked Pagan.

Pagan stretched out, her arms above her head. She was still very pale. With her curls spreading up over the arm of the sofa, Prana thought she looked like a Spanish painting: white skin, darkness swirling around her.

"I'm depressed," Pagan said. "But the odd thing is I feel better—physically. For the first time in months I don't feel nauseous, I don't feel like I have water on the brain."

Zeke put her feet up on the ottoman, as if she'd asked the important question and could now relax.

They had stayed off the subject of their mother because it

was uppermost in their minds, but now, when it was clear she wasn't coming, the afternoon seemed flat.

"So, what next?" Pagan asked. "Are we just going to hang around, waiting for her to get back?"

"I don't know what people do in situations like this," Zeke said.

"They hire private investigators," Pagan said.

"That's TV." Zeke was scornful.

"Do you think she's with a man?" Prana asked.

Pagan swirled the wine in her glass, watching it shimmer and coat the sides.

"But why wouldn't she tell us?" Zeke asked.

Prana bit at a tiny piece of skin on her thumb. Her mother had boyfriends as they grew up, but not very many. Most single men lived and worked in the city. She once heard her mother tell a friend that the men she met were either buying homes or getting divorced, neither of which made them very promising. With her usual aplomb, her mother did not seem nervous about dating while she had teenage daughters, nor did she ask for her daughters' opinions or approval. The men her mother dated didn't intrude on the circle of their life together. It was hard to imagine she would have left the country with someone they hadn't met.

"I wonder if this is a kind of huge delayed reaction, that she's always wanted to escape, and now she's finally done it," Prana said.

"Escape from what?" Zeke asked.

"You mean from us?" Pagan stirred.

"All those years she had to keep things together, maybe she finally just went off," Prana said.

"I don't think we're a huge burden," Zeke said.

"Not now, at least," Pagan said.

Prana played with the fringe of a wool blanket draped over the sofa, twisting the soft strands as she spoke. "Sometimes I thought she'd go back to playing music when we grew up, or go back to being the way she was."

"What do you mean?" Pagan asked. "You weren't even born then."

"You used to tell us stories about what she was like," Prana said. "Stories about living in Oregon."

"I did not!" Pagan seemed embarrassed.

"You did," Prana insisted. "When I was little, you told me stories about her playing the guitar, about her throwing a party on a blue moon."

Pagan merely shook her head.

"Maybe she wishes she'd kept playing music, or stayed more idealistic," Prana said.

"Nobody lives like that anymore," Pagan said.

"Of course they do!"

"She played the piano for a while," Zeke said, trying to soothe them.

"That's not what I mean," Prana said.

Zeke turned to Prana. "What are you saying? She's gone off to India to meditate or something?"

"I don't know. Maybe."

"The whole hippie thing was just a phase," Pagan said.

Prana was annoyed by her quick denial. Pagan could be so absolute—she didn't really know.

"If your father hadn't died, or Marco hadn't left, she might still be in that phase, don't you think?" Prana asked.

Pagan opened her mouth, as if to protest, then closed it. She scowled.

Prana felt an adrenaline rush of anger. She was tired of her ideas being automatically dismissed. "We never bought her an instrument," Prana said. "We should have bought her a dulcimer or something."

"A dulcimer? Come on." Zeke laughed.

Prana felt furious. They didn't want to make a space for her. They didn't want to listen. She tipped her head forward, pressed her fingers against her eyes, letting her hair fall around her like a curtain. "I just feel like I was the straw that broke the camel's back," she mumbled.

Zeke was still laughing about the dulcimer.

"What do you mean?" Pagan sat up.

Prana squeezed her eyes tight. She wouldn't say it. Not now. She didn't want to cry. She tried to take a breath, and the words squeezed out of her like dirty water wrung from a sponge. "If she hadn't gotten pregnant with me, Marco might have stuck around."

Zeke stopped laughing and looked over at her.

"Don't be ridiculous," Pagan said.

"Prana, what are you saying? We would have been better off growing up with Marco in Scarsdale or something?" Zeke asked.

"I feel like I sent everything into a tailspin," Prana sobbed.

Zeke swung her legs down off the ottoman and set both feet on the floor. She paused for a moment, then came over and put her arm around Prana. "Prana, something was going to send Marco off," Zeke said. "He's a charming guy, but he flits from one thing to another. He's still a little boy, even now."

"But it was all too much. I was too much." Prana didn't look up. She felt heavy and sick, her dinner churning inside her.

"Listen," Pagan said. Her voice was conciliatory, reasonable.

"I do remember some things, and honestly, you were the easiest, sweetest baby. God, we all loved you. Believe me, you have always been adored."

Pagan's words seemed to linger in the air. Prana couldn't speak.

Zeke, so rarely comforting, spoke in the soft tone she usually reserved for small children and animals. "You know, Prana, it's lousy about Marco, but we wish you'd tell us what you're really upset about. You think Mom's with a man because, well . . . that's what you've been doing all this time, isn't it? I wish you'd just tell us what's going on."

Prana tried to take a deep breath, but the room felt airless. She sat up and looked at her sisters. "How did you know?" she whispered.

Pagan looked helpless, then turned to Zeke as if she'd picked the lock to a door they weren't sure they wanted to walk through.

"We couldn't imagine there was no one." Zeke smiled wryly. "We figure he's either a senator or a spy."

"What?"

"Well, there had to be some reason you didn't tell us." Pagan sounded hurt.

Hearing her tone, Prana felt startled. She looked at Pagan's injured expression. Pagan felt left out. It was hard to believe.

"He was married," Prana said. "It's over now."

"The same man, for all this time?" Pagan asked.

Prana nodded.

"Whew!" Zeke stood up and shook her head.

"That's really the last thing I need," Prana snapped. "You're so damn smug! You think you know everything."

Zeke looked surprised. A grin slipped across her mouth, as

if admiring Prana's anger, even when it was aimed at her. She walked back across the room. When she turned to look at Prana, her expression was somber. "Prana, I don't feel smug. I finally meet someone I can really see being with, and she turns out to be a raving alcoholic. What does that say about me? How do you think I feel?"

Prana wiped her eyes, and her fingers came away smudged with charcoal-colored makeup. No one seemed to know what to say.

"Maybe it doesn't have anything to do with us," Pagan said.

"What do you mean?" Prana sniffed.

"Well, we cook up all these strange ideas, which are obviously kind of self-centered. Maybe it's not about us."

"It's always been about us," Prana said. She got up abruptly and went through the kitchen, out the back door.

Leaning against the deck railing, she pushed her hair from her face and lit a cigarette. She drew the smoke into her throat, her lungs, breathing deeply, and felt how perfectly the cool acridity filled the contours inside her. She shivered in the cold. It was early, already dark. She hated going outside to smoke. All this time her sisters had known. Pagan had felt left out. She couldn't believe it. She thought of the phone calls she hadn't returned, the thousand small evasions. She had worried that telling them about Stephan would separate her from them, and yet it was precisely her silence that had achieved the same effect. She finished her cigarette, started to light another, then changed her mind.

When she walked back into the house, she could hear, from the kitchen, Pagan and Zeke continuing the conversation without her. She went into the bathroom. Her mascara was smudged and runny; she wiped the makeup from her eyes and cheeks.

When Prana walked back into the living room, Pagan seemed to be prodding Zeke into trying to remember something. Zeke had a serious expression on her face, as if she were concentrating, trying to summon the memory up. Prana sat down next to Pagan on the couch.

"Do you remember that fight Mom had with her parents?" Pagan asked.

Zeke shook her head.

"Grandma said something mean. I don't know what it was, but Mom just packed us up and left. That minute. We were playing Parcheesi. Remember those little funny shaped pieces? It was already nighttime, and she just threw our stuff into suitcases and we took off."

"She wouldn't do that to us—would she?" Prana asked.

"Do what?"

"Just leave like that—I mean she blew off her whole family."

They were quiet for a moment, weighing the idea. Prana felt the darkness of it settle around them.

t w o

AFTER THANKSGIVING, ZEKE WAS GLAD TO GET BACK TO HER own place. Spending the day with her sisters had been tiring: keeping Maud out of everyone's hair, fetching things for Pagan, trying to reassure Prana when, uncomfortably, Prana had touched on something that was true.

Zeke could barely remember Marco's arrival in their lives. She did remember her mother's lightness and laughter, a feeling of electricity in the air. Marco would play tag, hide-and-seek; he was always ready to go somewhere. He took them to New York, and then he went off without them.

Growing up, Zeke seldom thought about him, but as an adolescent, she was annoyed by their yearly visits.

"I'm not dressing up for Marco's little Christmas charade," Zeke said.

Her mother faced her closet, considering different outfits, then pushed the clothes aside.

"Wear whatever you're comfortable with," her mother replied.

Zeke reappeared wearing a pair of ripped jeans.

Her mother turned and half-smiled. "Your knees will be cold."

"I'm not going skating. We're past that, don't you think?"

Her mother raised one eyebrow. Zeke had always been fascinated by her ability to do this. Without saying a word, she would lift one elegant eyebrow to convey her skepticism. Zeke had tried to practice it in the mirror, but simply couldn't do it. She dropped onto the bed, irritated because she knew her obstinacy was useless. Marco always charmed them.

"I don't get it. How does Marco get away with this?" Zeke asked.

The house was empty. Pagan had taken Prana somewhere on an errand, and her mother was quiet, as if listening to make sure they had not come back.

"What do you think he's gotten away with?"

"He gets to act like a big shot—when it's convenient for him. What exactly happened with him?"

Her mother looked at her, and suddenly she seemed tired. The first strands of silver lit her hair, but there was something truly fine in her mother; something enduring. She sat down on the bed and reached for a laundry basket resting in the middle.

"Marco had this vision of how we could all live cheaply, in a beautiful place." Her mother sighed and folded a worn dish towel. "But, of course, he dreamed it up while he was staring at the apple blossoms because, by the time we got to Somers, we were living in this tiny run-down cabin, and the charm of country living faded. Chopping wood, heating water on a woodstove, it was too much, especially when the reality of diapers kicked in.

"You won't remember this, but Pagan broke her arm when she was little, right after Marco and I met, and he paid every penny he had to the hospital. He'd known me for less than a month." Her mother looked at Zeke directly. Her eyes were large and blue-gray, like stones in a stream.

"Marco tried, he really did, but partly, I blame myself. I should have known that Marco couldn't do it. Your father was really capable. He knew how to fix things, and physically, he was strong. But living in a cabin with no running water and three small kids—it would have been a lot, even for him. Actually, your father never would have put us in that situation." She looked down at the quilted bedspread, and spread her hand against it. "Prana was about six months old, and Marco said the domestic scene was too much, three kids were just too heavy. He said the whole alternative scene was beat. Can you imagine? He bought a train ticket to Manhattan and left me with the last four hundred dollars he had. He did send money when he found work, but his only real responsibility was Prana." Her mother said this as if it excused him, then reached for the laundry basket. She picked up a sock and looked for its match, her face reddened. "Don't say it that way to Prana. I just say we were young. Marco had no idea what he was getting into."

Don't say it that way to Prana. Zeke sighed. She thought of Prana waving her out of the kitchen yesterday. Her sisters thought she was a jester, a clown. She wouldn't try to mediate between what they believed. Let them thresh it out. Prana was hung up on the sixties because she wanted to see their mother as a true believer, a spiritual seeker. Pagan resisted, because accepting that version meant that the responsibility of three children had forced their mother to abandon her beliefs. Zeke thought they were making it too complicated. Her mother had simply made a choice—a choice partly determined by how she'd been raised. Being poor, or going on welfare, simply wasn't part of her script. She wouldn't go home to her own uptight parents, so she had chosen to move to an upscale town, chosen a job that would pay decently. And to do that job well, she had assumed the clothes and demeanor that would work.

Zeke felt the beginning of a headache. She didn't like to think about things she couldn't see. Memory was like that, tricky and undependable, and her sisters were evidence that everyone's vision was colored by what she wanted to see.

ZEKE THOUGHT OF Prana weeping yesterday, *I was the last straw*. She remembered her mother leaning over Prana as she changed her diaper, letting her hair fall down to tickle Prana's face, Prana laughing and laughing. Watching them, Zeke had laughed too, the image of them widening to include her, knowing that she had also been cherished in this way. Closing her eyes, she could almost remember the feel of her mother's long hair washing over her.

THE DAY WAS unexpectedly mild for November, gray and slightly damp. After-holiday shoppers crowded the malls, and the streets in Pleasantville were quiet, the train station parking lot almost empty. Zeke kept expecting Marcie to call and yell at her for picking up Eleanor at school. Marcie must have returned by now, but there was no phone call, nothing.

Zeke parked downtown to run an errand at Plaza Discount. It was a store their mother didn't like, a jumbled precursor to Wal-Mart, but she had occasionally shopped there when they were kids. Zeke smiled to herself at one of Pagan's feeble jokes yesterday, *Pass the salt, plaza discount.* When they were small, with their mother's endless reminding about *please* and *thank you, please* had become "plaza discount," a silly way of getting in the requisite manners.

Zeke walked into the store, which was decorated for Christmas with cheap, tinsel garlands and cutouts of Santa and his reindeer in the window. The overnight change of holidays seemed absurd. Had they done this all in one morning? She needed contact lens solution and, scanning the aisles, she noticed a small, dark-haired girl comparing two boxes. The girl looked serious; something about her seemed familiar. She must be about Eleanor's age, and then Zeke realized it was Bert's daughter, Cecily.

"Hi there," Zeke said.

The girl looked up and eyed her suspiciously.

"I'm Eleanor's friend," Zeke said. "I met you at the farm."

Cecily bent to scratch her knee, then something in her seemed to relent. "Everyone at my house is sick, and my dad sent me to buy some cold medicine, but I don't know what to get—for kids or adults or what."

"Is he sick too?"

"Yeah, and my sister keeps throwing up all over the place."

"Where's your mom?"

"She's in Chicago, my grandma had an operation. My dad's

staying with us." Cecily blew upward with her bottom lip stuck out.

"How are you feeling?"

"I'm starting to get that weird feeling, you know?"

Zeke helped her pick out different kinds of cold medicine, nighttime and daytime, all for aches and fever.

"He gave me ten dollars, is that enough?"

"I have money." Zeke walked to the counter with her and paid for the rest of the medicine. "Where do you live? Do you need a ride?"

"We don't live far, just past the library." After she answered, Cecily looked startled and stared down at the counter, scrunching the top of her paper bag. Zeke realized what she was thinking.

"I know—you're not supposed to get in a car with anyone you don't really know. We tell Eleanor and Amy the same thing. Do you want to call your dad and ask if I can give you a lift?"

Cecily looked Zeke slowly up and down, then asked where the pay phone was.

When she returned, she said: "My dad said that would be great."

"Do you need anything else at your house? Do you have food and all that?"

"My dad made a huge turkey. I'm sick of it already." Cecily stuck out her tongue, making a cartoonish face.

Zeke laughed. "Maybe we should stop at the deli and get chicken soup or something."

Cecily shrugged. Zeke smiled and pushed open the door. She remembered feeling that adults were foreigners, almost unreal, a kind of impediment to real life.

She bought a large container of chicken soup and a box of saltines, the only comfort foods she could find. Cecily guided them back toward her house, and Zeke turned into one of the residential streets near the public library.

The homes were mostly colonials or Cape Cods, the occasional faux-Tudor, not grand, but well maintained. Cecily pointed to a boxy white colonial with green shutters halfway up the block, and Zeke pulled up in front of the flagstone path. She got out to help carry the soup, and when Cecily opened the front door, the dim lights, scattered boxes of tissue, the sick ward feeling of close air and suspended time swirled around them.

"Dad?" Cecily called out.

"Down in just a minute."

Zeke walked into the kitchen, which looked as if it were inhabited by someone who liked to cook, although its orderliness was obscured by dishes in the sink, half-full mugs of tea, glasses of juice and water scattered across the counter. A window over the sink looked onto a neat backyard.

She heard slow footsteps on the stairs, and then Bert appeared in the doorway, wearing a pair of old sweatpants and a sweatshirt. It looked as if he'd run a comb through his hair, but missed a spot near the crown of his head where a few strands stuck out at an odd angle. He sank down at the kitchen table.

"You look like hell," Zeke said.

"Yeah, I feel that way. How are you doing, Cecy?"

"I'm starting to feel kind of achy, but I don't look as bad as you."

Zeke moved to the kitchen table. "We went overboard on the cold remedies, but I figured it's better to have options." She opened the paper bag and he winced with the sound. "I got NyQuil and DayQuil."

"Oh, Florence." He smiled weakly.

"We also bought some chicken soup at the deli."

"You're wonderful." He cracked the seal and twisted open the DayQuil in one motion. He poured a dose and drank it like a shot.

Zeke felt uncomfortable. She wanted to offer help, but it seemed awkward, stepping into a role that wasn't properly hers.

"Where's Kim?" Cecily asked.

"She's asleep in her room. She got sick again after you left."

"Yuck. I wish Mom was here."

"I do too, sweetheart."

Cecily shuffled off, pouting.

"Do you want some of this soup?" Zeke asked.

"Oh, I'd love it." He started to get up slowly.

"No, sit," she said. "Where are the bowls?"

He pointed to a cabinet and she took out a bowl and poured some soup. As she carried it to the table, brothy steam rose into the air. She pulled a bag of saltines from the box.

"Oh saltines, perfect." Baggy skin puffed beneath his eyes, his hair was a bit greasy; there was nothing she could objectively say was attractive about him, but she felt a tenderness for him, that he would so clearly appreciate saltines.

She didn't want to offend him, but she looked around the kitchen and started putting dishes in the sink.

"No, don't bother with that," he said.

"I'll just clear then," Zeke said.

What was she doing—putting things away for a man? She wouldn't have thought twice about doing this for a woman; it would simply be helpful, doing what needed to be done. But somehow, she felt she was doing it for him. Of course that was silly, she was doing it because he was sick, not incompetent.

She turned around to see him leaning over his bowl with his head in his hands.

"Are you okay?"

"The soup helps. The medicine helps. I really do appreciate this."

"No problem," Zeke said.

The phone rang, a muted sound, and he waved it away with his hand. "The machine will pick it up."

He stood up slowly, still stooped over, and put his bowl in the sink. "I'm a lousy host, but I need to lie down while Kim's asleep. Poor thing. She's hardly ever sick, so when she throws up it frightens her."

She saw he felt awful; he was somewhere inside himself.

"Thanks again for getting Cecy home and bringing all the cold medicine. I really couldn't have gotten out the door."

Zeke nodded and moved toward the doorway. Her visit seemed half-finished, but she didn't know what else to do. She wanted to touch him in sympathy, put her hand on his arm or his back, but there was a necessary space between them.

"I hope you're all feeling better soon."

"We'll mend," he said, and closed the door behind her.

three

PRANA STRETCHED OUT ON THE CARPET IN A SUNNY SPOT IN Pagan's living room. She relaxed her arms and legs, trying to let her spine rest against the floor. She lifted her right leg, and as she lowered it toward her left side, she turned her head to the right, trying to crack her back. The pull in her right shoulder felt good. She rested there for a moment, letting the weight of her body help her stretch. She lifted her leg slowly, brought it back down, then reversed what she'd just done, lifting her left leg, and dropping it down to the right side. She turned her head to the left and breathed out. She lay still, feeling her ribs against the floor. She heard Pagan come into the room.

"You should take a yoga class," Pagan said.

Prana snorted. She lifted her leg slowly and brought it down. Her back felt as if it was just starting to relax.

"You must be feeling better if you're giving me instructions," Prana said. Her sister's listlessness had started to lift, and Prana was relieved. "You know better than to give me the other lecture now, don't you?" Prana raised her eyebrow. Her smoking bothered everyone; she didn't need to be told.

"You're thin, though," Pagan said.

"Don't." Prana sat up. "It's just—all this with Stephan, it was hard. I was partying too much. It's hard to eat when I'm upset."

"What was he like?" Pagan asked.

Prana ran her palm over the pattern in the carpet and thought of how many times she'd longed for this conversation. She had wanted to tell them all about Stephan: where he had been, what he had seen and done. Implied in this was the fact that his vision had rested on her for a while. Now it seemed childish. It didn't matter.

"He was remarkable," Prana said. "He'd been everywhere. But it went on for too long."

The sharp sound of metal clattering on the kitchen floor made Prana start, but Pagan waved her hand.

"It's that old percolator. She loves putting the pieces together. I just decided to let her trash it." Pagan grinned. "Path of least resistance."

Prana stretched her legs in front of her. "I think I'm going up to Mom's today."

Pagan looked over her shoulder, to make sure Maud was still occupied in the kitchen. "You know, I didn't mention this before, because it seemed too bleak, but when I was there I checked her computer." Pagan dropped her voice. "I found a copy of her will. She made it a few days before she left."

Prana felt a tumbling inside her. "Was there a note or anything?"

"No, not like that, and Tommy doesn't think it's anything to worry about. He says it's a normal thing to do before going on a big trip, but just the fact of it seems, I don't know . . ."

In the pause, Prana thought of the words on her mother's postcard. 'Don't let Pagan look for me, there's no point.' Did *there's no point* mean it was futile? She hadn't assumed the darker side of this.

"Was there anything about the will that seemed odd?"

"No. What you'd expect. Everything divided three ways. I didn't actually read it that carefully." Pagan shook her head. "By now I'm really pissed. I mean, I suppose it's all right that she goes off and does whatever she wants, but she had to know we'd worry about her."

"Maybe she just expected that we'd treat her like a grown-up," Prana said.

Pagan stood up and started to pace around the room. "I just feel like nobody tells me anything. You had this huge love, and never even told us. Zeke exists in a whole other stratosphere, and who the hell knows what's going on with Marcie, and Tommy, Tommy just. . ." Pagan stopped, and then Prana understood where this was all heading.

"How's Tommy doing with all this?"

Pagan seemed to crumple on the sofa. "He doesn't talk about it," she said. "I think he's still upset, but he just goes on as if nothing happened. You've seen how he is: he goes to work, keeps busy, works late. He's sweet with Maud, but there's this whole thing underneath that he doesn't want to say. It's terrible. I never thought we'd be . . . " Pagan studied her hands. She looked fragile, the blue vein at her temple more distinct. "It sounds terrible to say this, but I feel like he blames me for being willing to go through with it." She rubbed her wrist, kneading a pain that Prana couldn't see. "Or it's not quite that, but it's the whole God thing. When we got married, I didn't think religion would matter so much, but it does. We come at things from different planes. He really believes there's a God out there, watching over him, and that difficulties are some kind of test, or—I'm making it sound kind of simple and morbid—not a test, but something you have to go through. I don't know. All that Catholic crap lingers."

"So what do you believe?" Prana asked.

"I don't know. I spend so much time worrying, then it turns out I've worried about the wrong thing." Pagan looked as if she were going to cry. "I think shit happens, but I don't think it's punishment or retribution. People set themselves up for things to some extent. But now Maud is asking all these questions about God. Tommy wants to let her go to Sunday School, but I don't want her to get infected with all that guilt. Plus, how do I explain the dead guy on the cross?"

Prana got up from the floor and came to sit beside her.

"I'm sure you and Tommy will work it out," Prana said. She felt how carefully she made her voice reassuring, and hoped that she was right.

PRANA WANTED TO see the empty house for herself. She knew that Pagan and Zeke had both looked around, but she kept imagining she would find some trace of where her mother had gone. When she unlocked the door and stepped inside, the air was cool against her face. She turned up the thermostat, and the clanking sound of the furnace, a slowly waking metal animal, filled the house.

The emptiness spread out around her. She took off her coat and flopped into a chair that faced the large, living room window. She wanted a cigarette, then told herself it wasn't a cigarette she wanted, but more oxygen, breath, air. Was her mother prescient in naming her in such a way? When she was younger, she didn't realize her name was unusual, but as she and her sisters grew older, their names revealed them, became faceted. Pagan professed to be embarrassed about her name, but Prana felt their names were specifically chosen and rare, as if each of them had been born under a comet and their arrivals here on earth, as muddied as they had become, were somehow heralded.

She took a deep breath then let it out slowly. Smoking in the house, even in her mother's absence, would be a desecration. Once, as a teenager, she had complained about doing some household chore, and her mother turned to her and said, "I earned this house for us." That had been enough.

One of the last conversations she'd had with her mother had been right here. Her mother sometimes told stories about work that had a psychological turn: the gap between what the couple said they wanted and what they truly did want, what the family knew about themselves, and what they didn't. Over the years, her mother had noticed that newly renovated homes were often on the market shortly after the work was done, as if renovating the house, or redoing the kitchen, was an attempt to remedy an interior problem. Her mother had just sold a house she'd found for a couple less than a year ago. She guessed they were unhappy, even as they were looking, and then, when everything fell apart, they hired her to sell the house. Her mother said she felt guilty about profiting from their difficulty.

Through the trees, in the house next door, a light went off, another light went on. A light went off, a light went on. Prana thought of Stephan and felt an overwhelming sense of discouragement. She was learning everything so late. It was as if, for the past nine years, she had accumulated knowledge that hadn't coalesced until now. At nineteen, she hadn't known anything at all. Of course this wasn't something that people around her—even her sisters—would say. She knew how to dress. She was self-contained, not given to the gabby self-deprecations of many young women. But those things only gave the appearance of sophistication. She hadn't understood the larger world around her. She had once seen a bumper sticker on a friend's mother's car:

> It will be a great day
> when schools have all the money they need
> and the defense department
> needs a bake sale to raise money.

Prana had smiled, liking the idea, but it was years before she realized the slogan was an old cliché. She felt humiliated that she did not understand this then. When Stephan told her he was married, she had considered it only in terms of herself. His wife and family, the interior fabric of his marriage, were not real to her. She had reasoned that his wife must be used to doing without him; she had her children, had her own life. What did it matter if Prana took a little bit coming and going?

SHE CALLED MARCO and asked him to meet her for lunch. When she was younger, their visits had been a decorous holiday ritual, always accompanied by her mother and sisters. As a teenager, she had rarely initiated the idea of seeing him. Marco worked in advertising and had become very successful. He seemed to know he had behaved badly, but was only reformed enough to be contrite. She sensed he didn't regret his leaving so much as he regretted being the kind of person who had done such a thing.

She rose from the chair and went up to her mother's room. Tapping her fingers against her lips, she went to her mother's closet. What had her mother taken with her? She pushed the clothes along the rail. Her mother's clothes were understated and elegant: wool and linen and cotton. At the back of the closet, something long and dark caught her eye. A black dress. She touched the fabric, crepe de chine.

Gently, she pulled it from the closet. The dress was long and fitted, with a slit up one side and a low neckline. She tried to picture her mother in it, but it was not the kind of dress Prana had ever seen her wear. The tags were off. She put the dress to her face, the faintest scent of perfume, she couldn't place it. When would her mother have worn such a dress?

Prana unbuttoned her shirt, stepped out of her shoes and jeans, and looked at herself in the mirror. She pulled the dress carefully over her head, then worked to get the zipper up by herself. She gazed into the long mirror, humming a little tune. Gathering her hair in her hands, she twisted it into a chignon and stared at her reflection. She knew then. When her mother wore this dress, she could not have been alone.

four

AFTER PRANA WENT TO THEIR MOTHER'S, PAGAN FELT BEREFT. Tommy worked late almost every night. She wanted to talk, but there wasn't much to say. Her exhausted declaration from months ago, *this is the last time,* lingered in the air.

People said things worked out for the best, but if that were true, then someone, or something, must be governing them. She didn't necessarily believe things worked out for the best—they just worked out. Houses falling in. Irreparably ill children. You made the best of things—or not. Sometimes she envied Tommy's sisters, their clear beliefs and ready answers. Even when the answers weren't known, there was the idea of faith: the idea that God understood. She imagined Tommy was trying to keep busy, letting the meaning become clear later on, but she felt as if he were moving away from her.

Upstairs, Maud whimpered, waking from a nap, and Pagan went to get her. In the mornings Maud woke early, full of energy and demands, while Pagan stumbled groggily around the kitchen. But after a nap, she climbed onto Pagan's lap, her cheek warm against Pagan's chest, and rested there, before she felt awake enough to play. With Maud in her arms, Pagan sank into the sofa, felt her breathing, the peace of this slow waking. She hadn't felt sad about Maud getting bigger because there had always been the idea of another child to follow. She had imagined that, with two children, she would be overfull of the chaos and disruption of life with toddlers, and would be satisfied to move onto the next stage. Sometimes Pagan thought of a pair of pajamas Maud had worn as a baby: pale yellow with dark blue winking suns, and she thought about Maud's infant softness, her baby smile, and Pagan wanted to lie on the floor and weep.

She felt as if grief had carved out a space inside her, leaving something large and dark and clear. Had her mother felt this when her father died? Had she stopped believing in whatever she had believed in? Maybe belief had been irrelevant. She had two small children. She had to endure.

When she thought of her mother's will, Pagan allowed the unthinkable. It seemed so unlikely, but that was the problem. Anything seemed possible now.

MAUD NESTLED AGAINST her, then continued to sleep. Pagan wondered if a pattern was emerging in her life, a physical mirroring of something deeper: strong on the start-up, then weak on the follow-through, as if she were a flash in the pan. Her career, her pregnancies, her marriage. Pagan traced the soft line of Maud's cheek.

In grade school, when she started taking violin lessons with the other fourth graders, her music teacher had given her a great deal of praise and encouragement. By seventh grade, she was practicing seriously, and that year a new principal came to the high school. She was married to Carl Schulman, a violinist and composer, who spent most of the week in the city. He let it be known that he would take a few serious students in Shady Grove, and Pagan's mother had brought her to meet him.

Pagan knew immediately that he was a different kind of person. His accent didn't sound as if he came from the United States. Schulman was immersed in a world of ideas and history, aesthetics and music. He had lived in Israel and Europe, and she understood that, unlike most people they knew, Shady Grove was not a place he aspired to, but a place to hibernate. He looked like a mournful lion, with a full head of gray hair, and his speech was precise yet dramatic, as if he were speaking to an audience that included her, but was somehow separate from her. He was courtly with her mother, who dropped Pagan off for her lesson each week and then went to her office to make phone calls.

In his studio, Pagan came to understand that music was sacred. When Schulman spoke, the lives of great composers, their intentions for a particular piece, the complexities of tone, were concentrated into a lineage that extended into the present, into the very room they stood in. He used to say that she must work very hard at the violin or it would betray her.

One day she came to her lesson and, as she usually did, started to play a G scale in three octaves. Before she reached the second octave, he stopped her.

"You didn't practice yesterday, did you?" His tone was kindly, not angry.

She shook her head.

"You didn't warm up before your lesson did you?"

She shook her head again.

"All right, to work."

At the end of her lesson, he called her mother into the studio and gestured that they should both sit down.

"I must tell both of you something." There was something magisterial about him, with his long hair and broad nose, his serious expression. "I am not the right kind of teacher for Pagan. Probably, I am not a teacher at all. Pagan, you are a very sweet girl, and you are talented, but you are a nice, normal girl who should make music part of her life. I can't teach someone who is normal. I can only teach someone who is obsessed. It's healthy to skip a day of practicing, especially at your age, but I need students who practice *before* their lessons."

Pagan stared at his socks, sand colored with deep blue threads, different from any she had seen before.

"The fault lies with me," he continued. "I am married to an educator, so I know what a true teacher is. I don't have the necessary patience. I am a selfish man." He had been looking at her mother, weighing the effect of his words, but now he turned to Pagan, who wanted to look away. "Pagan, you should continue to play in your school orchestra, and you should play with a sense of joy, and try to remember me as a foolish man who took on a task he was not suited for."

Her mother clenched the muscles in the side of her delicate jaw. Schulman opened the door for them, his massive face sad. Her mother put her arm around Pagan's shoulders and guided her out the door, her violin case bumping the door jamb as they went out.

They walked silently out to the car, and when they got in, her mother turned to her.

"It's my fault. I shouldn't have sent you to someone who wasn't experienced teaching children."

"It's not your fault, Mom."

"It is." Her mother's chin trembled.

"Mom, I'm just not that good."

"You are. You're wonderful. Don't pay any attention to him."

She did continue to play, but something had gone out of it for her. His dismissal left Pagan with the sense that she could make a good impression, and then fail to live up to it.

WHEN MAUD FINALLY woke up, Pagan stirred too. She looked around and saw the house was orderly, but dusty in the corners. She hadn't really cleaned in weeks: a quick turn through the bathroom before Prana came to stay. Pagan made herself a strong cup of coffee and decided to straighten up. Maud started pulling pots out of the cupboard, and Pagan opened her mouth to protest, then thought better of it. She carried a pile of newspapers out to the recycling, tripped on the step, and cursed as the papers slid out of her arms. Gathering up the bundle, she set it on the stack, but the pile shifted again and something caught her eye. A paper from a week or so ago, a front page story about a doctor being shot. She pulled it out of the stack and carried the paper back to the kitchen. As she read it, she started to tremble. Bernard Slepian. Shot in his own home. Tommy must have hidden it. She thought of the doctor who had done her operation. He was an older man, perhaps in his early sixties. He must have known about this. She felt herself shaking. Oh, it could have been worse, much worse, and she felt grateful for her deliverance.

f i v e

IN THE EARLY MORNING HALF-DARK, BEFORE OPENING HER eyes, Zeke felt a dry place at the back of her throat, a feathery coolness on her arms and shoulders. Sitting up, she swung her legs out of bed, and the motion made her feel as if the water and blood in her body were shifting and tingling. She sat on the edge of her bed for a full minute. Monday. Who else could feed her animals? She tried to think of her dependable students. Names escaped her. The weeks after Thanksgiving were a precarious time. At the end of the semester, the fragile ones fell apart—they got mono, or had nervous breakdowns, or their roommates committed suicide, or their grandparents died. A professor once joked about how students' grandparents always died at a convenient time of the semester, and she had thought it was a cynical observation. After a few years, she realized it was simply a biological fact.

She hobbled to the bathroom and found some aspirin. The bottle was old, and she wondered if the aspirin would still work. She decided to do the morning feeding and get someone else to muck out. She would get phone numbers of reliable students and make sure the chores would get done for a few days. Maybe she wouldn't get too sick; maybe it would be all right.

As she drove to the farm, she felt as if she were riding on a roller coaster. Everything seemed swooping and hilly, rushing past her, the gray sky ominous.

She fed and watered the animals, stopping to rest every few minutes. She felt weak and chilled, her legs like rubber. She scratched Mr. T behind the ears, breathing in the tangy horse smell, then checked on Ebenezer. The new latch on his stall seemed pony-proof. She told herself to go home, but the barn was warm and sheltering, and she felt soothed by the rhythmic chewing of the horses. Her little house seemed solitary and cheerless. If Marcie were sober and back to her old self, she would take care of her. She would make Zeke rest in her guest room. The girls would wander in and out, and Marcie would bring her soup.

Zeke sat on a bale of hay, too tired to get up. Why hadn't she heard from Marcie? She didn't want to hear Marcie ranting, but a response would make it seem as if her actions counted for something.

When she got back home, the carriage house seemed impossibly hot. She turned down the heat, sank onto the couch and pulled a blanket over her. She'd let the fever burn itself out. Where was her mother? If her mother were here, she would stop and check on her. Where was Prana? Floating somewhere, hard

to pin down. Zeke dreamed her body was made of pipe clean-
ers. She was hollow, made of furred wire, thick and fuzzy white.
Day and night bled into each other. In the dark, she got up to
use the bathroom and brush her teeth, then went back to bed.
The following morning she felt weak, wanting something to eat,
but she didn't feel as if she could keep anything down. Someone
knocked at the door. She hoped it was Prana.

The knob turned. "Zeke, are you there?" Bert opened the
door.

Zeke wanted to pull the blanket over her head. "What are
you doing here?" she croaked.

"I heard we'd given you the flu." He closed the door and
came in.

"I feel like hell." Zeke pulled the blanket up under her chin.
He seemed large, as if she lived in a dollhouse and he took up a
lot of space. She gestured to a chair.

"I stopped by the farm to say thanks for giving Cecily a ride
home the other day, and one of the students told me you were
sick." He pulled a loaf of raisin bread and a container of lemon
sherbet out of a plastic bag. "This seemed like sick food to me."

She tried to smile, but felt herself wincing.

"I'll put this away," he said.

Zeke thought of the mess in her kitchen: days of stained coffee cups, plates in the sink. "Oh no, I can do it." She tried to
stand, but felt herself go suddenly light-headed, everything
becoming sparkly and black. He grabbed her by the arm to
steady her, but her knees buckled, and she felt herself going
down. He reached around and grabbed her under the arms, taking the whole weight of her.

"You need to stay down," he said.

He was stronger than he looked. He held her for a moment,

then gently let her back down on the couch. She slowly drew her legs up under the blankets. He leaned over and put his hand on her forehead.

"You have a real fever," Bert said.

She closed her eyes, feeling the coolness of his hand. She wished he would leave it there.

"Are you going to be okay here?" he asked.

"I'm fine."

He leaned over her. She thought for a dizzying moment that he was going to kiss her, perhaps he thought so too, but he looked at her, unafraid, studying her.

"Your eyes are glassy," he said.

She laughed, the air coming out of her in a rush.

"What?" He sounded concerned.

She waved her hand. "I'm hallucinating," she said.

LATER, HALF-DOZING, she dreamed about Cecily, unafraid, climbing the rope to the top of the gym. Zeke had done this too, waving from the top, just to watch the gym teachers freak out. She had always felt different from other people, that her heart beat a half-step slower. She didn't skitter at things the way her sisters did. Over the years, various women had accused her of being emotionally distant or forcibly calm, but mostly, it wasn't true. She wasn't holding anything in. When she discovered sex, it felt like a way to get up to speed, to move with the same pulse that others felt, but boys were so eager and transparent, their bodies so predictable, that she hadn't found them exciting.

In her freshman year at college she met Daria, who was dark-haired, gothic, although that wasn't the fashion yet. Daria was a women's studies major. Zeke hadn't known or cared about women's studies; it seemed like a lot of babble, but she liked the way Daria knew exactly what she was doing in bed. A very deliberate seductress, she specialized in getting women to go to bed with her a few times and then leaving them high and dry.

Zeke hadn't minded. In many ways, she had little to say to Daria, whose mind seemed always busy, defining her desires. Zeke felt it was the other way around. Physical sensation first, then the mind adapted to what the body wanted. She was bored by Daria's talky feminism, but she liked the excitement of something unexpected, someone new.

She hadn't slept with a man since college, a grad student in marine biology back in Santa Barbara. What was his name? Warren. The memory made her smile. He hadn't looked like a Warren. He was one of those earnest, backpacking types; his heroes were Muir and Chouinard. Warren spent most of his time at the ocean or in the mountains, and he smelled of woodsmoke and patchouli. He tasted like salt. She had liked the length of him against her. Warren was probably in his early thirties, which had seemed old to her at the time. Men, or boys, her own age bored her. Their bodies worked in spite of their heads. As far as sex, there was little to figure out. Women were different, more complicated that way.

She thought about what would happen if she got involved with Bert. Her friends would be pissed. In the women's community, to sleep with more than one woman was permissible—depending on the boundaries of the relationship. To sleep with a man was betrayal. Of course, those who knew Marcie would say Zeke was merely reacting to a difficult situation. Her mother, her sisters, they wouldn't care.

It was Eleanor and Amy she had to consider. The girls

would be bound to find out, through Bert's kids, if nothing else. She thought of how carefully Marcie had explained things to them. She had said that she and Zeke were a couple. The girls would distrust that, would distrust both of them, if she got involved with Bert. Once, Zeke had asked Eleanor if she'd ever been given a hard time because of her and Marcie. Eleanor had said no, but Zeke wasn't sure she was telling the truth. It would be like Eleanor to smooth it over. Zeke wasn't sure how much other kids actually cared. Eleanor has two mommies, big deal. In some parts of the country, kids might give her a hard time, but here in Westchester, kids were blasé, they knew it all.

The covers were too hot, she was sweating beneath them. She pushed them off, then quickly felt a chill. What would it be like to go to bed with Bert? She couldn't quite imagine. Well, actually she could.

six

PRANA DIDN'T WANT HER SISTERS TO KNOW THAT SHE WAS seeing Marco. Pagan would try not to comment, but would look worried and protective. Zeke would scoff. Prana took a cab to the train station, which had been the same since her childhood, with its dark wood wainscotting and benches like church pews. After the morning rush hour, the ticket windows were closed, the station empty.

Inside the train, she settled into a seat and pulled out her book. She liked reading on trains, the seductive rocking, the blur of disappearing landscape. She returned to her book in different places.

In the image, as Sartre says, the object yields itself wholly, and our vision of it is *certain*—contrary to the text or to other

perceptions which give me the object in a vague, arguable
manner, and therefore incite me to suspicions as to what I
think I am seeing. . . . It is precisely in this *arrest* of interpre-
tation that the Photograph's certainty resides . . .

Prana closed the book, holding the place with her finger. There
was no image of her mother's departure, no central fact they
could point to. She had no image for Marco's departure either—
both of her parents so present in their absence. She kept coming
back to the confiding voice. "The *almost,* love's dreadful
regime." The oblique, poetic chapters were like delicate boxes
made of Japanese paper, boxes within boxes. When she reached
the center, she would understand.

She had never called Marco "Daddy." He left before she
was old enough to speak. She thought of him as an exotic
guardian and imagined her mother had encouraged this, knowing he would never be more. She remembered summers at the
local pool, lying on the rough cement, the sun dipping behind
the clouds and the sudden chill, hearing kids playing in the pool:
Marco! Polo! Marco! Polo! They swam with their eyes closed
toward the answering voice, the call and response rippling out.
It did not include her.

Every year they went into Manhattan on the day before
Christmas. When she was little, she loved getting dressed up,
knowing Marco would make a fuss over all of them, that she
would be singled out as special. They got off the train in a dark,
steaming underworld, the platforms filled with grown-ups
carrying newspapers and colorful shopping bags. Her mother
held her hand and cut through the crowds, leading them into
the vaulted enormity of Grand Central Station: the high blue
ceiling with stars obscured by soot, the floors and corners filled

with homeless people. It was like a fairy castle, waiting to be transformed.

Marco always waited for them in Grand Central, and he looked like a picture in a magazine: freshly shaven, elegant, and good-humored. He would hail a cab and take them to Rockefeller Center, where they walked among angels fashioned from white wire and lights. The smell of roasted chestnuts and hot pretzels filled the air. They went ice-skating, ate lunch, then stood before the window at FAO Schwartz, gazing at the elaborate train tracks winding through Santa's workshop. He gave each of them a gift, usually something tasteful and expensive.

She thought of those visits like an old movie where the two people who are supposed to meet keep passing each other by. Her mother always dressed carefully, but Prana interpreted her preparations more as a matter of pride than desire. Their annual visit always left Prana with a vague, unsatisfied anxiety, an image of what they might have been like as a family with a father. So on Christmas Eve, by the time they returned home, she was stirred up, wanting, filled with lights and nice food and gifts, but relieved to be back on her own turf without the dazzle of male attention and the invisible threads of shifting allegiances.

Her mother's postcard. Rockefeller Center. Was it a sign she would return for Christmas? She thought of the bronze Atlas with the world on his shoulders, and felt like a child waking in the dark, her fears looming like shadows on the walls. Her mother might have cast them off, become some other self. If she didn't return by Christmas, something would have gone horribly wrong. Her mother might never come back.

· · ·

MARCO HAD GIVEN her the name of a Chinese restaurant on Second Avenue, which Prana suspected was his way of not having her come up to his office. She would be hard to explain while showing himself in a good light. Marco liked to orchestrate the atmosphere of even the smallest event. She felt a nervousness building in her throat and told herself it was foolish. He was nothing.

The restaurant was dark and quiet at noon; the lunch rush hadn't started. She gave Marco's name to the hostess, who led her to a booth at the back of the room. Marco stood up when Prana approached. His smile was bright in the dark.

Marco's curls were mostly gray, but he had the polished, satisfied look of a man who spent a lot of money on himself. He was tan, even in this weather, and looked as if he belonged to a gym. He took her arm and kissed her on the cheek.

Prana sat down and carefully unfolded her napkin in her lap. She let the silence build as Marco waited for her to speak. When the waiter appeared, she studied the wine list and ordered a glass of wine. Then she turned her attention to Marco.

"Have you spoken to my mother recently?"

Marco seemed taken aback. "No, I haven't. Why?"

"She's disappeared."

Marco's eyes grew wide, like a child feigning innocence. He pushed his menu off to the side. "What do you mean?"

"She sent each of us a note saying she was leaving the country for a while. When we tried to reach her, she'd already gone. I thought you might have some idea where she went."

Marco sat back against the booth and shook his head. "I have no idea."

Prana felt herself getting angry at the way he deflected things so easily. "I don't want a knee-jerk response," she said. "I want you to really think. Was there something she always wanted to see—the Great Wall of China, the Taj Mahal?"

Marco closed his mouth, trying to look adult rather than assuming the attitude of boyish impressionism he usually cultivated.

"You have to realize how little you all were then. Your mother's main concerns were getting everyone fed and clean."

"There must have been something," she insisted.

Marco opened his hands in a gesture of helplessness. "Everything was concerts then. Wanting to see Dylan, or the Dead. We weren't making big plans in those days."

Prana simply looked at him.

"All this about your mother . . . she's a strong person. I'm sure *she's* fine." Marco looked off to the side.

Prana wondered why they had ever found him charming. She waited, her silence forcing him to say more.

"But what about you?" he asked quietly. "You look tired."

Prana smoothed the thick napkin in her lap. How would Marco know what she usually looked like? She braced herself against the protective tone in his voice.

"I came up to stay with Pagan. She lost a pregnancy, right in the middle."

"Oh, I'm sorry to hear that." Marco's voice was sympathetic, but uncomfortable with the topic, he moved past it. "How's work?"

"I'm thinking of doing something different," she said.

"What's that?"

"I'm not sure yet." She wanted to say, *You can still be a father, it's not too late,* but knew she would never say it. She picked up her chopsticks and reached for the fragrant food.

* * *

THEY PARTED ON Second Avenue. Marco kissed her on both cheeks and moved off into the cool, gray air. She felt the way she had as a child, restless and unsettled, filled with a longing she didn't know she had until she had it. She had planned to walk around the city, go to a museum, but suddenly felt tired. She would come into the city again tomorrow.

When she walked into Grand Central Station, she noticed how the terminal had been restored. On her way into the city, she'd been too preoccupied to notice, but now, partly because this route mimicked the trips of her childhood and partly because Pagan had mentioned it, she looked up at the ceiling and saw the glittering stars.

BACK IN SHADY Grove, Prana called Zeke from the train station to see if she could get a ride. She would simply tell Zeke she'd gone to some museums. Zeke wouldn't ask for details. Prana was about to hang up when Zeke croaked "hello" into the phone.

"Are you okay?" Prana asked.

"I've got the flu. I feel like hell."

"Well, I'm calling from the train station, but I can take a cab," Prana said. "Let me pick up a few things, and I'll be at your place in a little while."

"Okay," Zeke said.

Prana knew she must feel terrible if she didn't protest. Zeke rarely got sick. It was part of her code: fresh air cured everything.

When Prana walked into the carriage house, she was taken aback. The apartment seemed lonely and bachelor-like, as if Zeke only changed clothes there. The furniture was mostly garage sale castoffs; there were no books on the bookshelves, just a stack of old magazines. She recognized some end tables her mother must have given to Zeke. Prana had forgotten them until now; the mahogany looked out of place with everything else in the apartment.

Zeke looked as if she'd just taken a shower and, exhausted by the effort, retreated to the couch. Prana put water on to boil.

"So you went into the city today?" Zeke asked.

Prana nodded.

"You saw Marco?"

Prana didn't answer. She got up as the kettle started to whistle. The sink was full of dirty dishes, and she opened the cupboard and took out the last two clean mugs. She found a box of tea, but the waxed paper had been left open, and the tea bags looked old and dried out. She set one in each cup, looked unsuccessfully for honey or sugar, then poured hot water into the mugs.

She carried them into the living room, and Zeke took the mug from her, muttering "thanks."

"You think I'm pathetic, don't you?" Prana said.

"I don't think you're pathetic. It's just—it doesn't get you anywhere."

"What do you mean?"

"You come in here looking like you've been kicked in the head."

"Gee, thanks."

"I know it's hard, but it does get tiring, you mooning around, acting all tragic."

"Zeke, what is going on with you?"

"I'm just tired of you feeling sorry for yourself over this whole Daddy thing. Marco may be a putz, but at least he's there, he's *real*." Zeke's voice cracked. "I can't tell you how crazy it makes me that I can't remember my father. Almost, but not quite, it's like that eye thing people have—you know, they can't see what they're focusing on, they can only see the periphery—that's what I feel like. It drives me crazy." Zeke put her head down on her arms and made a harsh noise that sounded like a cry.

Prana sank into a tattered plaid armchair. "I didn't know you felt that way," she said softly.

"Well, now you do." Zeke lifted her head, stirred the tea with the tip of her finger, then quickly pulled it out. She studied Prana. "You still eat food, don't you?"

Prana rolled her eyes.

"You're bone thin," Zeke said. "Are you a coke fiend, or throwing up, or what?"

Prana sighed. "I eat. I'm fine. I've been partying with this neighbor who always has stuff. I've been . . . I just wanted to get out of my head, I don't know. It's better up here. Keeps me out of trouble." She was dying for a cigarette and reached for her pack.

Zeke made a face, as if to say, *don't you dare.* Prana set the pack down.

"Are you going to get yourself in trouble when you go back?"

"No, not like that," Prana said. "The problem is, I don't care about anything. I'm done with Stephan. I don't care about work."

"Well, do something different."

Prana looked around at Zeke's paneled walls. "I could help you make this place look less like a pit."

"Interior decorating—there's a departure." Zeke's tone was flat.

Prana felt stung. She opened her mouth to say something snotty, then said, "You miss Marcie, don't you?"

"Yes," Zeke said. "I do."

s e v e n

TOMMY WAS WORKING LATE AGAIN. ALL EVENING, PAGAN TOLD herself to wait, let Tommy get in the door, relax a little, before she had a talk with him. Maud was asleep, and Pagan set the newspaper she'd found down on the table, then moved around the living room, picking up toys, books, odds and ends that Maud had carried in during the day. The phone rang and, as she moved toward the kitchen to answer it, she heard Tommy coming in the door. She blew out of her mouth, exasperated. She didn't like to be on the phone when Tommy came home from a long day.

"It's me." Prana's voice was teary.

"Are you all right?"

Tommy walked into the kitchen, his cheeks flushed with cold, and hearing Pagan's voice, gave her a quizzical look. She made a gesture with her hand, indicating it was all right, mouthing "Prana."

As he took off his coat, he noticed the newspaper lying on the table. He glanced at Pagan, then went upstairs to change.

"She is coming back, isn't she?" Prana sounded plaintive and childlike.

Pagan thought of how she talked to Maud when she was scared, how she reassured her reflexively, because the stark truth would be too frightening. She couldn't voice her own doubts now. "Of course she is, what's wrong?"

"Nothing. Well, nothing really. I went into the city to see Marco yesterday. And you know how that is, it's useless." Prana blew her nose hard.

"Did you call him?" Pagan felt awkward as soon as she asked, knowing how unlikely it was that Marco had called Prana.

"Yes." Prana sounded defeated. "I just thought I'd ask if he had any idea where Mom was. Of course he didn't."

"Good idea though," Pagan said. She listened for Tommy coming back downstairs.

"Zeke's got a crummy flu," Prana said. "I saw her yesterday."

"Is she okay?"

"She told me to get a life."

Pagan heard the discouragement in Prana's voice—Zeke's comment had struck home. "Oh, she's just crabby because she's sick," Pagan said.

"I'm afraid she has a point." Prana blew her nose again. "You know, I like being here at the house, but I rattle around. I think too much."

"Well, come down here tomorrow."

"Actually, I'm going into the city. I'm going to a few galleries."

Tommy came into the kitchen, got himself a beer, and went into the living room.

"Well, some night this week then."

"Okay. I'm sorry to call in such a state."

"It's fine," Pagan said. And even though she wanted to go to Tommy, she felt herself pause. "I'm glad you called," she said.

She hung up the phone gently and, picking up the newspaper, went into the next room to find Tommy sitting on the sofa, beer in hand, staring at nothing.

"Prana's freaking out."

"About what?"

"She's afraid my mother won't come back."

Tommy didn't answer. They had said all they could on the topic.

"Are you hungry? Do you want something to eat?"

"In a little," Tommy said.

"You knew about this, didn't you?" Pagan held up the newspaper. "Why didn't you tell me?"

Tommy looked surprised, then took a long pull of beer. "Why would I give you one more thing to worry about?"

His face seemed momentarily strange, a mask grown so familiar that someone new might have seeped up behind it without her knowing. She felt a sudden lack of affection for him, a coolness like a cloud passing over the sun.

"That's why people kept asking if I'd have any problem." She couldn't keep the accusation out of her voice.

Tommy sank down on the couch and, seeing his wide shoulders curve, she felt how easily she could pierce him.

"It just feels weird to think that everyone knew about this, and I didn't."

"I talked to my brother tonight," Tommy said.

Pagan heard the weight in his voice and knew something was coming. When Tommy turned to face her, his face was mottled red and white.

"Once, I got a woman pregnant. Just as we were splitting up." He looked away from Pagan. "I never would have known, but I ran into her at a party a few months later. She had an abortion after we split up." Tommy's features started to pucker, as if all drawn together in the middle of his face. "I feel like this is my fault, that it's . . . payback, I don't know. She didn't even tell me, and then it came back on you." And he leaned forward and started to cry in huge openmouthed sobs.

Pagan put her palm on his back. Men crying were so awkward, pent-up grief came from a buried place inside them. She felt a helpless distance. Everyone keeps things from me, she thought. My mother, Prana, now this. Tommy leaned into his hands, sobbing, and she heard what he could not say: *a son, a son, a son.*

Finally he stopped crying. He got up to find a tissue, then looked to her, as if for judgment.

"How could you be accountable for something you didn't know about?" Pagan asked softly. "That's such a Catholic guilt kind of thing."

Tommy nodded, but looked as if he'd start to cry again. She kept her voice even, trying to convince him. "Tommy, the two things aren't related."

He rubbed his hand across his face.

"I go around and around, wondering *why* the hell this happened, what happened to my mother, wondering what it's all about for fuck's sake. But one thing I do know: this is definitely not because of some girl you got pregnant. Don't take this on yourself."

Tommy's skin was returning to its normal color. She saw he was trying to believe her.

"She was on the pill and everything," he said.

"What did your brother say?"

"Basically what you said, except that I should tell you."

She touched the side of his face at the temple. How gray he had become in the past few weeks. Was she just seeing it now? They were quiet for a while, then Tommy leaned sideways and rested his head in her lap, facing her knees.

"It's impossible to go back," he said.

"What do you mean?"

He didn't answer for a moment and Pagan felt her heart pound.

"I used to believe that everything worked out for the best, you know?"

She knew what he wanted, knew how to reassure him, but couldn't bear to say it.

"There's something else," Tommy said.

"What's that?"

He rolled over so that he was looking up at her. "I want to go to church on Sunday."

His face looked odd, upside down. Pagan sighed. "Tommy, it's fine. Go to church. Take Maud to Sunday School if you want." Inside she felt as if she were screaming—*anything* to make their lives seem less oppressive. She felt their household was weighted by fear, a private little circle that didn't disperse but closed in on itself, pulling the world's worries into it. She tried to sound encouraging. "Maud asks about Sunday School because of Eileen's kids. They were talking about Advent calendars the other day."

She rested her hand on the side of his face and looked up.

If her mother would just return, the circle would loosen, disperse, and everything would be all right. Her absence felt like a pause that had gone on too long: a performance-art joke, an endless fermata. She imagined her mother somewhere far away, moving through the sunlit air, oblivious to how they all hovered without her.

ON SUNDAY MORNING she helped Maud dress while Tommy showered and shaved. She had bought Maud a dress made of fabric that was velvetlike and stretchy. Maud stood in front of the mirror, tipping her head to the side, admiring her reflection with her dress-up shoes and socks.

"How come you don't go?" Maud asked.

Pagan held up a coat her mother had bought last year; she slipped Maud's arms into the sleeves.

"This is something you and Daddy will do together."

Pagan kissed them good-bye, and watched them walk down the front path, hand in hand. Maud beamed up at Tommy. Pagan closed the door behind them, enclosing herself in the stillness of the sunny morning.

e i g h t

TRAITOR. THAT'S WHAT HER FRIENDS WOULD SAY. ZEKE HAD invited Bert and his daughters to go for a walk down to Hardscrabble Lake. When she opened the door, and saw only Bert, she was surprised.

"Where are the girls?" Zeke felt how blunt it sounded as soon as she said it, as if Bert himself were beside the point.

"Shopping with their mom."

"Oh." She stood in the doorway, feeling awkward. She had expected the distraction of the girls' company. Grabbing her barn coat from a hook by the door, she gestured behind her. "Well, you've seen the place, so I guess you don't need a tour. My younger sister came by the other day and basically told me my place was appalling."

"That's going a bit far," Bert said.

"So you agree?"

He grinned. "Let's just say it doesn't have those homey touches."

She closed the door behind her. "I rented it right before I met Marcie, and we mostly seemed to end up at her house." Zeke rubbed her mouth with her hand and got an unexpected whiff of the tiger balm she'd put on earlier; the smell reminded her of feeling sick and feverish. She studied her palm, which looked clean. She hoped she didn't have it on her lips.

She led them down the driveway. It felt good to be moving in the cool air. The entrance to the trail was across the road, obscured by brambles, but Zeke knew a place where the brush was thin. They followed a deer trail through a marshy hollow, and after a while, the ground became higher, the path more distinct, winding through the woods. In summer it was dark and leafy here, but now the sun shone through the trees. After a half mile or so, the trail ran into an overgrown gravel path that had once been a dirt road. They passed a dilapidated chicken coop covered with vines. "This must have been part of the farm." Zeke stopped to peer into the low, dark building.

"So are you and Marcie back on good terms?"

Zeke looked at him, startled by his assumption, then realized he was thinking of seeing Eleanor at the farm.

"No. Not at all. Eleanor faked a stomachache while Marcie was on a business trip. The school called me."

"Smart kid," Bert said. "Where's their dad?"

"He lives in Vegas. He works for one of the casinos."

"How did Marcie ever hook up with him?" His expression was curious; he seemed amused at the idea of Marcie married to a man who lived in Vegas.

"Well, first, he's not some pathetic type, he works in management, although I guess that just makes him a scammer. But Marcie met him when she was visiting some friends in Atlantic City. She worked at a hospital near there. To hear Marcie tell it, he's someone who doesn't mind taking advantage of people's weaknesses. Of course, Marcie's pretty expert in that area herself. But apparently she was young, and thought she'd try being a Jersey housewife for a while, can you imagine? I mean, she really wanted kids; and I think that, after she'd been married for a while, she thought, 'What the hell am I doing?' And she left him. At least that's her version, but Marcie knows how to make a story suit herself." Zeke kicked a small stone down the trail. The topic depressed her. "So why don't you vet show horses anymore?" she asked.

He smiled thinly at her question, but seemed to take her change of topic in stride. "Well, I do, but not for sale."

"Why?"

He stepped over a fallen tree. "When I first moved up here, I got a certain amount of pressure—subtle and otherwise. Some of the trainers are pretty handy with a needle, so vetting a horse for sale gets tricky. When a trainer's been buying big bottles of Phenylbutazone from me, I have no idea which horses are getting it. And it's awkward—if someone's giving me thirty or forty thousand dollars worth of business a year, he feels one hand washes the other. I just decided to make a cutoff point. If a horse comes from a barn around here, I won't vet it for sale if it's going to cost more than ten thousand dollars. People get the message."

Zeke cupped an apple she was carrying in her pocket. She liked the way he thought about things. People around here usually defined themselves emphatically, as if it took a combative stance to hold their ground. Marcie was like that. But Bert seemed different: he set himself up so he wouldn't be subject to pressures that many people felt were inevitable. There was an integrity to the way he made his own terms. In this part of Westchester, there was a steady stream of rich kids whose show horses cost large sums of money. Professional trainers handled the negotiations for these horses, and made money on commission, so it was in their best interest to move the horses and keep them sound. A horse that cost eighty thousand dollars and turned up lame was an expensive albatross. The horse still ate, needed stabling, and even the richest fathers didn't like paying hundreds of dollars a month to maintain a horse their kid couldn't ride.

"But you still do some nice stables."

"Sure. And I'll look over a horse if it comes from somewhere else, take X-rays, all that, but people form corporations to buy show horses these days, insurance companies have gotten into it." He shook his head. "It can get sticky."

Zeke looked off into the woods. A few years back, there'd been a huge scandal up in Bedford. Two riders were caught having horses killed so they could collect on the insurance. She'd been horrified when the story came out. The riders were professionals; she'd grown up watching them at Fairfield Hunt Club, at Boulder Brook, at the June show out at the Altshultul Estate.

"So doing the smaller barns works out okay?"

"Sure. I like the owners, and I still do the basic stuff at the big barns: inoculations, worming, although I'd like to give up floating teeth, I've got bursitis in my elbow."

She laughed.

"It's not funny, makes me feel old."

When they arrived at the lake, the water was dark and still, dappled with yellow fan-shaped leaves. She touched the toe of her boot to a thinly iced puddle.

"It's not a lake," he said. "More a pond."

"It's a lake," she countered. They sat down on some logs at the edge of a fire circle. She felt nervous, and noticed an old beer can, bottle caps, scraps of paper caught in the brush. She wanted motion to distract her, and wished she'd brought a bag to carry the litter out. She felt, in the silence, the tension between them. Bert stretched his legs.

"Did you ever go out with men?"

"Yes," she said.

"What changed?"

"Nothing really."

He smiled and looked at her straight on. He knew too much, she thought. This was not a good idea. She wondered if men could understand the world of women, how safe it could feel. Warm, full, ripe, women smelled right. She thought of Marcie, how nothing with her was safe or right. Still, Marcie herself was particular and amazing when she wasn't behaving like a lunatic.

She looked at his hands, wondered if he would reach for her. She was distracted for a moment, thinking of Marcie's mouth, and realized that she didn't want to kiss him, but wanted to feel him against her. Men were different, their bodies solid and predictable. Marcie was unexpected. Zeke thought of the graceful line of her back, her hips. With all the length of her, Marcie was unexpectedly light, as if her bones were birdlike and hollow.

"It would be easier to sleep with you if I didn't like you," she said.

He looked at her, drew a mark in the dirt with his boot. "I'm not quite sure how to take that," he said.

"It'd be like jumping out of an airplane."

"You're a thrill seeker, aren't you?" His tone was reflective. She had heard this before, but it was usually in the form of an accusation. "You know, if a woman lets herself be seduced by another woman, just for curiosity's sake, the women's community gets an attitude, as if—" and she searched for the right way to say it, "defecting from the hetero crowd is just playacting, toying with someone's feelings. But when it's the other way around—" and Zeke didn't look at him; she looked straight ahead at the lake. "It's even worse, you're a traitor." She brushed her bangs out of her eyes and grinned. "On the other hand, I've never been one to worry about what people think."

THE FOLLOWING DAY, sitting at her desk, she moved papers from one stack to another, thinking about Bert. Francis Bertelli. Why did she flirt with him? She was expecting his voice when the phone rang.

"Zeke?"

Marcie's voice sounded frightened, the last tone Zeke had expected.

"I'd really like to talk to you," Marcie said. "Could you come to the house?"

Zeke felt a leaping hope and then a wariness.

"Marcie, I do have a job. If you want to talk, you can come here."

"I can't." There was a long pause. "Zeke, I got a DWI. They took away my license.

"Are the girls okay?"

"They weren't in the car. I didn't hit anybody. I got stopped. Zeke—" Marcie took a deep breath. Zeke imagined it was for dramatic effect. "Please, I just got out of jail. It was awful."

"Who took care of the girls?"

"I called Agnes."

Zeke remembered Agnes, who had been a brief fling of Marcie's. Agnes was a nice woman. She should have told Marcie to fuck off.

"Eleanor knows everything." Marcie started to cry. "I really need to talk to you."

nine

PRANA BOUGHT THE *NEW YORK TIMES* AND, PULLING OUT THE gallery section, folded the rest of the paper into her bag. She could go up to the Metropolitan and see the Steiglitz pictures; she could go to MOMA; she could go downtown and see new work. Anything she pleased.

She took the subway downtown, rattling through the dark. Manhattan was overwhelming, multiplying, inexhaustible; it hummed with a different impulse from Washington, where the pale columnar buildings and monuments gave the impression of civilized spaciousness. She had found refuge in Washington's small museums, where she could linger in private. She loved the white marble and high ceilings at the Corcoran Gallery. Its grandeur made her think of a church, although a church without God. Art as God.

She and Stephan had gone there to see the Avedon exhibit. The large black-and-white portraits were stark, probing, as if the photographer had peeled back layers of the subjects' lives.

"It's as if their whole lives rose up into the moment the picture was taken," Stephan said.

He praised so little. She felt pleased they were seeing this together. She had loved being out with him, and at the same time craved being alone with him. She thought of how they were in bed, how she subsumed all that longing into the physical.

Getting out of the subway, she was pulled into the present. The underground stations were grimy and rich, secret places, their tilework a treasure in the dark. She stepped out onto Bleecker Street. The people looked spiky, biting, as if their exteriors revealed only a glimpse of their contained energy.

She walked into a gallery on Greene Street, which she remembered as a vast, shadowed room, but as soon as she walked in the door, she was confronted with a large white wall set slightly to one side. To see the exhibit, she had to walk through a maze of large panels. The first wall was completely empty except for four words in letters almost a foot high.

IT MUST BE ABSTRACT

She imagined there were images behind this injunction, so she walked around to the other side of the wall to find photos set in recesses, with scattered phrases around them. She had to step up close to read them.

But the priest desires. The philosopher desires.
And not to have is the beginning of desire.

> The first idea is an imagined thing.

The first idea is an imagined thing. The phrase was set precisely at her eye level. Prana felt like a tuning fork, struck. Standing there, reading the fragments, she felt an overwhelming sense of recognition. She had known all along. Stephan would say this was foolish. He would say art mustn't be abstract. Not at all. He would say that a photographer must be witness to something. A photo could be subjective, but it should represent some truth. She examined the photos: the undulant curve of a woman's back, a reflection of a glass roof taken in dark water. Prana felt something opening inside her. She turned to a second large wall.

IT MUST CHANGE

We have not the need of any paradise,
We have not the need of any seducing hymn.

> Music falls on the silence like a sense,
> A passion that we feel, not understand.

And below the words an elaborate cluster of images set in a kaleidoscopic pattern. She stared at the bright fragments. The circular pattern was familiar. What was it? The bright images rimmed dark resembled stained glass, and staring at the pattern it became clear to her, like a print emerging in the developer. The shape of the rose window. Notre Dame. The images were taken from many different photographs, cut and cropped, fragments of photos appearing and reappearing. A nail through a hand, Hebrew words, lines written in Cyrillic, a braid of thorns, gargoyles, the Wailing Wall, flying buttresses. The vaulted lines of church architecture shimmered as if blurred by hallucination. Photos of religious figures: statues of Mary, the Virgin of Guadalupe, Shiva, St. Bridget, Joan of Arc, Heloise, and Mary Magdalene. The photographer had selected the least clichéd of these figures, so the mélange of images was not sentimental, but slightly grotesque. She turned from it. She felt herself spinning, almost afraid of what she might find. On an adjacent wall, in smaller lettering:

> Two things of opposite natures seem to depend
> On one another, as a man depends
> On a woman, day on night, the imagined
> On the real. This is the origin of change.

The imagined and the real. All this time, she had thought of them as opposite. *Seem to depend on one another.* They were not in opposition; they were necessary to each other. She turned again.

IT MUST GIVE PLEASURE

> The complicate, the amassing harmony.

> To be stripped of every fiction except one.

Prana stood still, trying to make sense of it all. She felt an unbearable sense of recognition and looked at the gallery note in her hand. Who was the photographer? Only a name with initials: L. S. Roberts. No listing of other gallery shows, degrees procured, collections. The quotes were taken from a poet, Wallace Stevens.

She turned to look behind her. Three silverpoint photos hung on the back wall, different views of an old Nikon camera. The iris, dark and velvet, in the center. In two photos, a glimpse of hands at the edge of the frame, a man's or a woman's, she couldn't tell. In one, the fingers looked smooth, in another, the hand looked older. It must be the photographer, but then, maybe not. *To be stripped of every fiction except one.* She turned back to the mosaic of poem and images.

She felt a hot, uncomfortable feeling, one she didn't recognize at first. Then, standing in the quiet, she knew the feeling for what it was: jealousy. After the pleasure of recognition, a stab of knowing that someone else had conceived this, had articulated this vision, while she was arranging layouts for Martha Stewart clones. She saw herself small, like a tiny person standing in the center of a maze, and imagined the whole city blossoming around her, filled with people trying to make something coherent or beautiful from a world they couldn't know completely. It was time for her to stop merely admiring others. There was room for her to make something of her own.

ten

ZEKE DROVE TO MARCIE'S AFTER WORK. IF MARCIE WERE ON her own, Zeke would tell her to get better, get sober, call in a year, but what about Eleanor and Amy? How was Marcie going to get them around? There were no buses here.

When Marcie opened the door, Zeke was surprised at how good she looked. Her voice on the phone had sounded beaten down, humiliated, but here was Marcie, freshly showered, her dark hair brushing her face. Zeke wasn't sure how to greet her, but Eleanor ran up to give Zeke a hug. Amy was shy, but came up saying "Zekey, Zekey, Zekey," wiggling her fingers, and she reached up and clung to Zeke.

After a few minutes, Marcie said, "Girls, Zeke and I need to talk. You can play in your rooms, or go outside."

"Stay in," Eleanor said.

"Go out," Amy said.

Marcie sighed and hustled them out of the room. Zeke didn't like to see them go. Marcie, suddenly formal, gestured they should sit in the living room.

She brought Zeke a glass of soda with ice as if she were a guest. Zeke looked around the house and remembered how elegant it had seemed when they first met.

"These have been the worst few days of my life," Marcie said.

Zeke crossed her arms, and leaned back on the couch. She wondered how much of Marcie's distress was an act.

"I have a proposal, and I know you may not want to, but I'm going to ask you anyway." Marcie sat across from her, bouncing her foot rapidly, a tic Zeke had never seen before. Marcie took a deep breath. "I won't have a license for six months, and I want you to consider moving in with us for a while. I know it's asking a lot, but I can't even drive to buy *groceries*." Marcie leaned on this final fact as if it were particularly unjust. Zeke stared her down, and Marcie, chastened, continued. "I can probably find a ride to work, or I could take a car service. But I have to go to AA meetings, almost every night. I have to get a slip signed." She stopped and took a deep breath. "People have offered to take me back and forth to meetings. But who's going to watch the girls? I can't get a baby-sitter every night—or I could, but it doesn't seem like it would be good for them. I can't believe I'm saying this, but I have a probation officer, who'll be checking on me."

"So you're asking me to be a live-in housekeeper. Do I look like fucking Hazel?"

Marcie looked abject and twisted her hands in her lap. "Zeke, I'm asking you to be a friend."

"You haven't spoken to me for weeks, and now you've got

it all worked out. And so conveniently for yourself! Don't you think that's just incredibly selfish?"

Marcie looked as if she were going to cry. "I'm not just desperate. I *could* hire a housekeeper, although I don't know how I'd afford it. I can have groceries delivered, which somehow seems obscene, but that's not the point. I *have* to go to these damn meetings. And who's going to watch the girls?" Marcie's voice started to crack. "I can't mess up. They'll declare me unfit and send me to rehab. The girls would go to their father."

Checkmate, Zeke thought.

"If I agreed, I'd be sleeping in the guest room."

"Whatever you want," Marcie said.

Zeke felt hurt that she didn't protest.

"Look, if I'm just bailing you out, what's the point? It's just one more way you talk your way out of a scrape. It's still the same old shit."

"It's not."

"How do I know that?"

Marcie looked away as if embarrassed to meet her eyes. "I can't tell you what it was like to spend a night in jail."

"So what? It's just because you're a white bitch from Westchester that it seems so demeaning. Lots of people spend a whole lot more than one night in jail. You had some great revelation that night?"

"Yes, I did." Marcie set her chin defiantly.

"Well, what's that? What was your big revelation?"

Marcie looked down the hall, toward the girls' rooms, and lowered her voice. "How completely fucked up I am. How selfish I've been. I married Richard when I wasn't in the least interested in him. But I got what I wanted—I have these two lovely girls. I tried calling you the night I was arrested, but you weren't home.

I called Agnes, who had every right to spit in my face, who said she couldn't get the bail money that night. So Agnes called the baby-sitter's parents, and told them I'd been arrested for drunk driving. She asked if their daughter could stay overnight. So the Hansons know. God, it's humiliating. Agnes came to talk to the girls before picking me up, and told them that I was an alcoholic, that it wasn't their fault, that she hoped things were going to be better now."

Zeke raised her eyebrows and waited.

"I feel so *exposed*. Amy's walking around saying: 'Mommy is an alcoholic, Mommy is an alcoholic.' It's awful."

"But it's true." Zeke said quietly.

Marcie nodded, her eyes filling with tears. "I guess you have to think about this," she said. "If you don't want to, I'll hire a housekeeper. But when I think about the girls, you're the most sane person in their lives right now. Really, Zeke, I'll do anything. I'll pay the rent on the carriage house for all the trouble I'm causing."

Zeke felt light-headed. This all made sense, but it felt like a trap. It would suit Marcie so well.

"I'll think about it." Zeke stood up to leave.

"Talk to the girls before you go?"

Zeke went into Eleanor's room. She was sitting cross-legged on her bed, fiddling with a piece of lanyard. Amy twirled the dials of a worn-out Etch-A-Sketch. Zeke closed the bedroom door.

"Will you stay here?" Eleanor whispered.

Zeke looked down into her face, the soft sprinkling of freckles, her clear blue eyes.

"I don't know, Eleanor. Your mom makes me feel like . . ." Zeke wasn't sure how to say it. "Like a convenience. Like I would solve all her problems."

"You couldn't solve her problem," Eleanor said.

Zeke looked down at her and felt struck with the truth of this.

"Even if you wouldn't do it for Mom, would you do it for us?" Eleanor's fingers twisted in the plastic string.

Zeke felt tears swelling in her throat. She didn't want Eleanor to see her cry. She reached for Eleanor and hugged her, then whispered. "Okay, but don't tell your mother yet. I'm going to let her twist a little. I want to make my own terms."

Zeke kissed the girls and told Marcie she would call.

eleven

BACK AT HER MOTHER'S THAT NIGHT, PRANA FELT EXCITED BY her day, expectant, but the house was still empty. She climbed the stairs, set her bag in the room she had shared with Pagan, then walked across the hall and looked into Zeke's room, which still had trophies and ribbons, pictures from horse shows, all stored in boxes. She wondered if Zeke would let her fix up the carriage house. It could be fun. In spite of Zeke's prickliness, which Prana felt she could weather, it would be good for Zeke, who never seemed completely settled.

She decided to sleep in her mother's bed. Maybe she could will a dream, discover where her mother was. Prana smiled to herself, because she didn't really believe in such things. Her mail had finally been forwarded from Washington, and she carried a stack of it into her mother's room, climbing onto her mother's bed to sort it. Bills, announcements for openings, copies of magazines she had styling work in. She made little piles on the wide bed: Recycle. Keep. Pay. When she flipped open a magazine, one of the piles slid over and fell between the bed and the nightstand. She scrambled to pick up the papers and, as her fingers reached for a letter, she touched something soft and crumpled, a fallen newspaper clipping, half under the nightstand. She picked it up. It had been clipped from the *New York Times*. Carl Schulman, premiere of a new work in Tel Aviv. Zubin Mehta conducting. Why was the name familiar? Wasn't Schulman that violinist here in town? Pagan took lessons from him once, didn't she? But she quit. His wife was the principal at the high school. Didn't her mother sell them a house? Or sell a house for them? Prana couldn't really remember. She imagined this was the kind of thing realtors did—keep up with the accomplishments of their clients—but why would her mother clip it? Prana remembered the high school principal. She was crisp and bright, given to wearing red blazers. Schulman was a different, elusive story. She remembered him as a rich, black-and-white photo, with huge bushy eyebrows and a thick head of hair. He didn't seem to belong in Shady Grove.

ZEKE PREPARED HER ultimatum as she drove to Marcie's. Moving in, even for a few months, seemed constricting. She imagined sleeping with Bert while living at Marcie's. Marcie would just have to deal with it, but what about the girls? They'd be confused if they found out.

Marcie met her at the door, and when Zeke stepped into the house, the smell of baking bread wafted over her. Again, Marcie offered her something to drink, but Zeke declined, nodding toward the living room. She gestured that Marcie should sit down.

"First, I want you to give me visitation rights. I want you to sign a document, drawn up by a lawyer, that gives me the right to visit the girls at least twice a week. Second, I want you to pay for keeping my gas tank full. The money isn't really the issue, but this shouldn't cost me money as well as time. My last condition is that you go to those damn AA meetings six times a week. I mean it. You can miss one day a week, that's all. I talked to a friend last night. She said a lot of people—there was an expression—'identify out' in the beginning, but if I'm going to come here, I don't want to be a Band-Aid. I want you to get your shit together."

"You're really doing this for the girls, aren't you?" Marcie's face was pale.

"Yes," Zeke said. "I am."

BERT STOPPED AT the farm that afternoon as Zeke was closing up the barn. His expression was serious, as if he'd been considering something.

"I have a proposition for you," he said.

"You too?"

"You have offers everywhere?" He sounded amused.

"That's right." She tried to smile, but slammed the barn door.

"What's going on?"

"Marcie got her license taken away, and she wants me to move in with her so I can watch the girls while she goes to AA meetings at night."

"A romantic proposal."

"Exactly." Zeke sighed, then looked at him directly. "I'm going to do it though."

"Noble of you."

"Not really." She turned toward the paddock and leaned her forearms on the top rail.

"I hope Marcie's proposal doesn't negate all other offers."

"Try me."

He gave her a long look. "If I moved my horse over to Birch Hill, would you be interested in training him? Charlie's got a stall open. I think this horse has really got something, and I'd like to see him worked through the winter and spring. You could decide whether he'll be ready to show in the First Year Green division next summer."

Zeke was embarrassed to feel herself blush. She looked at him carefully, felt a sense of shock at how perfect this arrangement would be.

"Yes," she said. "Absolutely."

PAGAN HEARD A car stop in front of the house, and looked out the window to see an expensive sedan, it looked like a car service, idling in the driveway. She felt annoyed, wondering when the driver would figure out he had the wrong address, but as the car continued to idle in the driveway, she felt a pounding in her chest. She ran to the front door to see her mother getting out of the car, the shadow of a man still inside. The driver lifted two large suitcases out of the trunk.

Her mother turned to look at the house, as if sensing Pagan waiting. Pagan felt a burst of love and relief so strong she knew she'd weep, and she stared at her mother, trying to see what was different. Her mother seemed rested, lightened. She turned to close the car door and leaned in the window, saying something to the man in back. Pagan could only see his shadow, but the thick, leonine silhouette seemed familiar. She couldn't quite place it. Her mother's graceful movement was an unfamiliar, balletic gesture, as if leaning in to say good-bye, she was preparing to dance. Her mother turned. Her thick brown hair was loose down her back, sliding over her coat, the strands of silver bright in the autumn dusk.

Readers Guide to
Departures

DISCUSSION QUESTIONS

1. Each daughter's name carries its own meaning, relating to a stage of her mother's spiritual seeking. What traits in each woman's personality seem true to her name? What personality traits are in contrast to their names? How does each woman feel about the name she's been given? How do you think their mother chose their names?

2. Each daughter faces her own crisis. How do experiences with their mother affect how each deals with her own crisis? What have they learned from the difficulties their mother faced in her life?

3. Zeke discovers that her mother has taken a picture of all three of them with her when she left. Why do you think the mother chose that specific picture? How does the picture capture each woman?

4. How does the sisters' birth order affect their relationships with their mother and each other? Do Pagan and Zeke consider Prana differently given that she is a half-sister? Does Prana consider herself differently from the other two? Why? How does this affect her behavior toward her sisters?

5. What has held Prana back from finding an artistic path that would satisfy her?

6. Do you think Prana's affair with Stephan has anything to do with the fact that Marco abandoned her? How has she dealt with the fact that her father abandoned the family? How is this different from what her sisters face in dealing with the death of their father? How do they view Marco's leaving? Do you think it is easier to deal with the death of a loved one, or abandonment by someone you love?

7. Why do you think the mother leaves in such a secretive way, and why did she send a separate message to each of her daughters by different means, worded so differently?

8. What does the mother remember about her youth? What does she remember about her mother, and how do those memories affect how she feels about her father?

9. What qualities or characteristics make Bert attractive to Zeke? Why are these qualities appealing to Zeke and what do they say about Zeke's personality? Do you think that Zeke and Bert will ultimately have a romantic relationship? Why? Why does Zeke agree to take care of Marcie?

10. Pagan has a physical fear about the abortion, but she also faces a moral struggle. What is at the heart of the moral struggle, and how does it affect her marriage? How does the abortion affect her relationship with her sisters? How does it affect how she feels about Maud?

11. Before she finds out the news about her baby, Pagan tells Tommy, "This is it Tommy. This is the last time." Why does she say this? Is it the physical hardship of pregnancy? Do you think she will change her mind? Does the abortion damage their marriage? If so, how? If not, why not?

12. Pagan finds a prayer when she's first dating Tommy. What does it reveal about him? What does it mean to Pagan in terms of religion and how she feels about Tommy's beliefs? How does the prayer relate to Tommy's reaction to the bad news about the baby, and the decision to abort it? Why does Tommy want to start going to church again?

13. How are the three women different by the time their mother returns? How have they changed in the time she's been gone? What have they learned about themselves and about her? Will their relationships with her be different now?